DANIEL CORKERY was born in that county. He studied at and for over twenty years he t interested in the Irish langua, schools. Through his work became a university teacher and was Professor of English at University College Cork from 1931 to 1947. On his retirement he served on Seanad Éireann and the Arts Council, and devoted time to his painting in watercolours.

He wrote pamphlets, plays, and a novel, *The Threshold of Quiet*, a study of *Synge and Anglo-Irish Literature*, and a study of the Irish Munster poets of the eighteenth century, *The Hidden Ireland*. But he is best remembered for his four collections of short stories: *A Munster Twilight* (1916), *The Hounds of Banba* (1920), *The Stormy Hills* (1929), and *Earth Out of Earth* (1939).

Daniel Corkery died in 1964.

FRANCIS DOHERTY was born in Yorkshire in 1932. He read English at Sheffield University and in 1962 he was awarded an MA from Manchester University. He taught at University College Dublin from 1962 to 1963 and since then he has taught in the Department of English at the University of Keele, where he is Head of Department. He has published two books – *Byron* (Evans Brothers, 1968) and *Samuel Beckett* (Hutchinson University Library, 1971). He has also published articles on Beckett, Daniel Corkery and Flann O'Brien, and in the Norwich Tapes Series has produced audiotapes on Sean O'Casey, George Bernard Shaw, John M. Synge and Oscar Wilde. He was a founder of the British Association for Irish Studies.

NIGHTFALL
AND OTHER STORIES

Daniel Corkery

edited by
Francis Doherty

THE
BLACKSTAFF
PRESS
BELFAST AND ST PAUL, MINNESOTA

First published in 1988 by
The Blackstaff Press Limited
3 Galway Park, Dundonald, Belfast BT16 0AN, Northern Ireland
and
Box 5026, 2115 Summit Avenue, St Paul, Minnesota 55105, USA
with the assistance of
The Arts Council of Northern Ireland

Printed in Northern Ireland by
The Universities Press Limited

British Library Cataloguing in Publication Data
Corkery, Daniel, *1878-1964*
Nightfall and other stories.
I. Title   II. Doherty, Francis
823'.912 [F]

ISBN 0-85640-414-4

In
piam memoriam
patrum nostrorum

CONTENTS

INTRODUCTION

DANIEL CORKERY was a Corkman, lived all his life in Cork and travelled little, making Cork city and the countryside of Cork his especial location for storytelling. He lived a long life, being born in 1878 and dying in 1964, and this long life was bound up with teaching and the arts, with Ireland and the Irish language, with instruction and learning. A quiet man, crippled in one leg, he never married, but he taught and studied all his life. He worked for over twenty years in elementary schools, taught art (having studied in his own time at the Crawford Municipal School of Art), organised the teaching of Irish in schools, and graduated late into university teaching through his work on Synge and Anglo-Irish literature. He was Professor of English at University College Cork from 1931 to 1947, serving after his retirement on Seanad Éireann and the Arts Council, devoting time to his own painting in water-colours. He wrote pamphlets, plays and a novel, *The Threshold of Quiet*, a study of *Synge and Anglo-Irish Literature*, and a study of the Irish Munster poets of the eighteenth century, *The Hidden Ireland*. But he is best remembered for his four collections of short stories, from which this selection is taken.

Behind all that he did in his life and behind all that he wrote was a passionate belief in Irish identity, in the uniqueness of Ireland and in its permanent values which he felt were deep-rooted, long-lived and yet vulnerable to erosion or to being undervalued. He was a campaigner for the Irish language and traditions, yet, paradoxically, had a passionate and lasting love-affair with the English language. He had a real and deep engagement with people rather than with dogmas or doctrines. His enthusiasms led him to want to rediscover what he called *The Hidden Ireland*, and this book is in many ways the best introduction to him and his thought. It shows, first of all, an Ireland almost overwhelmed by foreign values, but an Ireland where on the fringes and in the margins another and richer life was lived. Ireland

> is the terrain of the common enemy, ruled by deputies of deputies of deputies, and sunk so deep in filth and beggary that its people have been thrust, as torpid and degraded pariahs should, beyond the household of the law.

There are two things here: the nationalism which is dangerous in its mystical belief in the *folk* and 'the spirit of the nation', ideas which can degenerate into sentimentalism or become the licence for violence; but more interestingly and of permanent value is the celebration of those who are outcasts, the alienated, the marginal people. In *The Hidden Ireland* we see that very important and omnipresent Corkery theme of hiddenness, of that mystery which lies at the heart of every person and of the world, so that often we feel that when he talks of the unknown truths which lie behind the scant historical details which we possess of the great poets writing in Irish, he is talking of himself. Just as we equally feel that he speaks of himself when, in *Synge and Anglo-Irish Literature*, he talks of *Riders to the Sea* and uses the phrase 'impassioned contemplation':

> Of itself the play is sufficient evidence of his gift of impassioned contemplation: it was that gift that enabled him to make use of such daily happenings as we ordinarily do not notice, to interpret the humanity of his characters. That gift, we may learn, is the be-all of the thaumaturgy the creative artist practises.

It is this quality of a hidden and mysterious heart revealed to 'impassioned contemplation' which gives life to all of Corkery's best writing, the best of which is itself to be found in the short stories. His four collections of short stories (*A Munster Twilight*, 1916, *The Hounds of Banba*, 1920, *The Stormy Hills*, 1929, and *Earth Out of Earth*, 1939) all have an intense focus on the solitariness of the individual who is put into circumstances which Seán Lucy speaks of as being 'beyond the ordinary everyday boundaries of his life'. It is there too that Corkery's training and practice as a watercolourist comes into its own, and Patricia

Hutchins points out that he always sees his characters as intimately part of a landscape, caught in light, colour and the vagaries of weather. But we feel that through writing of others he was able to write himself, and in the landscape and with his isolated figures he found ways which Deborah M. Averill says 'could best express his private self'.

Corkery was much influenced by the Russian tradition, quoting Chekhov's dictum on the pattern of the short story (in *Synge and Anglo-Irish Literature* while discussing *Deirdre of the Sorrows*) and modelling himself particularly on Turgenev, whose undemonstrative manner was devoted to the common people, whom he treats without patronisation and, when writing at his best, without giving them unearned qualities of heroism or grandeur. His peasants, farmers, fishermen of the country and his humble town-dwellers have each of them an importance and an inviolability which raises them above the level of the mundane; each has a soul and each a unique tale of suffering and endurance to tell. Corkery gives them space in which we are allowed to glimpse their realities but never completely to understand or possess them.

So, in a story like 'Nightfall' we see the complex and distressing emotional state of an elderly returnee whose youth and vigour have long gone, and yet who still sees himself as he was sixty years ago before he left Ireland. This is mediated to us delicately and painfully in a finely held tension between individual and community. Or, in 'A Looter of the Hills' Corkery re-writes Wordsworth's poem 'The Idiot Boy' from *Lyrical Ballads* as a tale of a seventy-year-old woman and her idiot son and the bonds which lie between them, all caught up in the old blind woman's country childhood and her love for the wildness of her lost world.

Many of Corkery's people are failures, incompetent or impotent, but each has dignity, each has worth undiscovered or unknown to others. Corkery can take us directly into the experience of the small child caught at a moment in 'Vision' where his world implodes because he is made to take an unwanted peep into the complex, unaccountable world of adulthood, but which he still has to try to maintain with the only weak tools he has, magical incantation and the imaginative creation of play. We can be made to inhabit the loneliness of the priest who, committed to his people, is yet condemned to minister to unlovely and grasping peasants whose hold on property is faster than their hold on God, and whose land is as mean and pinched as they are, with its 'terrible promiscuity of rock, the little stony fields that only centuries of labour had salvaged from them'. And we are led into other private worlds, the secret, unknowable significance of a blind fiddler's playing in a storm, a significance known only to the player, in 'The Serenade', a kind of 'spousal music' analogous to Wordsworth's 'spousal verse'. There is the violence of the storm in many of the tales, and there is that quiet which comes from suppressed violence, seen most powerfully perhaps, in a mysterious and bizarre yet compelling story of men driven beyond the limits of the possible in 'The Ploughing of the Leaca'.

All the tales are told in spare, economical ways, yet all are rich in suggestion and symbolism, and all are derived from a contemplation of the everyday which he called 'the homely', part of the programme which he set himself as a writer to accept open-eyed his own local world, the wild terrain of Munster, the brooding city of Cork among its hills. As a sympathetic anonymous reviewer in the *Times Literary Supplement* said in 1929 of *The Stormy Hills*:

> Here is to be found an implicit philosophy of life, a sense of continuity in character and setting, a grave pity and understanding by which the bitterness of human life is resolved.
>
> Synge discovered the larger rhythms of Irish idiomatic speech; Mr Corkery has developed the inward modulation and quieter cadence of idiom; and style and subject matter express one another.

Frank O'Connor contrasted the novel with the short story, and he suggested that the novel places man in society, but that the short story 'remains by its very nature remote from the community — romantic, individualistic, and intransigent'. He thought that the short story therefore had 'a sense of outlawed figures wandering about the fringes of society, superimposed sometimes on symbolic figures whom they caricature and echo – Christ, Socrates, Moses'. There are, indeed, occasional mythic figures in Corkery, but for the most part the figures are not mythic. It is as though Corkery holds as an axiom that if you take anyone at all, however plain, he or she can never be known and can never really know others. So the recurrent words in all his writing are words for silence, quiet and hiddenness. Seán O'Faoláin thought that 'some of the best things Daniel Corkery ever wrote were a few sketches of the Cork poor at the end of his first book of stories' and there is some truth in that. As one of Corkery's pupils at University College Cork remembers him saying in an aside on Shakespeare: 'Ah yes, Hamlet. A very complex character. But not as complex as an ordinary human being.'

FRANCIS DOHERTY
University of Keele, 1988

VISION

I

JIMMY'S MOTHER, sharply, told him once again to keep still; but how could he be expected to do that, ready for the road as he was, dressed up as he was. A thick woollen muffler bound him tightly together from his very lips to halfway down his chest. Within that, again binding him together, was a double-breasted overcoat, while his little legs, sturdy and strong, were bound in also, with gaiters. As he ran about the flagged kitchen his gloved hands seemed to herald his coming, the fingers wide apart. Dressed up like that, how could he keep quiet? Besides, it was only four o'clock in the morning, yet the whole house was up and about. The fire was blazing. His mother was busy at it, or was rinsing the teapot. The lamp on the wall was bright, brighter than he had ever seen it. Whenever the kitchen door opened a gush of cold entered, and he was astonished at the darkness outside, it was so close up against the door. He stared at it frightened; but when their man, Jackie, crossed the haggard with a swinging lantern, and its beams brought out the familiar objects, his terror changed to wonder, they seemed so strange. And there was such silence. The horse rattled his chains in it. The cart was being dragged from the shed. Everything flowed in upon him. To add to the wonder, their man rather noisily once again opened the door from outside and, with his hand on the latch, thrust in his head and said: 'Listen, ma'am,' and saying so turned and stared back into the darkness. The lamplight fell on his round head, his cheek, his shoulder, his hand; he looked like something cut out of paper. Jimmy made towards him, but his mother rapped out: 'Be quiet, can't ye.'

In the silence they heard a distant cart knocking its way down a treacherous hillside. The sounds were faint yet sharp; they widened the night for the boy: that cart, that horse, that man to be out in

I

the middle of all that darkness. He put his gloved fingers against his lips to think of it. But Jackie said:

'That's Miah Sullivan, 'tis no one else.'

'Isn't it early he's stirring?' the mother answered, adding with impatience: 'Tell himself to hurry, I'm after wetting the tea.'

When Jackie had gone Jimmy moved towards the door. His mother raised her voice:

'Look, there's your tea. Sit in. Drink it up or you won't go at all.'

So he sat at the table, and while with his two gloved hands he held the cup dawdling at his lips, his eyes were staring through the doorway, his ears keeping track of the lonely sounds of the distant wheels. His father came from the haggard, and at the sight of him comfort and courage returned to him. With his father he would go anywhere. When he saw him cutting the cake he forgot everything except that very soon they would be on the road to the fair at Dunmanway. Besides there was no other fair till after Christmas. His father would buy him something, he didn't know what, he wouldn't tell him. But whatever it was it would be all his own; and he would show it to his cousins when they came from Johnstown.

In the cart with them were six pigs. Only for the old soap-box, which had been put beneath his feet, he could have felt them moving about. He was quite comfortable. They had no light, but his father knew the way; he knew where to duck to avoid the branches that sometimes swished along the cart, unseen.

II

A buyer had come. Jimmy saw him hoist himself on the wheel, bend himself down over the pigs, rouse them:

'They're not much,' he said.

The boy was astonished. He flushed; he looked from the man to his father, but his father was only smiling; he heard him say quietly:

'Now, if you said they were handsome,' and he saw him shrug

his shoulders and look away. The buyer turned and made off, immediately came back and faced his father as if he hadn't said anything wrong at all! And his father didn't seem surprised. There was a little quiet talk, and then he saw the buyer grope for his father's hand, and slap his own right hand into it. He knew then the pigs had been sold.

After that his father put the horse, pigs and all, into a yard. The two of them then went into the house. The kitchen was full of people. They were all eating, sitting on long stools. There was noise, confusion, in the place, and he was glad when his father and himself were led into another room, a smaller room. After a while tea and rashers and eggs were brought to them on a tray. His father finished quickly, rose, and told him to sit on the sofa and wait until he came back: 'I'm not forgetting at all, Jim,' he said, and Jimmy knew he was talking about his present. When he reached the door the woman of the house looked in with him and said: 'What fear is of him?' He waited. He was glad he wasn't in the big room where all the people were; you could see the crumbs on their whiskers. But his father wasn't coming. After a long time the landlady again put in her head: 'Are you all right?' she said. He nodded, and was just about to ask where his father was, but she was gone and the door was closed.

He sat quite still: he felt that if he stirred or moved about, somehow his father would not come back so soon. But he listened carefully to the voices outside thinking he might catch his father's voice. The woman once more put her head in. At once he was on his feet. 'Where's my father?' he said.

She seemed surprised; she looked at him sharply. He heard her call out: 'Molly, Molly,' and as the servant girl entered she said: 'Take Jimmy here over to Stephen's.' Without a word, Molly, who was untidy, and flushed from cooking, caught up his hand roughly – he noticed it but it didn't matter – and hastened him across the street towards a very grand-looking doorway with a large round lamp above it.

'Did any of you see Ted Coveney?' she said boldly to the men standing on the steps.

A very tall man answered her: 'He's inside at the meeting.'

Another said: 'That's Ted Coveney's little boy,' astonishing Jimmy, who never before had seen him. 'Come on, Sonny,' he said, catching his hand. Jimmy felt himself being led down a long tiled passage; a glass door was opened; he was steered into a crowded room. There was a long polished table with a great many men sitting around it; behind them others were standing along the walls. The man who had brought him in spoke to one of those seated; and Jimmy felt himself being lifted on to the man's knee. 'Look at your daddy,' was whispered in his ear.

At once Jimmy saw him; he was at the other side of the table away down to the right. And his father had seen him too, was smiling at him. He saw him raise a papered-up parcel, a long box it seemed to be. He knew it was his present. As he looked at it he heard a sharp silvery bell ring, ding, ding, ding, ding, ding, and the noise lessened. He heard a man saying something about his father. First he said Mr Coveney, but afterwards he said Ted Coveney, and then again Mr Coveney. And he saw his father looking at the speaker. Then his father began to speak, turning again towards the crowd; he was now looking up along the table, looking almost at himself; but Jimmy soon understood that though his father was looking in his direction he was not looking at him or at anybody else or at anything else. It was queer. And everybody was listening. Jimmy's eyes ranged from face to face. Some of them frightened him: they were cross-looking, they were staring fiercely at his father, their mouths open. But his father wasn't cross-looking at all; he didn't mind them. His head was tilted very much, his brows were fixed, his eyes were intent, he was looking at no one, just talking on and on, and although he was tapping the table with the corner of the box, tapping it very gently, Jimmy felt his father didn't know that he had anything in his hand. Suddenly there was some stir, a chair moved, and Jimmy, terrified, heard some of the men cry out: 'No, no; 'tisn't so; 'tis not,' but the whole roomful cried against them: 'Ye know very well it is, it is; what fools we are.'

His father had taken no notice, kept silent for a moment, then went on talking, the box gently tapping the table. The boy was puzzled. The room was now quite still, listening. Suddenly his father stopped and said: 'That's what I think anyway.' The boy

4

saw him put the box this way and then that way in front of him, staring at it, and at last take his hand from it slowly, carefully, and fold his arms, and sit back. A hubbub of talk began and someone stood up; but to him no one would listen. Some were already leaving the room. Jimmy felt himself being deposited in a vacant chair. 'Your daddy will be over to you in a minute,' someone said to him. There was a crowd pushing through the doorway. Jimmy heard someone else say: 'Ted Coveney is a good judge, none better.' He swung round but he could not pick out who had said it. 'A good judge, none better,' he made his own of the phrase, and he looked intently at his father. He saw him in the midst of a group of men. They were asking him questions. He was answering them. They were looking up at him.

III

The papered-up box contained a toy lorry, a real lorry, because nothing was missing in it. It had a hood with a seat within it; a steering wheel that turned the front wheels; those wheels themselves had rubber tyres, you could smell the rubber. The backboard could be let down. That was how Tim Mason got the churns into his lorry. To note its wonders the boy felt himself trembling all over, his throat smothering. He held it in his two hands broadside to his eyes. He drank it in. He didn't know what to say until suddenly, in a sort of triumph, he found himself breathing out; 'My father is a good judge,' and he trailed his fingers along the toy. He would turn his cap back to front: Tim Mason always had his cap that way. He would race the lorry up the hill; he wouldn't blow his horn going up the hill, she'd make noise enough: Tim Mason had told him that. Coming down was different. He would blow his horn whenever he overtook the other lorries or a churn boy taking his milk to the creamery. You could bring meal in a lorry, a dozen sacks, he had seen them counted. You could take cattle in it, standing up. He'd put the young horse in it, with a halter on him.

5

As they jogged homewards darkness fell, and he began to feel cold. His father stopped the horse and wrapped an old coat about his son; his gloves he made him put on; and the lorry he stowed away safely beneath the soap-box. That certainly was the right place for it. How well his father had thought of it! Then surfeited with content, in a moment he was sunken in a deep sleep.

IV

When he awoke they were swinging into their own haggard. Familiar sounds had awakened him – the grinding of the wheels on the sloping rocks. Jackie was holding them a lantern, head high. He came forward, put it on a barrel top, took him from his father's grasp, and planted him on the ground. Through Jackie his father handed him his lorry. Jackie then caught the horse's head and led him in. He saw his mother coming from the house. She passed him as he stood there with his lorry in his hands, and made him no greeting. She went straight to the shed. She spoke to his father. He answered, his back turned to her. And then Jimmy heard her cry out angrily: 'Only twelve pounds for the lot?' He heard no reply. Something else sharp and high she said, and turned, was making for the house. Again she hadn't seen him. He saw his father go into the shed. 'My father is a good judge,' he whispered, in a changed tone, however, as if he were remembering things. He stood there in the darkness puzzled, as still as a stone; his brows were fixed, his eyes intent, his head tilted; as for the toy in his hands, it might as well have been a bit of an old ashplant. He was called twice before he crossed the haggard without a word out of him.

NIGHTFALL

H IS NAME WAS REEN, but they called him the Colonial: their
way of pronouncing the word, however, could not easily
be set down here. They had never used it, scarcely ever
heard it until the newspapers during the Great War had dinned it
into their ears. In New Zealand he had lived his many years. There
he had landed in his young manhood, toiled upwards, found
himself a wife, built his household, in course of years married off
his three sons and his two daughters, all to the wrong people, it
seemed; there at last he had buried his wife, upon which he had
thrown in his hand, sold off everything, and made straight back to
the rocks and the fields of his boyhood. Without warning one
summer afternoon he drove into his sister's house in west Cork, a
man still hardy, if grey-haired, erect enough, bright-eyed, and
with the firm voice and free ways of one who had not won
through without sweat and bitterness.

I

It was the quiet end of the farmer's year, a day in early October.
The Renahans since morning had been building what they called
the home rick. In the close beyond the cow sheds was its place
from time out of mind. More than two months earlier, in August,
before the corn was fit for cutting, they had built their main rick,
also in its traditional place – where the pathway that wound up
the side of the *cummer* towards the hill-top was widest.

It was a gully for the north-west wind, this close of theirs, and
they had been glad to put a crown on the day's work and get

themselves within to the warmth and merriment, the fire and the card-playing. They were a large family on whom the scatter for America had not yet fallen. Even without the others who had been assisting in the work – Phil Cronin, the labouring boy; Pat Lehane, a neighbour of theirs; Kitty Mahony, a neighbour's daughter; and one of the Lynch boys – the Renahans of themselves were numerous enough to fill the flag-paved, lamp-lit kitchen with bright and noisy life. They were all in their characteristically careless working clothes, patched and repatched and unpatched, stained with mire or sulphate of copper, many-coloured, loose-fitting; and one could not but notice all this because of this Colonial relative of theirs sitting on the settle between Kitty Mahony and the blaze of the fire. How different he was from the others! This ingathering he had foreseen, perhaps had foreseen Kitty Mahony's visit, and had made himself ready for it – had shaved himself, had put on his newest clothes – he had many suits of them – chosen his heaviest watch chain, his best linen; his boots he had polished; and his thinnish hair, after drenching it with odorous oils, he had carefully brushed and creased. The others, all of them, had contented themselves with bending their long backs and washing their hands in the current of water that ran from between two rocks swiftly across the close. It was their way mostly to keep their tattered everyday caps on their heads, indoors or out; and their hair was anyhow. Kitty Mahony was the only one who had taken any care with herself before coming across the fields from her father's house; she, however, always looked clean and tidy. Everybody knew that she was to marry the eldest son of the house, Mat Renahan.

Phil Cronin and Pat Renahan, the second son, were trying to recapture a way of dancing the 'Blackbird' they had seen at Dunmanway *feis* the Sunday before, three days ago. Again and again they had tried it. They would break down, begin to argue, resume the clatter, and break down once more. The musician – the youngest of all the boys, Tim – as soon as the rhythm of their feet went into confusion, would at once take the fife from his lips, lean down over his knees, and without a word, again begin his teasing of the sheep dog which, with stiffened limbs, lay stretched between his feet on the flags.

The old Colonial gave his head a critical shake: 'No,' he said, 'that's not it; that's not a bit like it,' and he turned and put his lips almost against Kitty Mahony's shapely ear: 'They're clumsy, see? They're clumsy, you know.'

'Isn't their own way just as good?' she answered him, carelessly, without turning her head. In the dance she was taking but little interest. She was eager for her lover to return from Dunmanway: she had had no thought that he would not be in his own house before her that evening. Her eyes were firm on the open doorway, on the chilly luminous space of sky that lay beyond the firelit figures moving and dancing on the flags. Yet even these few words the old man was glad to hear: 'Yes, but they're clumsy all the time. They couldn't put any finish on it even if they had the steps, not what you'd call finish.'

But the dancers had resumed.

Every now and then the father, John Renahan, without a word would plod slowly, bulkily, heavy-footed across the room, disappearing into the dairy for something or other. Massive, silent, heavy-featured, he thought but little of disturbing the laughing group in the middle of the flags. He would hulk through them in a straight line like a surly bull making through a herd of milkers. Without breaking the rhythm they would draw aside, lifting up their chests. They were so used to his ways that they took no anger from them. Once again he entered from the close and passed through them without a word, without a sign. As he did so, the girl's thoughts took on sudden and passionate life. All those about her, the dancers, the others, were nothing to her either. They were there in that kitchen and he she would have there was elsewhere. 'I wish he'd come, oh, I wish he'd come' – her passion spoke within her so earnestly that she feared she had said the words aloud. She looked from one to another, turning her eyes only, and when she caught the annoying voice again in her ear she was almost relieved: 'There's a great change in everything, in everything. They're awkward.'

She nodded twice, and he was encouraged. He raised his voice this time, speaking to the whole room: 'You may give it up. You can't master it. You're that awkward.'

The dancers slackened off, and Pat Lehane, an onlooker leaning against the wall, took the pipe from his mouth: 'Of course we're awkward, and as you'd say, damn awkward too. And 'tisn't for want of instruction we're awkward. Our little priest, down from the altar itself he's at us; and I'm afraid 'tis little improvement he's making in us. And the master, he says our equals for awkwardness isn't in Munster. And the returned Yanks, and they doing nothing at all themselves only strealing round, they're the worst of all. The awkward squad, that's what we are. The awkward squad that can't learn nothing.'

He was big, bony, high-coloured, with large flashing eyes, like an excited horse's, and a drooping moustache of strong hairs with dew drops pendulous at the tips of them; when speaking he threw up his head as if to give the voice free passage from the strong gristly throat. In gurgles and splashes it gushed from him; and the moods of his impetuous heart were felt in the uneven flow of it. 'The awkward squad that can't learn nothing,' and he threw his hand carelessly in the air as if there never could be question of amendment.

They were puzzled how to take him, but Tim, the musician, pointed his fife straight out at the dancers: 'The awkward squad,' he said, and throwing back his head, went into uncontrollable laughter. It was a way out. It took hold of them all; and the dancers began to look around for corners of seats to sink upon. The whole floor space in the centre of the room then lay vacant, the light falling on it.

Phil Cronin had already risen to get down the pack of cards when, whatever madness had seized on him, the old Colonial rose and stepped deliberately into the gaping space. 'Play it up, Sonny,' he said to the boy, with such a motion of the hand as he might use to call a porter in a railway station.

The boy gave him a swift glance, tightened his fife with one firm twist, blew in the hole of it, and started the tune, his eyes looking straight out from under his brows at the waiting figure. Very erect he stood, silent, in the glow of the fire, his arms stiffly downwards, his head raised, and an inward expression on his features: he was listening, listening – delaying to let the music take full possession of him. As silently they all stared at him. Then he sprang out. With a lightness, even daintiness, with a restraint that puzzled them, he was tapping out the rhythm as he had learned it more than sixty years ago before decay had come upon the local traditions. But the onlookers were not impressed. They were soon aware how limited his steps were; and to them who had often seen prize dancers from Cork city or Limerick, where the dancing is even better, his style seemed old-fashioned and slow. And of course after a few minutes there was but little life left in the aged limbs. They sagged at the knees. Noticing this they took to encouraging him, whispering wondering remarks on his skill and timing. The old fool danced and danced, would dance until he dropped, it seemed, although by now his performance was little better than a sort of dull floundering.

Pat Lehane then took to letting yells of delight out of him as if he could not help it: 'Whew! Whew!' he cried: and soon the others were joining in. In the midst of the bedlam John Renahan, the father, entered in his silent way, made across the room, brushing almost against the floundering figure whom, perhaps, the touch of a finger would now overturn. Silence fell upon them all. The fife still sang out, but not so boldly. The dancer floundered more helplessly than before. The tapping had become a sort of scraping and sliding.

As the father reached the door of the dairy room he looked along those ranged against the wall and without raising his voice said: ''Tis a shame for ye.'

Their eyes followed his rounded back as he went from them; then they looked at one another shyly. But the dancer held on. Somebody began to clap gently. They all took it up, and Pat Lehane reached his hand to the tottering figure and led Reen back to the settle.

The creature was trembling violently – one noticed it as he wiped his streaming face. His chest was heaving.

II

They heard the son of the house turning his horse and cart into the yard. Soon afterwards he entered, a bag of bran dragging heavily from his right arm.

As he sat eating his supper, he was given in whispers a glowing account of the Colonial's skill as a step-dancer. The Colonial himself, now in the centre of a little circle who, at the other side of the room, were shuffling and dealing the cards, let on not to hear what was being told to the young man. Yet they knew he was taking in every word of it. For all that whenever he played a card he raised his lips towards Kitty's ear, telling her that he was winning because she was there beside him.

When she saw that her lover had finished his meal she stood up from beside the Colonial. She could not further restrain herself. Her eyes were hot and flashing, her colour heightened. But the Colonial also stood up. He said with some huskiness in his voice, with some difficulty in making it carry: 'Maybe Mat is tired after his journey?'

Mat had been through three or four years of guerilla warfare, captaining his district. There were but few places in Munster he had not been in. He moreover had been in prison and following that in an internment camp. He had learned to shift for himself. From the colour in Kitty's cheeks, her angry eyes, her eager, parted lips, he guessed that the old man had been pestering her. He too took fire; yet he held himself in. He looked at him silently, and his smile broadened like the cold sunshine of a March day across a tract of bare countryside: 'Do I look tired?' he said.

Old Reen was confused: 'But if I went along with you, along with you, some of the way?'

The lover had put a cigarette between his lips. He leant across the table, stretching out his head until he had the tip of the cigarette above the chimney of the lamp that hung on the whitened wall. Kitty was standing uneasily in the middle of the floor. They heard the Colonial's voice again: 'My hat is upstairs.'

The cigarette had reddened: taking it from his lips Mat said nonchalantly: 'Up with you then.'

Stumbling in his eagerness Reen made up the stairs for the hat. He glowed to think what a surprising lot of things about dancing he would say to the two of them, things they could never have heard of. When he had disappeared, the lover impulsively flung open the door, held it open for the girl, put his arm about her shoulders passionately, and turned to those within: 'Give us half a mile start on that champion dancer of yours, half a mile – that's all we ask.'

They were gone, their spirits leaping within them.

When the Colonial came down with his new black hat in his hand, the roomful were very intent on their cards. He made straight out, pulling the door to behind him. Then the card-playing ceased and there was a blank silence.

The father broke it saying: 'I wish to God that old idiot would go back to where he came from. And I don't like what that pair is after doing either. I don't like it at all.'

His words took the merriment out of the gathering. Soon afterwards all except the sons and daughters of the family made out, but it was through the back door they went out. Their heavy boots were heard clamping up the rocky passage that led to the bohereen. That way they would not chance to come on a poor flustered creature groping in the darkness, making onward in sudden and reckless starts or standing still listening for any little stir that might let him know whether the lovers had gone east or west. Only in a dull way those neighbours felt that they should not care to come upon an old man so bothered in his thoughts. What a fool he was! – sixty-nine years of age, if a day, yet willing to let it slip from his memory that his life had been lived out, that his hair was grey, and that his arms would be empty for ever more. They gave no thought to the lovers. Yet, and for no reason it seemed, the spirits of the two of them as they made onwards began to leap with so astonishing an energy within them that their limbs for trembling could hardly keep the ground. Swifter and swifter they made on, whispering, wondering why they could no longer maintain their laughter.

THE AWAKENING

I

IVOR O'DONOVAN knew it was Ted Driscoll had called him: raising himself above the edge of the bunk he was just in time to see him manoeuvring that bear-like body of his through the narrow little hatchway, to see the splintery shutter slap to behind him. At the same moment he heard the Captain clearing his throat. The bunk opposite was his, and now Ivor saw him, all limbs, mounting awkwardly yet carefully over the edge of it. What between the sprawling limbs, the ungainly body and the hovering shadows above them, the place was narrowed to the size of a packing case. The timber work of the cabin had become so dark with the smoke of the stove that neither shadows nor limbs seemed to stir except when their movements were sudden and jerky. Ivor soon heard the Captain gathering his oil-cloths from the floor with one hand while with the other he dragged at the bunk where the cabin boy was sleeping; this Ivor knew, for as he sat up he caught the familiar words:

'Come on, come on; rouse up; they'll be waiting.'

The Captain he then saw disappear through the toy-like hatchway.

Ivor O'Donovan himself with a stifled groan descended life-lessly from the bunk to the floor. He drew on his sea boots – they had been his father's – drew his oil-cloths about him and in turn thrust his hand into the warm pile of old coats and sacking in which the sleeping boy was buried. He shook him vigorously: 'Come on, come on; they'll be waiting,' he said, and then hurried aloft into the drizzling darkness and took his place with the others.

The tightness that he felt on his brain from the moment Ted Driscoll had roused him seemed natural, not unexpected;

nevertheless he groaned to recollect the cause of it. Now, how-ever, as he settled down to his night's work, planted in the darkness there at the gunwale, braced against it, facing the Captain, the dripping fish-laden incoming net between them, he noticed that the tightness had somehow slackened, was still loosening its grip of him, so much so that he had some fear that it would again suddenly pounce on him with its first heat and violence.

Ted Driscoll and Tom Mescall were forward at the windlass; beyond them the boy, bending down, was coiling the rope they passed to him.

It was very dark. Everything was huge and shapeless. Anchored as she was, tethered besides, clumsy with the weight of dripping fish-spangled net coming in over the gunwale, the nobby was tossed and slapped about with a violence that surprised him; flakes of wet brightness were being flung everywhere from the one lamp bound firmly to the mast. Yet the night was almost windless, the sea apparently sluggish: there must be, he thought, a stiff swell beneath them. What most surprised him, however, was to find himself thinking about it. That evening coming down the harbour, he would not have noticed it. The whole way out, his back to the sea, he had stood upright, his feet set wide apart, his hands in his belt, glum, silent, gazing at the cabin boy who, sprawled upon the deck, was intent upon the baited line he had flung over the stern. But as far as Ivor was concerned that patch of deck might have been free to the sun: his own anger, his passion, was between him and the world. That afternoon he had waited for Chrissie Collins for two hours. At the very start he knew, he *knew*, so at least he had told himself she would not come. For all that he had gone hot and cold, again and again, while waiting for her. He had broken from the spot impulsively: a moment later he had trailed back again, giving her one more quarter of an hour to make good in. Then when his rage was at the peak, hurrying down to the jetty, he had suddenly caught sight of her, all brightness, stepping briskly up the hillside, the schoolmaster walking beside her, as eager as herself. Her head was bent, her eyes were fixed on her dainty toe-caps, and she was listening complacently to the schoolmaster's blather. Only that he should have to tear through the village and it filled with the gathering crews, he'd have told her what he thought of her.

With his eyes downwards on the sprawling limbs of the boy, he had indulged, as if it were the only thing for a man to do, the heat of the passion that that one glimpse of her had aroused in him.

Now, ten hours later, braced against the timbers, swaying and balancing, freeing the net, freeing the rope, grabbing at the odd dog fish, the odd blob of seaweed, the tangle of seawrack, flinging them all, as they came, far out, clear of the rising meshes – he was puzzled to contrast his present indifference with his stifling anger of the afternoon. Yet he was not pleased with himself. This calming down of his seemed like a loss of manhood. His mind could not, it appeared, stay fixed on the one thought. He found himself noticing what he had never noticed before – how the mackerel, entangled in the meshes, would catch the light of the worried lamp and appear just like a flight of shining steel-bright daggers hurtling by him from gunwale to hold. Never to have noticed so striking a thing before, how curious! But had the Captain ever noticed it? He glanced shyly at the aged face opposite him and started, for the Captain, he saw, had had his eyes fixed on him, all the time, perhaps! And Ivor recalled, reddening slightly, that also that afternoon while lost in his own passionate thoughts he had caught him observing him with the selfsame silent gravity. Why should he do it? He was Captain. But the boat was his, Ivor's; and one day when he was somewhat older, and when his mother was willing to trust him, he would sail it. But this was unfair, he felt, for the Captain, this Larry Keohane, had been ever and always his father's dearest friend and shipmate, had sailed with him till he was drowned, had indeed been with him that very night; and afterwards he it was who had undertaken the management of the boat for them; and in such a way that not a penny of the fish money had ever gone astray on them. Later on, now two years ago, he had taken Ivor on board as one of the crew, and taught him whatever he now knew of sailoring and deep-sea fishing. There was surely plenty of time yet for thinking of playing the Captain. Besides, the selling of the fish was trickier work than the catching of it. His eyes fell on the claw-like hands of the

Captain, they were twisted with rheumatism, and a flood of kindly feeling for this grave and faithful friend suddenly swept over him with such power that he found his own hands fumbling at the net without either skill or strength in them. To glance again at the Captain's face he did not dare.

'Up, boys, up!' he impulsively cried to the windlass men as if to encourage them. In the clinging darkness, although the drizzle was becoming lighter and lighter, he could make out only the shapeless bulk of themselves and the windlass: two awkward lumps of manhood rising and falling alternately, their sou'westers and oil-cloths catching some of the flakes of the wet brightness that were flying around everywhere. 'Twas curious work, this fishing. Like a family they were, confined in a tiny space, as far almost from the other boats as they were from the houses on the hills where the real families were now huddled together in sleep. The real families – each of them was different from the others. Tom Mescall's was the most good-for-nothing in the whole place. Others had quite nice houses, clean and well-kept. But most strange of all was it to have him, Ivor, thinking of such things, his head calm and cool (and he thereupon grabbed a huge dog-fish from the passing net and with a gesture deliberately sweeping sent it far out into the splashing darkness).

II

The work went on and on and Ivor could not help all kinds of thoughts from crossing his brain, nor help noticing the onward rush of them. The dragging of the net was done in silence, no one speaking until they each and all were sure that they had had a fairly good catch, and that all the nets were heavy. Ivor then was aware that some dull and lifeless conversation was passing to and fro between the men at the windlass. He was hailed suddenly by one of them, Ted Driscoll: 'Look where Leary is, east.'

Far off, east, Ivor saw a tiny light. As he watched it the other voice came through the darkness, half speaking, half calling:

' 'Aith then he wouldn't be long swinging on to the Galley in there.'

'Is it Leary, do you think?' Ivor asked the Captain, and he was answered:

' 'Tis like the place he'd be.'

Ivor then sent his gaze ranging the sea noting the disposition of the boats. They were far off, nearly all of them. Some were miles beyond Galley Head. Others were away towards the west. Here and there a pair of lights seemed to ride close together, only seemed, however, while an odd one, like Leary's, played the hermit in unaccustomed waters. Far to the west the great light of the Fastnet every few moments threw a startling beam on the waters and, quenching suddenly, would leave a huge blackness suspended before their very eyes, blinding them. He noticed how, little by little, the timid lamps of the fishing fleet would in time manage again to glimmer through that darkness. He bent himself once more on the work, thinking over and over again what a curious way they had of making a living. On the land at this time of night every one of the houses was a nest of sleep – chilly walls and warm bedding. After all Chrissie Collins was a farmer's daughter, a small hillside farmer, a 'sky' farmer. Farm houses had ways of their own. Fishermen also had ways of their own. The next time he met her he would hold his head as high as hers.

The dragging went on and on. The unending clanking of the windlass, the wet mass of the net, the grip of his feet on the narrow way between gunwale and hold while the boat tossed and tugged, the sudden flashes of the lamp, the long silences of them all, the far-off lonely-looking lights of the other anchored nobbies and ketches, the bold startling blaze of the Fastnet, and above all the stream of shining daggers sweeping by – for the first time in his life he reckoned up the features of the fisherman's calling, and felt some sort of pleasant excitement in doing so, as if he had heard some good news or come upon some unexpected treasure. He could not understand it.

When the last of the nets was in they tidied the decks, pitching the seawrack into the sea. He heard the Captain say to Driscoll, whose head was bent down on the confused mass of fish and net in the hold: 'Good, and a fair size too. I'm very glad.'

'I'm very glad,' repeated Ivor in his mind, wonderingly, yet feeling that the words fitted in. He noticed Driscoll and Mescall, their arms hanging heavily after their night's work, their sea boots lumping noisily along the deck, going aft to the little cabin, making down the hatchway without a word. The boy had gone down previously. The waft of the smell of boiling fish, of boiling potatoes, that came from the smoke pipe told of his toil below. To Ivor it was very welcome. He was hungry; and besides they would presently all meet together round the little stove. 'I'm very glad,' he whispered, not knowing why. And the smoke, he saw, was like a lighted plume rising from the top of the iron pipe.

The Captain drew closer to him. He took the fragment of pipe from his mouth and, smothering the glowing bowl in his fist, pointed sou'west:

' 'Tis Casey that's going in.'

'Is it?' Ivor said, also picking out the one craft in all the far-scattered fleet that had got under weigh, that, very slowly, for there was scarcely a breath of wind, was making for the land.

'Maybe 'tisn't,' the Captain then said.

'I'm sure 'tis him all right,' Ivor said, though he was not sure at all.

They stood side by side following with their eyes the distant slow-moving light. There was scarcely a morning that some boat or other did not hoist sail the moment their catch was made and hasten in. There was always some special reason for it. And the other craft, every one of them, would make guesses at the boat, as also at the cause of her lifting anchor in such haste. The others were content to make the pier any time before the buyers had received from other fishing ports and from Dublin itself their morning telegrams fixing the day's prices. Ivor thought how it was nearly always something having to do with the real household, with the real family, that brought a fisherman to break that way from the fishing grounds before the others. Sickness, or the necessity for some early journey, or the emigrating of a son or daughter. 'I remember your father, one time we were out, and far out too, south the Galley, ten mile it might be, how he called out and we not ready at all: "That'll do, boys, we'll make in."'

The Captain's quiet husky voice stopped, and Ivor wondered if that was all he had to say; but the tale was taken up again:

'That was twenty-two years ago this month.'

Ivor was once more astray, he could not find reason in the words.

'Yes,' he said, quietly.

'That night he expected a son to be born to him; and he wasn't disappointed.'

Ivor knew that he himself was the child that on that night came into the world; but what kept him silent was the Captain's gravity. Such matter among them had always been a cause for laughter. Ivor was nevertheless glad that the Captain had spoken seriously; for all that, fearing to betray his own state of mind, he answered:

'That's not what's taking Casey in anyhow.'

The Captain did not seem to hear.

'All night long,' he said, 'I'm thinking of things that I saw happen out here on these waters for the last fifty-four years.'

Ivor raised his head in astonishment. Why should such recollections have set the Captain examining him the whole night long?

'Strange things,' the Captain resumed, 'strange voices, sad things too, very sad, things that should not happen.'

After all, the Captain was in the humour for spinning a yarn, that was all. But, instead of the yarn, the Captain, scanning the sky, merely said:

''Tis going south; the day will be fine, very fine.'

Ivor too felt a slight stir in the air, and from the hatchway Driscoll called them down.

'With God's help 'twill be a fine day,' the Captain said once more, throwing the words over his shoulder as they moved aft, one behind the other, sauntering along in their heavy sea boots.

The air in the cabin was reeking with the smell of fish and potatoes, and so thick with fire smoke and tobacco smoke that one could hardly make things out. There was hardly room for the five of them there. The boxes they sat on were very low and the men's knees, on which they held the plates, seemed to fill the whole space. One felt the warmth against one's face like a cushion. Yet Ivor welcomed it all – the heat, the smell of the good food, the close companionship – not alone for the comfort it all wrapped him round with but for the memory it raised in him of those many other nights on which he had experienced it, his body as cold as ice and his fingers unable to move themselves. The others were already eating lustily and noisily.

'Not too bad, not too bad,' he cried out cheerily, planting himself between Driscoll and Mescall, just because they were head to head and nose to nose in earnest argument. They took no notice of him, continuing it still across his very face. Driscoll, who was the simplest of them, was showing how Mrs O'Connor, the shopkeeper who supplied them with all and sundry, had done him out of two-and-elevenpence, and Mescall, who, in spite of his harum-scarum wife and family, was their merrymaker, was explaining how she had tried the same trick with him and how he had laid a trap for her and caught her – a trap so clever that Driscoll had no idea how it worked or how by using it he could recover his two-and-elevenpence. The boy was heard plunging vessels in a bucket of water. All the time the Captain held his peace, and Ivor, noticing it, glanced at him, wondering if he were still recalling what he had seen happen on the fishing grounds during his long lifetime upon them.

Leisurely yet ravenously the meal went on, and when they thought of it, or at least so it seemed, first Mescall and then Driscoll, who had had no sleep till then, threw off their sea boots and disappeared into the darkness of the bunks. In the same haphazard way Ivor, the Captain, and the boy returned to the deck.

At last they had her moving: her sails were flapping, coming suddenly between their eyes and the dazzling flood of light out-welling from sea and sky. When they filled, when she settled down, Ivor heard the Captain say in a voice that sounded unusual:

'I suppose I may as well go aft.'

Unable to account for the words Ivor answered in mere confusion of mind:

' 'Tis better, I suppose,' as if the matter was not quite clear.

Silently the Captain went aft to the tiller, and Ivor, as was his custom, threw himself on the pile of rope in the bow: there was no more to be done. He felt the streaming sun, into which a benign warmth was beginning to steal, bathing his body from his hair down. After the work of the night, after the food, a pleasant lassitude, as thick as his thick clothing, clung to him. The cabin boy was already fast asleep on the deck, cuddled up like a dog, his face buried in his arms. Ivor felt sleepy too, yet before he yielded to it, he recalled the memory of the handful of them, cut off from all other company, working silently in the drizzling darkness, the tossing lamp momently flashing in their eyes and lighting up their dripping hands. He recollected too the rise and fall of the awkward bodies of the two men at the windlass, the clanking of the axle, and the uncompanioned boy beyond them working away in almost total darkness. Clearer than all he recalled the flight of glittering spear heads sweeping by between himself and the Captain. Then also the group in the smoky cabin, the hearty faces, the blue and white plates, the boy plunging the vessels in the water. How different from what was now before his eyes! The sea was wide, wide; the air brisk, the seagulls screaming, quarrelling, gathering in schools, dashing at the transparent crests of the waves or sweeping in great curves to the east, the west, everywhere, their high-pitched cries filling the air with a rapture that opened the heart and at the same time alarmed it. Yes, very different, yet his pictures of the night-time – the groups silently working in the darkness, the gathering in the little cabin – these were dearer to him just now than the bright freshness of the morning. He recalled the unexpected words of the Captain – 'I'm very glad.'

At last the drowsiness that he would keep from him over-powered him.

He awoke to find the boy's hand timidly unclutching his shoulder:

'Himself wants you.'

Rising up he caught the Captain's eyes resting upon him with a calmness that surprised him, that disturbed him. He went aft.

'You're wanting me?'

'Sit down there, Ivor, there's a thing I have to say to you.'

Fearing some reference to Chrissie Collins, some questioning, some good advice, Ivor sat down without a word. The Captain blurted out:

'Ivor, boy, 'tis time for you to sail what belongs to you.'

As he spoke his hand lifted from the tiller – an instinctive giving up of office. Instantly however it fell upon it again. Ivor perceived the action with his eyes, not with his mind, for the words had sent a thrill of delight through his whole body. Everything he had been noticing that night of nights was in that overwhelming sensation – the darkness, the clanking windlass, the shining fish, the cabin, the seagulls, everything – but he caught hold of himself and said:

'But, Lar, why that? Why that?'

'Because 'tis time for you.'

'But why so? 'Tisn't how you're going from us; what's after happening?'

'Nothing. Nothing. Only all the night I'm thinking of it. 'Tis the right thing. Herself is at me too. If there's a touch of wind in the night, she don't sleep a wink.'

'Oh! If the boat goes we all go.'

'You can't talk to them like that. Anyway 'tis right. 'Tis your due. We got on well, Ivor. Them that's gone, they deserved as much. We done our best, all of us.'

'Lar, 'tis better wait till my mother hears of it.'

'If you wouldn't mind I'd give you Pat to be in my place. He'd be better for you than a stranger.'

Again that thrill of delight went through him. He thought at once if the Captain had not offered his son, a stranger would have

23

to be brought into the boat, one of those unlucky creatures perhaps who had given the best of their lives sailoring the wide world over, creatures who were not trustworthy, who had bitter, reckless tongues, who destroyed the spirit of goodwill in any boat they ever got footing in. That danger the Captain had put aside. There was therefore a clear way before him, and a boat's crew after his own heart.

'I'm thankful, Lar, and herself will be thankful; but what will you be doing with yourself?'

A little smile grew upon the Captain's face, and both of them raised their eyes to scan the hillsides they were approaching. In the sun which now lay thick upon their brown-green flanks, nestling in the zig-zag ravines they saw the little groups of houses where the fishermen lived. Some of the cottages, snow-white, faced full in the eyes of the morning, sunning themselves. Others were turned aside, still asleep in the shadows, catching a bright ray only on chimney head or gable.

'Wouldn't I want to sit in the sun and smoke my pipe as well as another; that will do, Ivor. Ted's coming up. He's after smelling the land. In the evening I'll fix up with your mother.'

V

It was a Saturday morning. That night and the next they would all sleep in their own houses, not in the boats.

In the evening the Captain went to Ivor's house, and, as he said himself, fixed things up with his mother. Then he shook hands with them all, with Mrs O'Donovan, Ivor, his two sisters, and his young brother, who was only a boy. He then set off up the hill for his home.

Afterwards, standing up before the bit of glass nailed against the wall, Ivor stood shaving himself. His heart was blazing within him, his cheeks burning, for the Captain had been speaking his praises, and all his people had been staring at him.

It had been a day of uninterrupted sunshine, and now a bright heaven, slow to darken itself, although the sun had been a long time sunken, darkened to blackness every ridge, bush, tree clump, roof and gable that stood against it. On the roads and fields it still threw down a persistent glow; and Ivor went in and out the doorway praying for the dusk to thicken. In the midst of the Captain's praise of him he had felt a burning desire to see his boat once again with his own eyes, to be sure it was still there at the pier, where, with scores of others, it was fastened. He wanted to feel the tiller beneath his right hand – that above all. And yet he would not care to have any of his neighbours see him doing so. Nightfall was never so slow in coming. At last, however, with a yearning look at the still livid sky he set off down the path towards the roadway. He could gambol, he could sing, only that at the same time he had thoughts of the heavy responsibility that in future would rest upon him. He strove to calm himself, to walk with the appearance of one who had no other business than to breathe the cool air of the evening. He knew there would be groups of men still in the public houses as well as along the sea wall; and these he wished to escape. Before entering the village he vaulted over the wall, descended the rocks, and made along by the edge of the waters. At a point beyond the farthest house he climbed on to the road again, and, more assured, made towards the deserted pier. At its extreme end, almost, his *Wildwood* was moored. The pier itself, the debris on it, the fish boxes, the ranks of barrels – as well as all the conglomeration of boats along its sheltered side – the whole had become one black mass sharply cut out against the livid waters of the harbour. On a standard at its very end a solitary oil lamp, as warm in colour as the waters were cold, was burning away in loneliness. Towards it, and as quietly, almost as stealthily as if on a guilty errand, he steered his way. He was glad when the piles of barrels so obstructed the view that no one could spy him from the road. Doubtless the news was already abroad; by now the men were surely all speaking about it; as for himself, it was very strange coming at the time it did, coming, without expectation, at the tail-end of the night when for the first time he knew what it was to be a true fisherman. He was glad Chrissie Collins had her schoolmaster. It left himself as free as air. And thinking the thought he breathed in the pleasant coolness of the night, yet could not, it seemed, gulp down enough of it. Glad of the darkness, of the loneliness, he suddenly threw out his two arms wide apart, stretching them from him, and drew the keen air slowly and deliciously through his nostrils. And breathing still in the selfsame manner went forward a few steps. Then suddenly, he saw a figure, outlined against the tide, seated on some fish boxes, gazing silently at the nobby for which he himself was making! He knew it was the Captain. His arms fell and he stood quite still. 'Oh!' he said, in a sudden stoppage of thought. He turned stealthily and retraced his steps, fearful of hearing his name cried out. But nothing was to be heard except his own careful footfall; and before he reached the road again he had recovered himself. It surely was a sad thing for Larry Keohane to have his life drawing to an end. Why was it that nothing can happen to fill one person with happiness without bringing sadness and pain to somebody else? Yet the Captain, he remembered, that evening in his mother's house had been quite cheerful, had told them how glad he was that they had made quite a good catch on his last night, and what a peaceful night it had been! And what a fine boat the *Wildwood* was; and how happy he was to be leaving her in hands that would not treat her foully; indeed he could well say that he was flinging all responsibility from his shoulders; and that was a thing he had been looking forward to for a long time. And saying that, he had gone from them cheerily and brightly. Yes, yes, but here surely was the real Captain, this seaman staring at his boat.

Ivor waited, sitting on the wall in the darkness, for a long time. At last he heard the slow steps of the old man approaching, saw him pass by – saw him very indistinctly for the darkness, yet knew that he had his hand covering his pipe in his mouth and his head on one side, a way he had when he was thinking to himself. He waited until the footsteps had died away up the hillside; then he rose to resume his own quest towards the nobby. He found he could not bring himself to do so. He did not want to do so.

With slow lingering steps, with stoppings and turnings, at last he too began to make towards his home. His head was flung up, almost flung back. More than once he told himself that he didn't ever remember the sky to have been so full of stars. Somehow he felt like raising his hand towards them.

CARRIG-AN-AFRINN

I

DUNERLING EAST was its name, the model farm in all that countryside. Only after many years it had come to be so; and Michael Hodnett, the farmer who had made it so, lay fast asleep in his armchair on the right-hand side of the front door. As of its own weight his big strong-looking head had sunken itself deep into his deep chest. The sunshine of the October afternoon was depositing itself lavishly upon him, thickening upon him, it seemed, while slumber bound him there, so huge and lumpish, so inert, so old and fallen. Dunerling East just now was looking more model-like than ever before. The house itself had had all its sashes, its doors, its timber work painted afresh; its blinds and curtains had been renewed; its ivy growths trimmed; and the whole farm, even its farthest fields and screening thickets, spoke of the same well-being, the same skilful management. The sleeper might lawfully take his rest, his spirit had so indisputably established itself everywhere within the far-flung mearings. Even were he to pass away in his sleep, and stranger folk as reckless as might be, to come into possession of the land, many years must needs go by before Dunerling East became hail-fellow-well-met with the farms round about it, shaggy and scraggy as they were, waterlogged in the bottoms and bleached or perished on the uplands, unsheltered by larch or beech.

All this cleaning up had been done in preparation for the first coming together, after many years, of all or nearly all that were left of the family. The arrival of Stephen Hodnett, the third youngest son, from the States had been the occasion. He had brought with him his young wife, and, as well, an elder sister of hers, a young widow, for whose distraction indeed the voyage had been undertaken. Of all the sons of the house this son, Stephen, perhaps had done best: he was now manager of a large bakery store in New

York. But the brother next to him in years, Finnbarr, had done well too. He was come, also accompanied by his wife, from Kerry, where he managed a very successful creamery. The son to whom the care of the farm had fallen, to whom indeed the farm now legally belonged, Nicholas by name, had maintained it in the condition to which his father, this old man asleep in the chair, had brought it; perhaps he had even bettered it, but, of course, the land had been got into good heart long before it fell to his turn to till it. Nicholas, though older than Stephen or Finnbarr, had never married: he would wait until his father's death. The only other son of the house was up in Dublin – Father Philip Hodnett, a curate in St Multose's parish. He was the one living member who was not at present in Dunerling East. Within the house lurked somewhere the eldest living of all the old man's family, Ellen, the second child born to him. She looked old enough to be the mother of those mentioned, even of Nicholas, the eldest of them. She was sixty and looked more. Her cheeks were thin and haggard, colourless, her hair grey, and her eyes stared blankly at the life moving before them as if it were but an insipid and shadowy thing when compared with what moved restlessly, perhaps even disastrously, within the labyrinths of her own brain. On her the mothering of the whole family had fallen when Michael Hodnett buried his wife in Inchigeela.

From the feet of the sleeping figure the ground fell away downwards to a bracken-covered stream. Beyond the bracken it rose again; much more suddenly however, so suddenly indeed that the red earth showed in patches through the tangled greenery. Those reddish patches looked like corbels supporting the cornice-like ledge of the upward-sloping grazing grounds above. Just now, along that sun-drenched ledge, a procession of shapely deep-uddered cattle was moving from left to right, the beasts in single file or in pairs or groups, deliberately pacing. Thirty-one milkers were to pass like that, making for the unseen bridgeway across the stream in the hollow. Presently they would dip from sight and again be discovered in the tree-covered passage trailing up towards the milking sheds, the rich sunshine catching their deep-coloured flanks and slipping swiftly and suddenly from their horns and moving limbs. Anyone who had ever come to know how deeply the sight of that afternoon ritual used to thrill the old man, now so sunken in his sleep, could hardly forbear from waking him to witness it.

Behind the cattle sauntered Nicholas. His head was bent, and in his right hand a sliver from a sally tree lazily switched the cattle along. Although a working day, he was dressed in his Sunday clothes. His gaiters were new, rich brown in colour, and had straps about them; his boots also were new and brown. All day since morning his visitors, his brothers Stephen and Finnbarr and their people, had been away motoring in the hills towards the west – around Keimaneigh and Gougane Barra – and he had found the idle day as long as a week. 'Stay where you are,' he had said to one of the labourers who were digging out potatoes in the fields behind the house; 'stay where you are, and I'll bring them in,' and he was glad of the chance to go through the fields one after another until he was come to where the impatient cattle were gathered, anxious and crying, about the fastened gate. Their time for milking was overdue, and they needed no urging towards the sheds. When they were safe across the bridge he left them to themselves: by that time the first of them were already head-bound in the stalls. Closing a gate behind them he made diagonally up the sloping field. At his approach his father suddenly raised his head.

''Tisn't Sunday?' he said, and then, recollecting himself: 'They haven't come back yet?'

'Any moment now,' Nicholas answered. He then turned his back on him and gazed across the countryside where a couple of roads could be picked out. The weather had been very fine for some weeks and little clouds of sunny dust wavered above them.

'Are the cows in?'

'I'm after bringing them across.'

'Is Finn after looking at them?'

'Yes, he'd get rid of the Kerry, he said.'

'Didn't I tell you! Didn't I tell you!'

He had filled up with passionate life. As he blurted out the words, he raised his heavy stick in his blob of a hand. Nicholas glanced away from him, and again searched the countryside with his eyes:

'They won't be long now: 'tis as good for us to be going in!'

He put his arm beneath his father's. He lifted him. The old man's right foot trailed uselessly along the ground. But his thoughts were on the cows:

' 'Tis often I do be thinking on the two beasts we had and we coming hither from Carrig-an-afrinn. Scraggy animals, scraggy, splintery things.'

II

Mrs Muntleberry, the young American widow, and her sister, Stephen's wife, were both thoughtful gentle women; it was plain in their quiet eyes, their quiet faces. After the meal, homely in its way, but good, they now sat bent forward earnestly staring at the old man who was keeping himself so alert and upright in their midst, ruling the roomful with word, gesture, glance. Of his power of work, of his downrightness, they had, of course, often heard from Stephen: in Stephen himself they had found something of the same character: until to-day, however, they had not realised how timid in him were the strong traits of his father's character. They had been motoring in a world of rock-strewn hillsides; they had swung into glens that struck them cold, so bleak they were, so stern-looking even in the softest tide of the year. Carrig-an-afrinn they had not actually passed through: it would have meant threading slowly up many twisting narrow hillside bohereens in which their car could scarcely turn: perhaps also Stephen had not cared to have them actually come upon the bedraggled homestead – little else than a hut – from which the Hodnetts had risen. They had, however, gone as close to it as the main road allowed them, had seen, and felt almost in their bones, the niggardliness of life among those hillsides of tumultuously tumbled rocks. That wayfaring in bleak places had brought them to understand Stephen's father; even if he were no different this evening, had remained as he had been ever since their arrival – drowsing between sleep and waking, mumbling old songs, sometimes losing count of who they were – they would nevertheless because of this day's excursioning have more deeply understood the tough timber that was in him. But all the evening he had been quite different. The names of old places, of old families, had been in the air about him. He grew young to hear them, to bethink himself of them. They had aroused him. Stephen had forgotten many of them. He would say, ' 'Tis north from Inchimore,' and his father had enough to catch at: ' 'Tis the Sweenys were north of Inchimore. 'Tis Keimcorravoola you're thinking of.' And of itself either the place name or the family name was enough to spur the old man's brain to all manner of recollections. So it had been with him all the evening, alert as they had never seen him, a new man, and not a bit modest about his powers when young, whether at fighting or hurley or farming. His stick was in the air about their heads: and once without warning he had brought it down on the table, making them all leap to their feet and grab at the dancing tea things – down with all his force lest they should not clearly understand how final had been the stroke with which he had felled a Twomey man in a faction fight at Ballyvourney. And when in speaking of some other ancient wrestling bout he referred to his adversary's trunk, how he had clasped it and could not be shaken off, the two women looked at himself, alert yet lumpish before them, noted his body's girth and depth, and felt that 'trunk' was indeed the right word to use of such bodies.

Finn's wife, the Kerry woman, was enjoying it heartily. Her Kerry eyes, deep hazel in colour, were dancing to watch the old man's antics, grotesque and unashamed, were dancing also to note the quiet, stilly, well-schooled Americans opening the doors of their minds to comprehend adequately this rough-hewn chunk of peasant humankind. The expression coming and going on the faces of the three sons, she also enjoyed. She watched to see how they took every gross countryside word and phrase that would unconcernedly break from the old man's lips. Her own Finn she held for the cleverest of them because he had the gift of slipping in some contrary word that would excite his father to still more energetic gestures or more emphatic expletives.

In time old Hodnett had exhausted the tale of the great deeds of his prime: a gentler mood descended on him: 'Like you'd shut that door, or like you'd tear a page out of a book and throw it from you, I put an end to all that folly and wildness. Listen now, let ye listen now, this is what happened and I coming over here from Carrig-an-afrinn.'

III

He told them how on that day, which of all the days of his long life stood most clearly before his mind, he had made swiftly home from the fair at Macroom. Michael, his eldest son, a boy of about sixteen years at the time, had hastened down from the potato field on hearing the jolting of the returning cart. As usual with him he examined his father's face. He was at first relieved and then puzzled to discover from it that his father had scarcely taken any drink during that long day of absence from home, of boon companionship in the town. More than that, his father was going about in a sort of constraint, as if he had had something happen to him while away, or had come upon some tidings which now must be dwelt upon within himself. Yet he did not seem gloomy or rough, and he could be gloomy enough and rough enough when the fit was on him. Often and often after a long day in Macroom, he had turned in from the road, flung the reins on the horse's back, and without preface begun to heap maledictions on the head of the villain pig buyers from Cork with whom he had been trafficking. To-day he was different:

'Is Johnny above?' he questioned his son as he loosed the horse from the shafts. The boy nodded.

'Up with you then. Up with you while there's light in it.'

The boy, climbing up to where he had left old Johnny, who was helping them to dig out the potatoes, was still wondering over the mood his father had returned in.

'What is he after getting?' the labourer asked him.

'Four ten.'

'He'd get more in Dunmanway last Friday.'

'He's satisfied. He says he is.'

Before long they saw himself coming through the gap. 'What way are they up along there?' he asked them, nodding his head towards the sloping ridges they had been digging.

'Small enough then,' his son answered.

The father stooped and picked up one of the potatoes. He began to rub it between his finger and thumb.

'They'll be different in Dunerling East,' his son said, complacently tossing his head.

As if that were the last thing he had expected to come from the boy's lips his father looked sharply at him.

Dunerling East was the farm he had been for several weeks negotiating the purchase of. It was ten miles away towards the east, ten miles farther from the hardness of the mountains, the cold rains, the winds, the mists. In those ten miles the barren hills that separate Cork from Kerry had space to stretch themselves out, to die away into gentle curves, to become soft and kind. So curiously his father had looked at him the boy wondered if something had not happened to upset the purchase. He was not surprised when his father, peering at him under his brows, spoke to him in a cold voice:

'The potatoes might be better. The grass too. And the cattle. Only the Hodnetts might be worse.'

Michael glanced at the labourer, then back at his father. He found him still skinning the potato with his hard thumb. But he could also see, young and all as he was, that his thought was not on the potato, big or little. The labourer had once more bent to his digging; and Michael, withdrawing his eyes slowly from his father's face, spat on his hands and gripped the spade: yet he could not resist saying:

'They're poor return for a man's labour.'

He scornfully touched the potatoes hither and thither with the tip of his spade, freeing them from the turfy earth, black and fibrous. They were indeed small.

The father seemed careless of their size. He stood there, a solid piece of humankind, huge, big-faced, with small round eyes, shrewd-looking, not unhumorous. He said: 'If I hadn't that fifty pound paid on it, I'd put Dunerling East out of my mind.'

He turned from them and made for the gap through which he had come. They questioned each other with their eyes and then stared after the earnest figure until the broken hillside swallowed it up.

It was a soft, still evening. Here and there a yellow leaf fell from the few scattered birch trees growing among the rocks which, on every side, surrounded the little patch of tilled earth. A robin was singing quietly, patiently – the robin's way. The air was moist; and because a break in the weather seemed near, they worked on, the two of them, until they could no longer see the potatoes. Then Johnny straightened his back, lit his bit of a pipe and shouldered his spade. Together both of them, taking long slow strides, made down towards the house. Suddenly the boy said:

'Look at himself!'

They saw him standing upright on one of the numerous ledges of rock which broke up through the surface of their stubble field. He had his back towards them. He was staring downwards, overlooking his own land, towards the straggling road, staring intently, although little except the general shape of the country-side could now be distinguished.

'Is it? Is it him at all, do you think?' old Johnny asked.

'' Tis sure,' Michael answered. Then he cried out, sending the vowels travelling:

'Ho-o! Ho-o!'

His father turned and after a pause began to make towards them. Awkwardly they awaited him; they did not know what to say. He said:

'' Tis at Carrig-an-afrinn I was looking.'

Carrig-an-afrinn was the name of the whole farm, a large district, mostly a hillside of rock and heather; they were standing in Carrig-an-afrinn: but they understood that what he had been looking at was Carrig-an-afrinn itself – the Rock of the Mass, the isolated pile of rock by the roadside from which the ploughland had got its name.

They walked beside him then.

'I'm after hearing a thing this day I never knew before,' he said, and then stopping up and examining their faces he added:

' 'Tis what I heard: in any place where a Mass was ever celebrated an angel is set on guard for ever and ever.'

' 'Twould be a likely thing,' the old labourer said.

'I never heard tell of it,' Michael said.

'Myself never heard tell of it,' his father snapped out.

' 'Twould be a likely thing,' old Johnny said again, 'remembering the nature of the Mass.'

'Who was it told you?'

'One who was well able!'

The three of them turned and looked downwards towards the rough altar-like pile of rock where Mass used to be said secretly for the people in the penal days when it was felony to celebrate Mass in public. Only the pile of rock was visible, and that not distinctly, so thick the light had become.

'You know very well that Mass was said there hundreds and hundreds of times.'

The father spoke to his son almost as if he had been contradicting him. He received no reply. Then he added in a suddenly deepened voice:

'Likely that place is thick with angels.'

The labourer uncovered his head without a word.

In stillness they stood there on the lonely hillside; and in the darkening rocks and fields there was no sound, except of small things stirring at their feet. After a few seconds, the farmer faced again for the house. Without thought, it seemed, he avoided the rocky patches. Indeed even at midnight he could have walked unperplexed through those rock-strewn fields. The others heard his voice coming to them in the dusk over his shoulder:

' 'Tis a strange thing that I never heard of that wonder until I'm just leaving the place for good and all. A strange thing; and it frightens me.'

When they found themselves free of the fields and in the *poirse*, or laneway, that led up to their yard, he said again with sudden passion:

35

' 'Tis a small thing would make me break the bargain.'

The boy flared up:

'A queer thing you'd do then.'

'Queer!'

'It may be years and years before we have the chance of buying a place like Dunerling East.'

He spoke the name as if that of itself were worth the purchase money.

'Carrig-na-afrinn is not a bad farm at all.'

At this Michael burst out:

'Johnny, do you hear him? And he raging and swearing at them rocks as long as I remember – raging and swearing at them as if they were living men and they against him! And he praying to God to take us out of it before his eyes were blinded with the years. And now he'd stay in it!'

Of that incident and of the night that followed it, the old man, forty-four years after, remembered every detail – every word spoken and every thought that disturbed his rest.

IV

Having given them to understand all that has been here set down, he went on: 'I tell ye, I didn't shut an eye that night, only thinking and thinking and I twisting and turning in my bed. When I looked back through the years and thought of what a poor place Carrig-an-afrinn was – there was scarcely a poorer – 'twas little less than a miracle to have me able to buy out a big place like this – a place that had been in the grip of the gentry for hundreds and hundreds of years. And up to that I always thought that I had no one to thank for it but myself – the strength of my own four bones, but after what I was told in Macroom that day, how did I know but that maybe it was in Carrig-an-afrinn itself the luck was? and that good fortune would follow whoever lived in it like good Christians, and that maybe secret friends would help them, and they at the ploughing or waiting up in the nights for a calf to come, or a young foal or a litter of bonamhs itself? Who knows? Who knows? And what puzzled me entirely was that I should be ignorant of all that until the very day, as you may say, I was settled on leaving it. It frightened me. While we were in Carrig-an-afrinn no great sickness befell us or misfortune, except a horse to break his leg or a cow to miscarry or a thing like that; and I thought of all the strong farmers I was after seeing in my time, and they having to sell off their places and scatter away with themselves into Cork or Dublin, or maybe to America itself. Sure this place itself, if ye saw it when we came hither, the dirty state 'twas in, the land gone back, exhausted, and the house and sheds broken, everything in wrack and ruin – 'tisn't with a light heart ye'd undertake it. But of course only for that I couldn't have bought it all at all. So I said to myself, and I listening to the clock ticking at the foot of the bed, I'm undertaking that big place, and maybe 'twon't thrive with me. And if it fails me, where am I? That's what I said. If it fails me, where am I? I tell ye, I was broken with thinking on it. And all the time, and this is the queerest thing of all, I heard someone saying, "Carrig-an-afrinn, Carrig-an-afrinn. Carrig-an-afrinn, Carrig-an-afrinn." And not once nor twice nor three times, but all the night long, and I thinking and thinking. Of course, there was no one saying it at all, only maybe the beating of my own heart to be like a tune. But I was afraid. I thought maybe music might come rising up to me out of the *cummer,* and it thronged with angels, or a great light come striking in at the window. And sure enough at last I started up and I cried out, "There it is! There it is!" But 'twas no unnatural light at all, only the dawn of day breaking in on top of me. 'Tis how I was after dozing off for a little while unknown to myself, and I woke up suddenly in confusion and dread.

'That morning and I rising up, my limbs were like wisps of straw. I was terrified of the long day before me, and that's the worse way a man can be. But when I came out and stood in the broad sun, and 'twas a morning of white frost, I drew in the air to myself, and I took courage to see my poor animals grazing so peacefully on the hill, just like what you see in a picture. If the big farms broke the men that were born to softness and luxury, Dunerling East wouldn't break me, and I reared hard and tough!

That's what I said, with great daring in my breast.

'Not long after that we moved our handful of stock east to this place. I laughed to picture the two scraggy beasts, and all the deep feeding of Dunerling East to themselves. And that same evening myself and Michael, Michael that's dead, God rest him, went over and hither and in and out through the length and breadth of this estate and round by the boundary ditch; and 'tis a thing I will not forget till my dying day what he said to me, my son Michael, that same evening, and we killed from the exertion. He stopped and looked up at me before he spoke:

' "Look," he said, "why have you your hands like that?"

'My two hands, clenched, and stiff, *stiff*, like you'd have them in a fight, watching your opponent, watching to catch him off his guard, or for fear he'd spring on you. That's how I had my hands. And 'twas natural for me to have my hands like that, for what I was saying to myself was: I'll break it! I'll break it! And I was saying that because if I didn't break it I was sport for the world. Like a bully at a fair I was, going about my own land the first day I walked it!'

In recalling the labours of his prime he had become a new man. When they looked at him they saw not the stricken old creature whose days were now spent in the drowsy sun, but the indomitable peasant who had wrung enough from the rocks of Carrig-an-afrinn to buy out Dunerling East from the broken gentry, and who then had reclaimed Dunerling East from its hundred years of neglect. When he could not find words to fit his thought his left eye would close tight, and one big tooth, that he still retained in his upper gum, would dig itself into his lower lip, until the struggling words came to him. And they noticed that his two hands had clenched themselves long before he needed them clenched to illustrate how it was he had tackled the reclamation of the sluggish marshlands of Dunerling East. His own sons quailed before him. The two Americans had drawn together, shoulder touching shoulder: they watched him across the table with wide eyes, their faces drawn. The creamery manager from Kerry dared no longer to put in his jocose word. He wished rather to be able to draw off the old man's mind from this renewal of the unrelenting warfare of his manhood. But no such word could he find: his father was abroad in a passion of fictitious energy: it would indeed be a potent word that could stay or hinder him. Every now and then the timbers of the heavy chair groaned beneath the movement of his awkward carcase. He was unconscious of it. It meant as little to him as his own exposing of the shifts, the meanness, the overreaching, the unintentional tyranny he had practised while he worked out his dream.

'My poor boy, Michael,' he went on, 'was the first to go. He was great for the work. For a boy that was slight and tender I never saw the equal of him. 'Twas how he had great spirit. A word was worse to him than a whip. When we'd be cutting the deep grass in the inches, half a dozen of us all in a line, and he'd fall behind, being young and soft, I'd say to him, "Ah, Michael," I'd say, "God be with the little fields of Carrig-an-afrinn, you could cut them with a scissors"; that would bring him into line I tell ye. The poor boy. 'Twas pleurisy he got first; and we thought nothing of it: maybe we didn't take it in time. But what chance was there to be taking him into Macroom to the doctor, or from one holy well to another? The time he died too, it could not be a worse time. Herself was after bringing little Stephen into the world – and before she was rightly fit the harvest was upon us; and 'twas the first real good harvest we got out of Dunerling East. When I looked at it standing I said: "'Tis my doing and my boy's doing, and my boy is dead!" But herself was better than any man in a harvest field. Maybe she overworked herself. She wasn't the one to give in. The day she was laid in Inchigeela 'tis well if I didn't curse the day I came hither from Carrig-an-afrinn. Father O'Herlihy was standing by. "The Lord giveth and the Lord taketh away," he said, and his hand on my shoulder, and 'twas all I could do to say "Amen" to that. There I was with a houseful of them about me and only herself, that poor thing inside, only herself to do a ha'p'orth for them. I don't blame her for being as she is – knitting, knitting, knitting, or looking into the fire and thinking – I don't blame her at all. What she went through after that, pulling and hauling and slashing and digging, 'twould kill half a parish. Up at four in the morning getting the pigs' food ready, or the mash for the calves; and milking the cows, and keeping the children from mischief. The only other girl I had, she was second after Nicholas there, I lost her just when she was rising to be of use to me. 'Twas a fever she got from drinking bad water. And the two boys I lost after that, one of them was the terror of the countryside. He turned against herself inside; he was wild and fiery. Mind you, he dared me to my face. He said what no son of mine ever said to me. I won't repeat it. I won't repeat it. The eyes were blazing in his head. The delicacy was showing in him. The brains of that kind is a terror. He went off with himself and left me in the lurch. And then he came back – one twelvemonth after – and 'tis like herself inside he was. Only bitter, and the health wasted. The same as any labouring boy he walked in to me. Not a shirt to his back, or what you could call a shirt. He shamed me, the way he was. And he dying on his feet. 'Twas a dead man was patrolling the fields for months before he took to the bed entirely. And I daren't say a word to him because he had a tongue would raise blisters on a withered skull. The other poor boy, his name was Laurence, was a handsome boy. Everybody used to say he'd make a handsome priest. But sure at that time I couldn't dream of such a thing. It takes a power of money to make a priest. He died of pneumonia, and not a thing to happen to him only a bit of a pain in his side. Only for that I hadn't time to be thinking on it I'd be saying there was a curse on top of us; but no, because year after year the produce was getting better and better; and in spite of all the sickness and deaths and funerals – and funerals are the greatest robbers of all – the money began to rise up on me, and I could get in the help when I wanted it – 'tis often I had a score of men at the harvesting, besides what neighbours would come of themselves. Those there' (he nodded at his three sons, all of them sitting with bowed heads, with pipes in their mouths, not daring to break across his speech) '– those there, they only knew the end of the story. Ah boys, ah boys, the softness comes out of the hard, like the apple from the old twisted bough, and 'tis only the softness ye knew of. And then in the end of it all, the great change in the laws came about and I bought out the land and 'twas my own, as you may say. The day I signed for it, a sort of lowness came over me,

40

and I remembered my poor dead boy saying, and he my first born, "Look how you're holding your hands!" Let ye listen to me now; I cried down my eyes to my own self that night because herself was in the clay. That poor soul inside, you might as well be talking to a cock of last year's hay, dull with the weather and the sun, you'd only get "yes" and "no" for an answer. And the rest — those here — were too young. What I did was: to send over for old Johnny, old Johnny I would have helping me an odd time in Carrig-an-afrinn, to come over to me, that I wanted him. God knows all I wanted him for was to keep me in talk against that terrible fit of darkness and loneliness would fall on me again. He came over and together we walked the land, every perch of it. He knew what sort it was when we came hither, and 'tis he was the man could tell the difference. What he said was, now, let ye listen, let ye listen to what he said, and he only a poor ignorant man: "After all, 'twas only a rush in your hand!" Now that was what a wrestler would say of another in the old times, "He was only a rush in my hands," meaning by that that he had no trouble in breaking him. That was great praise and yet it couldn't rouse me for I was after walking the land field after field; and one field I found was the same as another. That's a strange thing to say. Maybe 'tis how I was old and I coming hither. 'Twas in Carrig-an-afrinn I grew up. There was never a man drove a handful of cattle of his own rearing to a fair that hadn't some favourite among them; and he sees the dealers come round them and strike them and push them, and knock them about, and he knows that they are all the same to him, that he sees no difference between one and the other, except one to be riper than another, or a thing like that. And 'twas so with me. I walked my fields and one was the same as another. There was no corner of them that I could make for when the darkness would fall on me. I knew 'twould be different in Carrig-an-afrinn. And that's what I was thinking of when old Johnny said to me that after all Dunerling East was like a rush in my hands. I opened my heart to him. I told him I felt like the steward of the place, and not like the owner of it. He said 'twasn't right for me to be saying a thing like that, and 'tis down on my two knees I should be and I thanking God, but that the heart of man was only a sieve. The very next day and I still going about like that, counting up the great improvements I was after making since I came in, and arguing with myself, and yet dissatisfied with myself, I wandered up the hillside opposite, and whatever turn I gave or however the sun was shining, 'twas about four o'clock in the evening, I saw Doughill and Douse rising up in the west and snug away down at the foot of Doughill I saw a little shoulder of a hill, and "Honour of God," I said, "if that isn't Carrig-an-afrinn itself!" Let ye listen to me, I fell down on my knees in thanksgiving like a pagan would be praying to the sun! And from that day forward I had a spot of land to turn to when the black fit would fall on me. Mind you, 'twas a good time I found it, for while I was breaking the place and wrestling with it I didn't think of anything else, only to be going ahead and going ahead. But 'twas different when I could pay for the help, and I had time to look around, and the rent wasn't half what it used to be. Ah, the soft comes out of the hard, and the little lambs from the hailstones. If Dunerling East is a good property now 'twas many the hot sweat fell into the sods of its ridges. But sure them that could witness to that, they're all dead, except that poor thing inside, God help her; and 'tis she took the burden as well as the next.'

V

His voice fell and the glow of exaltation vanished from his features.

'They're all dead?' Mrs Muntleberry said, quietly.

'Dead!' the old man answered her, and having said it, his head kept on moving slightly up and down to some pulse in his brain.

'Then these,' she said again, and indicated the three sons with her eyes, 'these are a second crop.'

'A second crop,' he said, 'except that poor creature inside.'

They found it hard to break the silence that had fallen on them. Earlier in the evening both Stephen and Finnbarr had been, as one might say, themselves – Stephen, the bakery manager, a hustler, and Finn, the creamery manager, not unable to hustle also. But as the story went on, and, though they had heard it all in a fragmentary way before, they had scattered from the homestead without ever having made themselves one clear unified picture of what coming hither from Carrig-an-afrinn had meant for their father. They had never seen him clearly as one who would not be beaten, no matter who by his side fell worsted in the struggle. Only the oldest of them, Nicholas, the farmer, could recall any of the dead, and he was a soft quiet creature, strong of body, but inactive of brain. The one mood, however, had come upon all three; they were not much different from what they had been before they had scattered, from what they had been when Ellen would still them by whispering the one word: 'Himself.'

It was Finn who first rose. He went and lightly beat the inverted bowl of his pipe against the bars of the fire grate. Then drawing with his strong lips through the empty stem, head in the air, he took a few steps towards the window and drew back one of the heavy curtains. The colour, the glow had gone from the day. Instead there were now everywhere filmy veils of mist. Beyond the sunken stream the hillside looked near and the screens of trees, ash and beech, seemed tall and unsubstantial: in the twilight softness the homely features of farming and cattle trafficking were hidden away. The scene was gracious and tender. They all stared through the window.

'It looks fine, so it does,' Finn said.

'It does; it looks fine,' his wife added, letting the words die away.

The old man was listening.

' 'Tis what a traveller said, and he a man that had recourse to all the places in the world, 'tis what he said: that it had the appearance of a gentleman's place out and out.'

Mrs Muntleberry turned and let her eyes rest softly on his face:

'Still you liked Carrig-an-afrinn too?'

He lifted his head; such words he had not expected: 'Ah, ma'am, ah, ma'am,' he said, making an effort to move his trunk so that he might face her directly, 'Carrig-an-afrinn, Carrig-an-afrinn, the very name of it, the very name of it!' And he stared at her with a fixity of expression that frightened her, stared at her in blank hopelessness of saying even the first word of all the words that rioted within him. He recovered. He swept his hand across his brow, toying with his hair. 'They tell me Pat Leary, who's there ever since we came hither – there's only the one year between us – they tell me he sits in the *cummer* an odd hour at the foot of the rock where the Chalice used to stand. His work is done. He'll catch hold of plough nor snaffle no more, same as myself. 'Tis a great comfort to him to sit there.'

She was sorry she had brought Carrig-an-afrinn back to his thoughts.

'The heart is a sieve,' she said, watching him to see how he'd take old Johnny's word. But he was not so easily moved from mood to mood.

'You saw it to-day?' he questioned earnestly. 'You saw it to-day?'

'We went quite close to it. Did we see the Rock itself? Did we, Stephen?'

Stephen said as boldly as he could:

'Oh yes, we went quite close to it.'

'Ah, ma'am, Nicholas there, some day he's going to pack me into the motor car; and over with us to see it. It can't be long I have to stay.'

Before he had finished, almost indeed at the first word, Nicholas had risen and quietly taken down a shabby-looking old violin from the top of a heavy cupboard that stood in the corner. While they all looked at him he tuned it without a word, and to him tuning was no easy task. Then he stretched his two long legs out from the chair and began to play.

The instrument was almost toneless, and the player almost without skill. He played the old songs of the countryside, going straight from one to another, from a *caoine* to a reel, from a love song to a lively rattle about cattle-dealing or horse racing. Nerveless, toneless, yet the playing was quiet; and it was the music itself, and not the instrument or musician was in the fiddler's mind. After a while this the Americans noticed. Then the scratching, the imperfect intonation, the incongruous transition from melody to melody disturbed them but little. He played on and on; and they

44

were all thankful to him. The room darkened, but the sky was still bright. At last he lowered the fiddle, a string needed to be tightened. The others at once broke into talk. Mrs Muntleberry was nearest to Nicholas. She had her eyes on the instrument. He noticed how at the word 'Carrig-an-afrinn' which was again on the lips of the old man, her head had raised itself. He whispered to her, without taking his eyes off his task:

'He'll never see Carrig-an-afrinn again.'

'No?' she whispered back, with a little gasp of surprise.

'Nor nobody else,' he went on; 'they're after blasting it away to make the road wider: 'tis how two lorries couldn't pass on it. I'm in dread of my life he'll find it out. 'Twould be terrible.'

She turned her eyes on the old man's face. The music had restored him again to confidence. His eyes were glowing. He had re-established his mastery. 'Let ye listen, let ye listen to me,' he was saying.

THE EMPTIED SACK

I

URGED TO IT BY HIS SON, John Connole made up his mind to do as the other potters had done; to throw aside the ancient methods, the antique gear he had inherited from his fathers, as they from theirs, and to install – it was his son's word – to install instead a modern scientific furnace in which the heat could be regulated to the hundredth part of a degree. Old Tadhg Kinnane, that dwarf-life creature, stooped and venomous, more than eighty years of age, whose body some intensity of brain rather than warmth of heart kept alive – what would *he* do then? With his heaped-up donkey-load of furze branches piled higher than his head he would no more be seen in the streets of Youghal, for furze was not the tinder used in the new-fashioned furnaces.

'And the poor creature,' Jack Tattan, one of the potters, began, half smiling, his hands under his clay-white apron, ''tis little use he's now for anything else.'

'He's eighty, he must be eighty-three,' Fred Lincoln said, his eyes twinkling against the sun; he had just come from within.

'Why should he be working at all? What is he working for? All he earned his whole life long, what did he do with it?'

''Twill be worse for him than the *Calliope*.'

'It will that.'

Forty years ago when the *Calliope* lay along the jetties all the windows of the hillside town gazed wide-eyed at her bright shapeliness. Her gilded points and lines, her whiteness, her sparkle, her shining newness, had bespoken welcome for her from the townsfolk; her crew, from captain to cabin boy, were given the run of the port. Tadhg Kinnane was then in the prime of life, forty years of age, yet had for all that already buried his household – parents, wife, children, all except one daughter – had buried them in

Ardmore of the Saints across the water. That daughter he had taught to keep house for him – if house it could be called. In due course she had grown into the custom of accompanying him to the town with his load of furze; still later, whenever he was busy working for the neighbouring farmers at the harvest or ploughing, she was become venturesome enough to undertake herself the delivery of the furze branches at the potteries. She would start off before the sun had risen, would pilot the ass and cart down the rough mountainy *poirsin*, along the white roads, and, at last, through the cobbled streets of the town; would look, it seemed, neither to right at the sailormen nor left at the 'prentice potters, but make straight on for one or other of the yards – there were many of them then – would sedately receive the payment, would make her household purchases, always at the traditional shops and in the traditional way, and arrive, oftentimes late at night, at the lonely cabin in the hills with a mouthful of gossip for the sun-burnt, sun-drowsed exhausted man stretched along the settle patiently awaiting her, his pipe in his mouth. He was not sharp enough in eye or brain to notice that those visits were having more and more attraction for the rich-blooded ripening girl. Her lips were girlish, soft, and full; she had a tender grace and innocence about her, her brows were light, well-shaped; her eyes timid and as dark as berries. She could not speak without blushing. Reared apart from womenfolk, she felt awkward when alone with them. She feared their questioning.

Forty years ago, then, after a long day's threshing in Pierce Fielding's barn, Tadhg Kinnane lay stretched in that patient attitude on the settle awaiting his daughter's return from the town. He saw the dusk thicken, the bats make their own of the sky, the earth darken, grow heavy and cold after the going of the sun; and then, one by one, he watched the stars coming into the heavens silently, silently. From the settle it was that he saw the night fall. At last he arose slowly, and slowly went out, sitting on a block of wood by the door. The pale wide glare of the afterlight startled him, so frank it was, so untender. Yet the coolness, after the labour of the day, found welcome in his limbs; he stretched out his legs, rested his back and head against the wall, and sleep fell on

47

him. When he awoke, suddenly, as if a whirring bird, with a cry, had struck him one stroke, a dark-blue silent night, gemmed with stars, was standing upon the earth. His hands were cold, and a soundless wind was feeling softly at his features. It was some moments before he realised that the fear he felt all about him, like a chilly, invisible garment, was due to his daughter's delay in the distant town. He groped his way into the hut, making for where the last spark of fire was still visible among the ashes; this, with the fire-wheel, he fanned up vigorously, indeed passionately. As suddenly he stopped and glared at the clock's face: it was ten minutes past one. It could not be so late, he thought; but from far away he heard a calf roaring, and the cry shook the heart in him, for it opened the spaces of the silent night, made it seem vast and lonely, vacant of any living soul to comfort one in trouble. No, it could not be so late, he reasoned with himself, yet again came that unrestrained cry of animal distress; and he felt he could not wait any longer. He plunged the candle into the fire, and set it lighting on the dresser. He reached for his coat, it hung on a hook in a roof timber, and as he flung it on he suddenly stretched an ear for other sounds that he fancied he had caught – the jolting of the ass cart as it made up the difficult, rocky passage towards the house. 'Ah!' he breathed, and the comfortable warmth of anger began to replace the chilly fear within him. Oh, he would speak to her, he would speak to her, and never again would she go alone into that cursed town of tradesmen and sailors. He buttoned his coat hurriedly, it would show her what he had been about to do; and, waiting, he stood on the threshold, alert, stiffened up, filling the opening, the night-blue sky before him, the glowing interior behind. Again, and more clearly, he heard the homely, drowsy, unhurried rattling, and he drank comfort from it. Then it ceased. But almost at once, again began. Once more stopped, for some time too. Once more began, stopped once more. 'God guide us, God guide us,' he breathed, and made hurriedly down towards the rambling, uncertain noises. He found the cart dragged obliquely across the passage, the ass cropping the long dew-cold herbage by the edge of the way. As for his daughter – she already was far on the sea in the arms of the wild young skipper of the *Calliope*.

Tim Tobin, then, had said the word that had renewed for them the story of Kinnane's far-off day of trouble. Bitter and all as old Tadhg was he had suffered his share, and had, as they said, shrunk into himself, closing not only his mouth but his heart. When one is come to that what is left except to bend upon the work of the day? And this he did. He would labour for the farmers round about, sometimes rising at dawn and travelling ten or fifteen miles to a harvesting or ploughing, and, come home, would be heard late in the night hacking and hewing in the furze thickets by the river bed or along the hills. He took on pottery after pottery, and kept them going, and neither the driving sea winds nor mountain floods nor rains ever hindered him or even delayed his coming to them at the right time. They it was that failed him, one after another giving up the ancient way. By this time, however, himself was getting old, was now more than eighty years; and for one so old the hacking out and the gathering and the piling of one load of furze branches was a full week's work.

'Do you know, I'm sorry for the old creature – in a way.'

'Um, um, you needn't then. He won't starve.'

'That's true. Still, what'll he do with himself?'

'Lie down and die; and indeed they're a long time waiting for him, his people in Ardmore.'

'Will he come to-day, I wonder?'

II

As if unaware of any change whatever, the old man dragged his little donkey, rather viciously, one thought, into the yard. Animal, tackling, furze branches, cart – and then the old man himself – face, whiskers, hair, hands, clothes – they all were of one texture and one hue – a rough, hodden grey upon which the dust of the long distance he had come was scarcely noticeable. As always, the animal made to swerve to the left where, it remembered, long tufts of bluish grass were to be cropped between the cobblestones; and, as ever, the old man snarled at it, 'Come on, you!' Then, 'Whu-ee!', 'Whu-ee,' his hard old lips blew out, and he threw the reins

49

carelessly on its back. He stopped suddenly, his head down, even more than usual, his brows bent, even more than usual, to that intensity of purpose by which he seemed to live. At last, fixing his thought, he hobbled forward quite briskly towards the open-air stairs which led up to John Connole's office. But again he paused, hesitating for a moment; and, as precipitately as he had gone from it, made back to his cart, from which, hurriedly, he began to fling the furze branches off about the yard. John Connole, who must have seen him, came on to the wooden platform at the head of the stairs: 'Take them up again, take them up, I say. And be off with you, be off with you, you old deceiver. You were told not to bring them.'

The old man stopped as he pulled one from the pile; he held it in his hand, awkwardly, like a defeated flag; such words he had heard before in other potters' yards. Timidly, quietly, he put the branch on the ground. 'Take them up, I tell ye. Didn't I tell you I was done with you? Be off with yourself.'

John Connole turned his back and went into his office. The old man raised his eyes towards where he had been speaking on the platform.

A little group were standing under a low wide archway: the autumn sun was playing about their feet, not on their heads or faces: 'There you are, Tadhg. There you are,' one of them called to him, not roughly. He could think of nothing else to say.

John Connole's son came across the yard. He was well-dressed, well-combed. He had some papers in his hand. He was puzzled for a moment to see the old man slowly replacing the branches on the cart: when he understood, he made a gesture with the papers towards the group in the archway: 'Give him a hand with them,' he said, and with the lightness of youth in his limbs bounded up the wooden stairs.

The men began quickly to fling the branches on to the cart, old Tadhg looking at them suspiciously. For them during the long, long years he had always been little more than a butt for their joking; they would begin again at any moment, he felt; but no; they helped him to swing the cart about on the rough cobble-stones, to set it going, and all without one word of impatience. They then drew back, they had played their part. He peered at them, still suspicious, but, making sure they had no thought of gibing at him any more, he took a step towards them; 'Whisper,' he said, 'did ye ever hear this?' and he hissed out an Irish saying, which, translated, is 'Petting the dead and the dead laughing!' They could only keep their silence, staring at him. And he looked back at them, and smiled!

He grabbed the mouthpiece and led his swaying, carelessly built load through the gateway and out into the traffic of the main street.

III

It took him only a moment to make up his mind as to what he should do. He turned down a narrow sunless street of long-deserted warehouses. At the farther end was a glare of light – the wide sky, the bright waters of the estuary. He made straight for the edge of the jetty, dragging the donkey after him with a callous vigour, its head screwed sideways up. He swung the cart about until its tailpiece was towards the waters. Then, muttering and growling he began, still with something of a false strength in his limbs, to pitch the branches into the sea.

If he had drawn his cart in at any other point of those all too spacious jetties, he might have finished without interruption, but now, suddenly, he heard, 'Look out!' shouted at him in an un-Irish accent. A sailorman with a noose of stout new rope across his guernsey, around his shoulders, was coming towards him labor-iously: pressed forward at a sharp angle, his thin and worn shoes showed the play of the feet within them. It was not he who had shouted: it was another, whose duty it was to lift the rope over whatever quayside debris lay about. Again, this man shouted 'Look out! Look out!' and failing to raise the cable high enough above the cart, about half the load was swept off on top of old Kinnane: when the rope had passed by, himself, too, had been thrown and was sprawling in the midst of the branches. He had to turn on his face and hands to rise up. He did so as if there were need for haste, as if he had no time to think of what had befallen, or of the wet rope, the labouring sailorman, or the ship that like a dazzling vision was gliding to its moorings. He resumed without a thought, it seemed, and with the same surly vigour, his task of pitching and kicking the branches into the water. The last he flung in with all his strength. 'Take them with you, me fine salt water,' he snarled, and turned away. He at once began dragging his cart from the quayside. The men on the ship, some of them standing with mooring cables in their hands, thought doubtless that he had been fulfilling some daily task and now was setting off for home. He did not seem to have given one glance at the ship: her spars were bright against the rich blue of the sky; all about her were gleams, points of sun-fire, lines of light. One glance perhaps he had given her, no more, when, sitting in his cart, he started for his lonely nest in the hills.

IV

How many, many hundred times he had thus in the gathering twilight made homewards! The falling night, the cool airs, the silent winding road, showing dimly before him, the rocky heathery hills, now closing in on his path, now opening out again, all the time, however, rising higher and higher, growing darker and darker – it was easy for him in such surroundings to forget that this was the very last of all such journeys: that he would never see the potteries again. And so, now wide awake, shouting and pulling at the little animal, and now drowsing into sleep, his head bobbing and his hands hanging limp, resting on his knees – on and on he journeyed, mile after mile. His voice was sometimes heard: 'Go on, go on, can't ye,' and no weakening seemed to have overtaken it. But, swinging around into that rising, stone-strewn, winding passage that led to his house, he suddenly felt afraid and cold and lonesome. Only a dismal and empty hut lay before him – as if it had not been empty and dismal for more than forty years! A cold and empty house! but as suddenly he saw out before him the ever-rising masts of a sailing ship, her spars, her cordage, shining in the sun! 'Go on, can't ye!' he called out bravely, with a new ring in his voice, and from that until he threw the reins on its back, he gave the animal but little peace.

He removed the mouthpiece and left the ass to its haphazard grazing, the cart still tackled to it.

Meanwhile he had lit a candle, had closed the door, and soon was searching and poking in all the holes and corners of the room. Little cries broke from him. Sometimes he stopped, listening. He climbed up on chairs and fumbled at the roof timbers. At last he satisfied himself that no more remained to be done. In the middle of the place half a loaf of bread was hanging from a rafter by a string: it was his way of baulking the rats of it. From this he broke off some junks and began hastily to chew them, still moving about as if unable to rest. He suddenly quenched the light, locked the door behind him, and made once more for the cart. He restored the mouthpiece, sat in brightly, and vigorously urged the animal back towards the town. It wanted an hour to dawn. 'Ah! ah!', 'Ah-h-h,' he breathed out, showing his teeth – a cry that was full of triumph.

When he once more entered Youghal town, the pale morning was playing upon it; nevertheless, everything was still fast asleep, churches, shops, and houses deep in their dreams. Not a sound, not a movement – no door, no window stirring, no blind raised. The rattling of the wheels, even old Tadhg himself noticed how sharp and loud the sounds were. He was glad to turn once again into that deserted lane among the vacant warehouses. Again he made for the jetties. He tied his beast by the reins to some iron bars in a window frame. He hobbled forward, as with purpose, towards the dreaming ship. Silent she was, disdainful, yet his yeart filled with warmth as he gazed up at her. Seagulls were flying about her topmasts, gliding and wheeling, crying out sharply their long melancholy notes. Her grey-painted side was high above his head: he had not foreseen the difficulty of waking so huge a mass into life. But soon he noticed that a young sailorman, smoking quietly, lazily, had been watching all the time. By way of greeting he raised hand and stick to him. He was afraid he might suddenly disappear into the depths of that huge contrivance. He drew nearer, hobbling, 'Whisper,' he said, cautiously beckoning the sailor to come closer – 'Whisper, what's the name of her?'

'The name?'

'Yes, her name, what's on her, the ship?'

'The *Hispaniola*. 'Tis all along her.'

'The *Calliope*?'

'No, the *Hispaniola*.'

'Whisper, whisper now: are they after changing it?'

'Change what?'

'The name of her. For why did they change it?' He was whispering up, his left hand at his mouth.

'They haven't changed it. *Hispaniola*, that's the lady's name.'

'Ah, ah, I'm telling ye now, whisper, 'tis the *Calliope* she is. Isn't it I that should know that? 'Tisn't so easy to deceive me. The *Calliope* – and the Master – Captain Hinchion – that's the name. Look now, like a good boy – go in and tell him there's one here would like to make speech with him – and, whisper, 'twould be no harm to tell him that he won't be sorry at all if he's said by me. Go on now.'

'But he's not aboard, your Captain Hinchion; he never was.' As he spoke in his somnolent voice the sailor raised his eyebrows, his two hands, the smoking pipe in the fingers of one of them, held loosely.

'He never was,' he repeated.

'Ah, he's not. He's not. You tell me that?' Perplexed, he stared piteously at the sailor.

'*Calliope*,' he whispered again, in a sort of staring vacancy.

'No, *Hispaniola*, Portland, Maine.'

The old man waved his hands with sudden joy.

'Portland, Maine – that's it. A hundred times they said it to me, 'tis there I'd find her.'

'Was she from there?'

'Portland, Maine, Portland, Maine.'

'Hold there a while now, will you?'

'No, no; stop! Come back.'

'I'll be back presently.'

'Ye will?'

'Certain.'

He vanished from Tadhg's eyes; but the old eyes never shifted; they were fearful the sailor might not return. When he did return he was accompanied by an oldish, blear-eyed scrubby-bearded seaman, vicious-looking, scowling. His limbs were twisted with rheumatism. He fastened his gaze on Tadhg:

'The *Calliope*?' he muttered huskily, absently, his weary worn-out voice offending the freshness of the morning.

'Yes, yes.'

'Portland, Maine?'

'Yes, yes.'

'Captain Hinchion?'

'Hinchion – young. A bold lad. A bold lad.'

'Right you are. I seen her often. I seen her in Portland, Maine. In Caleta Buena. In Sydney. . . She went. . .'

He stretched his hand out over the ship's side, he lowered it slowly, the fingers wide apart one from another. 'She foundered. Crew, Cap'n, cargo. Cap'n's wife. All of 'em. All.'

'They were drownded? All drownded, ye're saying?'

'You have it,' he nodded affably.

The old man glared at him, his jaw hanging foolishly. The seaman took no notice; he raised his head: calculating how long ago it was since the *Calliope* had foundered, he was, unseeingly, staring into the windows of the little town, blindly, although every one of them was a living torch against the sun.

'It's forty years ago.'

'Forty?' Tadhg repeated, in a dull and stupid voice.

'Forty, I said,' the seaman rapped out at him. He was a chronicler of the seas. Tadhg's head swung up in answer: 'The Captain's wife. . . she was my daughter. Maybe now, ye wouldn't believe that?'

Their eyes were fixed on him. There was something like a snarl of victory in his way of saying the words; and something like disdain in his abrupt turning away from them.

The young man laughed quietly. 'Queer old thing,' he said; but the other flung a string of filthy words after the retreating figure.

The spark of fire the truculence of the sailor had induced in old Tadhg lived but a moment; in a sort of stupor he got into his little cart and, almost without thinking, set out from the still-dreaming town towards his home. He had lost a whole night's sleep and, bright morning though it was, he had gone only a little way when his head dropped on his breast. It did not matter. Often and often before it had happened to him. All those who travelled that road were acquainted with him; had known him even in their child-hood. To see him pass with his head fallen on his breast gave them scarce a thought. It was a little group of stranger tinkers that at last gathered about the cart, waking him up and telling him he had better be careful. Their wild faces, sun-dark, dirty, passionate, were about him in a ring. He stared at them stupidly. A middle-aged, bedraggled woman, with a child at her breast, folded into a shawl, was still shaking him, fearing he would drop off to sleep again. 'Good man,' she was saying, 'you'll come to mischief, you'll come to misfortune. For the love of God mind yourself. 'Tis many a good man met his death and he going the road like that.'

He gathered his wits. Anyone who had known him for the past forty years would, as answer to her words, have expected from him a snarl, nothing else: but no, his voice sounded weak, uncer-tain of itself:

'And, *a laogh*, 'twould be all one. 'Tis how, whisper, *a laogh*,' he drew the woman towards him away from the others. ' 'Tis how, they used to tell me they always come home in the end, and they broken, and every hand raised again' them, and they dark in themselves, and like a dirty slut upon their father's floor.' He raised his head and looked at her straight in the eyes: 'Let me tell you, let me inform you, 'tisn't like that she'd be with me, 'tisn't, 'tis not so, far from it, but in silks and satins, with bangles and ear rings, and – and –' Words failed him, and he gave up, with an impatient gesture, the attempt to find them. 'Whisper, what a mistake they were making! 'Tis I could dress her out. 'Tis so. And, whisper, not a soul knew it, not a soul knew it – and I laughing at them! Laughing at them in my heart of hearts! All the years of my life, laughing at them in my heart of hearts!' And he shook his head with satisfaction to think how he had been laughing at the world all the years of his life!

The tinker woman nodded to show she understood, but indeed all she understood was that the old man was simple-minded and couldn't keep his thoughts to himself. Suddenly she saw all his strength go from him, saw him trembling and trying to control his tongue. 'But 'tis all one now,' he began to glaum his breast. 'My heart,' he said, 'is a cage without a bird, I'm an emptied sack! There is no spirit in me any more, nor strength nor life nor anything. But God's Will be done, the Will of God be done,' he gathered up the reins weariedly. He did not care how long the road was, nor how cold and lonely his cabin.

The tinkers drew away from him, moving quickly on. The woman began to speak: 'He's very old, that poor creature is. I didn't notice it at first. But I'd say he was a firm man in his day. A firm man. And he had the look of a miser. He was laughing, he said, in his heart of hearts. Look at that now – his heart of hearts.'

But even as she spoke she was racing ahead eager to catch a glimpse of the town they had been making for since the break of day. Her bare feet as they swiftly padded along threw up clouds of dust from the sunny roadway.

The donkey cart meanwhile went on towards the distant hills, aimlessly, it seemed, straggling about the road. Every now and then the grey old head of the drooping figure in it would move from side to side, and 'Vo! Vo! Vo! Vo!' – the traditional Irish cry of sorrow – would break from the lips. Sometimes the cry was loud and unrestrained; sometimes smothered, only a groaning.

THE PLOUGHING OF THE LEACA

WITH WHICH SHALL I BEGIN – man or place? Perhaps I had better first tell of the man; of him the incident left so withered that no sooner had I laid eyes on him than I said: Here is one whose blood at some terrible moment of his life stood still, stood still and never afterwards regained its quiet, old-time ebb-and-flow. A word or two then about the place – a sculped-out shell in the Kerry mountains, an evil-looking place, green-glaring like a sea when a storm has passed. To connect man and place together, even as they worked one with the other to bring the tragedy about, ought not then to be so difficult.

I had gone into those desolate treeless hills searching after the traces of an old-time Gaelic family that once were lords of them. But in this mountainy glen I forgot my purpose almost as soon as I entered it.

In that round-ended valley – they call such a valley a coom – there was but one farmhouse, and Considine was the name of the householder – Shawn Considine, the man whose features were white with despair; his haggard appearance reminded me of what one so often sees in war-ravaged Munster – a ruined castle-wall hanging out above the woods, a grey spectre. He made me welcome, speaking slowly, as if he was not used to such amenities. At once I began to explain my quest. I soon stumbled; I felt that his thoughts were far away. I started again. A daughter of his looked at me – Nora was her name – looked at me with meaning; I could not read her look aright. Haphazardly I went through old family names and recalled old-world incidents; but with no more success. He then made to speak; I could catch only broken phrases, repeated again and again. 'In the presence of God.' 'In the Kingdom of God.' 'All gone for ever.' 'Let them rest in peace' – (I translate

58

from the Irish). Others, too, there were of which I could make nothing. Suddenly I went silent. His eyes had begun to change. They were not becoming fiery or angry – that would have emboldened me, I would have blown on his anger; a little passion, even an outburst of bitter temper would have troubled me but little if in its sudden revelation I came on some new fact or even a new name in the broken story of that ruined family. But no; not fiery but cold and terror-stricken were his eyes becoming. Fear was rising in them like dank water. I withdrew my gaze, and his daughter ventured on speech:

'If you speak of the cattle, noble person, or of the land, or of the new laws, my father will converse with you; but he is dark about what happened long ago.' Her eyes were even more earnest than her tongue – they implored the pity of silence.

So much for the man. A word now about the place where his large but neglected farmhouse stood against a bluff of rock. To enter that evil-looking green-mountained glen was like entering the jaws of some slimy, cold-blooded animal. You felt yourself leaving the sun, you shrunk together, you hunched yourself as if to bear an ugly pressure. In the far-back part of it was what is called in the Irish language a *leaca* – a slope of land, a lift of land, a bracket of land jutting out from the side of a mountain. This leaca, which the daughter explained was called Leaca-na-Naomh – the Leaca of the Saints – was very remarkable. It shone like a gem. It held the sunshine as a field holds its crop of golden wheat. On three sides it was pedestalled by the sheerest rock. On the fourth side it curved up to join the parent mountain-flank. Huge and high it was, yet height and size took some time to estimate, for there were mountains all around it. When you had been looking at it for some time you said aloud: 'That leaca is high!' When you had stared for a longer time you said: 'That leaca is immensely high – and huge!' Still the most remarkable thing about it was the way it held the sunshine. When all the valley had gone into the gloom of twilight – and this happened in the early afternoon – the leaca was still at mid-day. When the valley was dark with night and the lamps had been long alight in the farmhouse, the leaca had still the red gleam of sunset on it. It hung above the misty valley like a velarium – as they used to call that awning-cloth which hung above the emperor's seat in the amphitheatre.

'What is it called, do you say?' I asked again.

'Leaca-na-Naomh,' she replied.

'Saints used to live on it?'

'The Hermits,' she answered, and sighed deeply.

Her trouble told me that that leaca had to do with the fear that was burrowing like a mole in her father's heart. I would test it. Soon afterwards the old man came by, his eyes on the ground, his lips moving.

'That leaca,' I said, 'what do you call it?'

He looked up with a startled expression. He was very white; he couldn't abide my steady gaze.

'Nora,' he cried, raising his voice suddenly and angrily, '*cas isteach iad, cas isteach iad!*' He almost roared at the gentle girl.

'Turn in – what?' I said, roughly. 'The cattle are in long ago.'

''Tis right they should,' he answered, leaving me.

Yes, this leaca and this man had between them moulded out a tragedy, as between two hands.

Though the sun had gone, still I sat staring at it. It was far off, but whatever light remained in the sky had gathered to it. I was wondering at its clear definition among all the vague and misty mountain-shapes when a voice, quivering with age, high and untuneful, addressed me:

''Twould be right for you to see it when there's snow on it.'

'Ah!'

''Tis blinding!' The voice had changed so much as his inner vision strengthened that I gazed up quickly at him. He was a very old man, somewhat fairy-like in appearance, but he had the eyes of a boy! These eyes told me he was one who had lived imaginatively. Therefore I almost gripped him lest he should escape; from him would I learn of Leaca-na-Naomh. Shall I speak of him as a vassal of the house, or as a tatter of the family, or as a spall of the rough landscape? He was native to all three. His homespun was patched with patches as large and as straight-cut as those you'd see on a fisherman's sail. He was, clothes and all, the same colour as the aged lichen of the rocks; but his eyes were as fresh as dew.

Gripping him, as I have said, I searched his face, as one searches a poem for a hidden meaning.

'When did it happen, this dreadful thing?' I said.

He was taken off his guard. I could imagine, I could almost feel his mind struggling, summoning up an energy sufficient to express his idea of how as well as when the thing happened. At last he spoke deliberately.

'When the master,' – I knew he meant the householder – 'was at his best, his swiftest and strongest in health, in riches, in force and spirit.' He hammered every word.

'Ah!' I said; and I noticed the night had begun to thicken, fitly I thought, for my mind was already making mad leaps into the darkness of conjecture. He began to speak a more simple language:

'In those days he was without burden or ailment – unless maybe every little biteen of land between the rocks that he had not as yet brought under the plough was a burden. This, that, yonder, all those fine fields that have gone back again into heather and furze, it was he made them. There's sweat in them! But while he bent over them in the little dark days of November, dropping his sweat, he would raise up his eyes and fix them on the leaca. *That* would be worth all of them, and worth more than double all of them if it was brought under the plough.'

'And why not?' I said.

'Plough the bed of the saints?'

'I had forgotten.'

'You are not a Gael of the Gaels maybe?'

'I had forgotten; continue; it grows chilly.'

'He had a serving-man; he was a fool; they were common in the country then; they had not been as yet herded into asylums. He was a fool; but a true Gael. That he never forgot; except once.'

'Continue.'

'He had also a sire horse, Griosach he called him, he was so strong, so high and princely.'

'A plough horse?'

'He had never been harnessed. He was the master's pride and boast. The people gathered on the hillsides when he rode him to Mass. You looked at the master; you looked at the horse; the horse knew the hillsides were looking at him. He made music with his hoofs, he kept his eyes to himself, he was so proud.'

'What of the fool?'

'Have I spoken of the fool?'

'Yes, a true Gael.'

''Tis true, that word. He was as strong as Griosach. He was what no one else was: he was a match for Griosach. The master petted the horse. The horse petted the master. Both of them knew they went well together. But Griosach the sire horse feared Liam Ruadh the fool; and Liam Ruadh the fool feared Griosach the sire horse. For neither had as yet found out that he was stronger than the other. They would play together like two strong boys, equally matched in strength and daring. They would wrestle and throw each other. Then they would leave off; and begin again when they had recovered their breath.'

'Yes,' I said, 'the master, the horse Griosach, the fool Liam – now, the leaca, the leaca.'

'I have brought in the leaca. It will come in again, now! The master was one day standing at a gap for a long time; there was no one near him. Liam Ruadh came near him. "It is not lucky to be so silent as that," he said. The master raised his head and answered:

' "The leaca for wheat."

'The fool nearly fell down in a sprawling heap. No one had ever heard of anything like that.

' "No," he said like a child.

' "The leaca for wheat," the master said again, as if there was someone inside him speaking.

'The fool was getting hot and angry.

' "The leaca for prayer!" he said.

' "The leaca for wheat," said the master, a third time.

'When the fool heard him he gathered himself up and roared – a loud "O-oh!" it went around the hills like sudden thunder; in the little breath he had left he said: "The leaca for prayer!"

'The master went away from him; who could tell what might have happened?

'The next day the fool was washing a sheep's diseased foot – he had the struggling animal held firm when the master slipped

62

behind him and whispered in his ear:

' "The leaca for wheat."

'Before the fool could free the animal the master was gone. He was a wild, swift man that day. He laughed. It was that selfsame night he went into the shed where Liam slept and stood a moment looking at the large face of the fool working in his dreams. He watched him like that a minute. Then he flashed the lantern quite close into the fool's eyes so as to dazzle him, and he cried out harshly, "The leaca for wheat," making his voice appear far off, like a trumpet-call, and before the fool could understand where he was, or whether he was asleep or awake, the light was gone and the master was gone.

'Day after day the master put the same thought into the fool's ear. And Liam was becoming sullen and dark. Then one night long after we were all in our sleep we heard a wild crash. The fool had gone to the master's room. He found the door bolted. He put his shoulder to it. The door went in about the room, and the arch above it fell in pieces around the fool's head – all in the still night.

' "Who's there? What is it?" cried the master, starting up in his bed.

' "Griosach for the plough!" said the fool.

'No one could think of Griosach being hitched to a plough. The master gave him no answer. He lay down in his bed and covered his face. The fool went back to his straw. Whenever the master now said "The leaca for wheat" the fool would answer "Griosach for the plough."

'The tree turns the wind aside, yet the wind at last twists the tree. Like wind and tree, master and fool played against each other, until at last they each of them had spent their force.

' "I will take Griosach and Niamh and plough the leaca," said the fool; it was a hard November day.

' "As you wish," said the master. Many a storm finishes with a little sob of wind. Their voices were now like a little wind.

'The next night a pair of smiths were brought into the coom all the way from Aunascawl. The day after that the mountains were ringing with their blows as the ploughing-gear was overhauled. Without rest or laughter or chatter the work went on, for Liam was at their shoulders, and he hardly gave them time to wipe their sweaty hair. One began to sing: "'Tis my grief on Monday now," but Liam struck him one blow and stretched him. He returned to his work quiet enough after that. We saw the fool's anger rising. We made way for him; and he was going back and forth the whole day long; in the evening his mouth began to froth and his tongue to blab. We drew away from him; wondering what he was thinking of. The master himself began to grow timid; he hadn't a word in him; but he kept looking up at us from under his brow as if he feared we would turn against him. Sure we wouldn't; wasn't he our master — even what he did?

'When the smiths had mounted their horses that night to return to Aunascawl one of them stooped down to the master's ear and whispered: "Watch him, he's in a fever."

'"Who?"

'"The fool." That was a true word.

'Some of us rode down with the smiths to the mouth of the pass, and as we did so snow began to fall silently and thickly. We were glad; we thought it might put back the dreadful business of the ploughing. When we returned towards the house we were talking. But a boy checked us.

'"Whisht!" he said.

'We listened. We crept beneath the thatch of the stables. Within we heard the fool talking to the horses. We knew he was putting his arms around their necks. When he came out, he was quiet and happy looking. We crouched aside to let him pass. Then we told the master.

'"Go to your beds," he said, coldly enough.

'We played no cards that night; we sang no songs; we thought it too long until we were in our dark beds. The last thing we thought of was the snow falling, falling, falling on Leaca-na-Naomh and on all the mountains. There was not a stir or a sigh in the house. Everyone feared to hear his own bed creak. And at last we slept.

'What awoke me? I could hear voices whispering. There was fright in them. Before I could distinguish one word from another I felt my neck creeping. I shook myself. I leaped up. I looked out. The light was blinding. The moon was shining on the slopes of new snow. There was none falling now; a light, thin wind was blowing out of the lovely stars.

'Beneath my window I saw five persons standing in a little group, all clutching one another like people standing in a flooded river. They were very still; they would not move even when they whispered. As I wondered to see them so fearfully clutching one another a voice spoke in my room:

' "For God's sake, Stephen, get ready and come down."

' "Man, what's the matter with ye?"

' "For God's sake come down."

' "Tell me, tell me!"

' "How can I? Come down!"

'I tried to be calm; I went out and made for that little group, putting my hand against my eyes, the new snow was so blinding.

' "Where's the master?" I said.

' "There!" They did not seem to care whether or not I looked at the master.

'He was a little apart; he was clutching a jut of rock as if the land was slipping from his feet. His cowardice made me afraid. I was hard put to control my breath.

' "What are ye, are ye all staring at?" I said.

' "Leaca-na—" the voice seemed to come from over a mile away, yet it was the man beside me had spoken.

'I looked. The leaca was a dazzling blaze, it was true, but I had often before seen it as bright and wonderful. I was puzzled.

' "Is it the leaca ye're all staring —" I began; but several of them silently lifted up a hand and pointed towards it. I could have stared at them instead; whether or not it was the white moonlight that was on them, they looked like men half-frozen, too chilled to speak. But I looked where those outstretched hands silently bade me. Then I, too, was struck dumb and became one of that icy group, for I saw a little white cloud moving across the leaca, a feathery cloud, and from the heart of it there came every now and then a little flash of fire, a spark. Sometimes, too, the little cloud would grow thin, as if it were scattering away, at which times it was a moving shadow we saw. As I blinked at it I felt my hand groping about to catch something, to catch someone, to make sure of myself; for the appearance of everything, the whiteness, the stillness, and then that moving cloud whiter than everything else, whiter than anything in the world, and so like an angel's wing moving along the leaca, frightened me until I felt like fainting away. To make things worse, straight from the little cloud came down a whisper, a long, thin, clear, silvery cry: "Griosach! Ho-o-o-oh! Ho-o-o-oh!" a ploughing cry. We did not move; we kept our silence: everyone knew that that cry was going through everyone else as through himself, a stroke of coldness. Then I understood why the master was hanging on to a rock; he must have heard the cry before anyone else. It was terrible, made so thin and silvery by the distance; and yet it was a cry of joy – the fool had conquered Griosach!

'I do not know what wild thoughts had begun to come into my head when one man in the group gasped out "Now!" and then another, and yet another. Their voices were breath, not sound. Then they all said "Ah!" and I understood the fear that had moved their tongues. I saw the little cloud pause a moment on the edge of the leaca, almost hang over the edge, and then begin to draw back. The fool had turned his team on the verge and was now ploughing up against the hill.

'"O-o-h," said the master, in the first moment of relief; it was more like a cry of agony. He looked round at us with ghastly eyes; and our eyeballs turned towards his, just as cold and fixed. Again that silvery cry floated down to us "Griosach! Ho-o-o-oh!" And again the stroke of coldness passed through every one of us. The cry began to come more frequently, more triumphantly, for now again the little cloud was ploughing down the slope, and its pace had quickened. It was making once more for that edge beneath which was a sheer fall of hundreds of feet.

'Behind us, suddenly, from the direction of the thatched stables came a loud and high whinny – a call to a mate. It was so unexpected, and we were all so rapt up in what was before our eyes, that it shook us, making us spring from one another. I was the first to recover.

'"My God," I said, "that's Niamh, that's Niamh!"

'The whinny came again; it was Niamh surely.

' "What is he ploughing with, then? What has he with Griosach?"

'A man came running from the stables; he was trying to cry out: he could hardly be heard:

' "Griosach and Lugh! Griosach and Lugh!"

'Lugh was another sire horse; and the two sires would eat each other; they always had ill-will for each other. The master was staring at us.

' " 'Tisn't Lugh?" he said, with a gurgle in his voice.

'No one could answer him. We were thinking if the mare's cry reached the sires their anger would blaze up and no one could hold them; but why should Liam have yoked such a team?

' "Hush! hush!" said a woman's voice.

'We at once heard a new cry; it came down from the leaca:

' "Griosach, back! Back!" It was almost inaudible, but we could feel the swiftness and terror in it. "Back! Back!" came down again. "Back, Griosach, back!"

' "They're fighting, they're fighting – the sires!" one of our horse-boys yelled out – the first sound above a breath that had come from any of us, for he was fonder of Lugh than of the favourite Griosach, and had forgotten everything else. And we saw that the little cloud was almost at a stand-still; yet that it was disturbed; sparks were flying from it; and we heard little clanking sounds, very faint, coming from it. They might mean great leaps and rearings.

'Suddenly we saw the master spring from that rock to which he had been clinging as limp as a leaf in autumn, spring from it with great life and roar up towards the leaca:

' "Liam! Liam! Liam Ruadh!" He turned to us, "Shout, boys, and break his fever," he cried. "Shout, shout!"

'We were glad of that.

' "Liam! Liam! Liam Ruadh!" we roared.

' "My God! My God!" we heard as we finished. It was the master's voice; he then fell down. At once we raised our voices again; it would keep us from seeing or hearing what was happening on the leaca.

' "Liam! Liam! Liam Ruadh!"

'There was wild confusion.

' "Liam! Liam! Liam! Ruadh! Ruadh! Ruadh!" the mountains were singing back to us, making the confusion worse. We were twisted about – one man staring at the ground, one at the rock in front of his face, another at the sky high over the leaca, and one had his hand stretched out like a sign-post on a hill-top, I remember him best; none of us were looking at the leaca itself. But we were listening and listening, and at last they died, the echoes, and there was a cold silence, cold, cold. Then we heard old Diarmuid's passionless voice begin to pray:

' "*Abhaile ar an sioruidheacht go raibh a anam.*" "At home in Eternity may his soul –" We turned round, one by one, without speaking a word, and stared at the leaca. It was bare! The little cloud was still in the air – a white dust ascending. Along the leaca we saw two thin shadowy lines – they looked as if they had been drawn in very watery ink on its dazzling surface. Of horses, plough, and fool there wasn't a trace. They had gone over the edge while we roared.

'Noble person, as they went over I'm sure Liam Ruadh had one fist at Lugh's bridle, and the other at Griosach's, and that he was swinging high in the air between them. Our roaring didn't break his fever, say that it didn't, noble person? But don't question the master about it. I have told you all!'

'I will leave this place to-night,' I said.

'It is late, noble person.'

'I will leave it now, bring me my horse.'

That is why I made no further enquiries in that valley as to the fate of that old Gaelic family that were once lords of those hills. I gave up the quest. Sometimes a thought comes to me that Liam Ruadh might have been the last of an immemorial line, no scion of which, if God had left him his senses, would have ploughed the Leaca of the Saints, no, not even if it were to save him from begging at fairs and in public houses.

STORM-STRUCK

I

O N AN AUGUST AFTERNOON the fishing village of Cuandor
on the west Cork coast is like a dream-village; it is so still.
Its rocky street is then a strip of sunshine, a strip of shadow;
and not a soul crosses from the one to the other: the men are far on
the sea, they have sailed in their nobbies and ketches for the Manx
fishing-grounds; and the women are at work in their gardens, bent
over the violets they grow in ridges, like potatoes, for the London
markets.

On such a day John Donovan arrived home from Butte City,
Montana. It looked as if he had stolen home. Even so, the news was
not long spreading from hedge to hedge – an empty story.

Nightfall brought no relief. Instead of his coming into Lavelle's
public house, there came Jack Kiniry from Ringogreine. On his way
he had passed the Donovans' house, and his tale was that the place
was dark and silent. And as he said so, his questioners saw it in
vision – a windy, stony place, just where the good land ended and
the cliffs began. Because it was so poor, the boy, John Donovan,
had sailed six years before for America.

The following day was Sunday. The church bell had tolled for
Mass; yet still, as was customary, the dark-cloaked women and
the sun-tanned men from the hills lingered in groups. They
whispered in low voices that the boy of the Donovans had come
home – a blinded man. But when, at the end of the rocky street,
the group they had waited for appeared, the blind man and his
aged father, the peasants moved silently into the church, where
already the priest was praying on the altar.

As the old man, bent almost double from years and the slavery
of his toil, led his son over the uneven ground, he looked up from
under his brows, to right, to left, and spoke no word. He looked

like one who had done something wrong. But his son was more than erect, his head flung nervously up in that sorry posture common to blind men and dreamers, his blank eyes sweeping equally landscape and sky and sea.

This had Butte City, Montana, done for him. A flash of light in the gloom of a copper mine, a rumble, a tremor; then, silence. Afterwards, amid a whispering of nun-like voices, the gradual return of consciousness in a bed of snow-white sheets, snow-white to judge by the feel of them. 'I want to go home,' he whined, like a boy who fails halfway in an adventure. Then recalling the explosion, he fainted again, and, as he did so, he heard someone whisper that his sight was gone.

The first night at home he scarcely spoke a word. His father and mother in their lonely house had lived more or less always in silence; and he, since his loss, had become acquainted with it. Perhaps, this first night, he was listening to the loud ticking of the weight-clock or to the crying seagulls. But after a long pause he blurted out: 'Where's Kitty Regan now?'

The old man and woman looked at each other, neither quite ready to answer; they knew what Kitty Regan had meant to him before his departure to America; they knew why there he had chosen the slavery of the copper mines and had hoarded his earnings. The father thought it better to speak carelessly, as if it now was all an old story:

'Oh, she married into Kilvonane parish.'

'I thought so,' said the blind man.

And in spite of his effort at control a quiver crossed his face, such as might happen in a dream. It went through his mother like a sword. She rose, putting an arm around his shoulder, laying her hand on his:

'Don't mind, boy,' she said: 'maybe 'tis she wasn't worthy of you – and look at the man she got; God help us, 'tis a hard life she has.' And the mother pressed the son to her breast.

He sprang to his feet.

'What's this? Bless me! We're not going to have scenes, sure we're not.'

And forgetting himself, he flung forward from her hands and

fell on the chair she had risen from. Steadying himself, he cursed several times in a voice that was hard and strange to them; it was his Butte City voice.

At first he took to sitting outside the door in the sunshine, and by dint of short and bitter answers soon rid himself of the gossips of the place. It seemed he could satisfy himself for ever with listening to the seagulls and rooks. However, after some weeks, he made friends with a boy named Conny Maher, and the two of them would go for long rambles on the cliff-tops. One day they got as far as Fylenashouk, the most windy, the highest of all the cliffs; and ever afterwards this was his favourite resting-place. It stands sheer above the sea: eastwards there is the long promontory running out to the Galley Head, in summer time a strip of gold terminating in a white point; westwards the coast is fringed with groups of rocky islets, pearly in the sun. Perhaps he remembered west and east in the touch of the wind.

One day in the late autumn, sitting there alone, he felt the sun darken; then a large rain-drop stabbed the back of his hand. In a second the whole shower was pelting on him. He bent his head waiting for it to pass; but the whole face of the day had changed – afar off he heard the dull rolling of thunder. He began to fidget. Carefully he stood up, crouching his back to the rain. He must not move, he might walk over the cliff; besides, Conny would soon come seeking him. But, as if it had leaped through a great distance of space, the thunder suddenly crashed about him. 'My God!' he said, listening to its rolling off. 'Conny, Conny,' he then cried out, and anger and anxiety struggled in his throat. Again and again he started, feeling that lightnings were playing about him. And 'Conny, Conny,' he screamed between the thunderclaps.

Unexpectedly a hand, wet with rain, caught his, and a coarse voice, yet a woman's voice, said 'Come.' Hastily they made forward over the rough ground, so hastily indeed that soon his breath went from him, and in spite of the rain he grew hot and sweaty. 'Stop a moment,' he gasped, 'I'm bate out, 'tis long since I went so fast.' He made to smile, but it flickered out at once, for he thought that he might be staring at a rock or tree. His hand had been dropped, and the stranger's silence stung him. 'Do you see a little boy anywhere? Dan Maher's little boy. Conny Maher?'

'No,' was the sullen answer.

'We'll go on,' he said, bitterly; his blindness had never so come home to him. The stranger again gripped his hand firmly, almost fiercely, and in the same headlong haste they made on through the pouring rain. 'Oh, oh,' he said, whenever the thunder burst; but his helpmate kept her silence. And so he stumbled on, until his limbs were staggering and his heart thumping.

'If there's e'er a shelter anywhere, I could wait; Conny will be coming –'

'Where's the shelter?'

Drooping, he stood fetching short breaths: 'You'll be all wet,' he said.

'Where's the harrum in it?'

'I'm all right now,' he said, and stretched out his useless hand once more.

When he found himself being dragged through some bushes he knew where he was.

'The road?' he said.

'Yes,' came a gasping reply.

More swiftly now they stumbled down the hill. He was gaining hope, reckoning that his house could not be far off, when his hand was suddenly flung down, seized, and dropped again, and 'Oh!' the voice cried, as if in terror. 'There's someone coming,' and the woman rushed from him.

'Kitty, Kitty Regan, for God's sake –' he cried, all in a breath, his voice wild and high with surprise and despair, his hand glauming at nothing. Only with her last word had her own voice broken from her, letting him know whose hand had led him. Too late; there he stood, his empty hand stretched out, the rain drenching it. His father came panting up to him. 'In the name of God, Shawn,' he said, 'how did 'oo come so far?'

'Whisht,' said the blind man, struggling with his thought.

''Tis a miracle from God, 'tis so,' said the old man, and 'Whisht, I'm telling ye,' was again his son's savage reply.

That night John Donovan sat like a dazed man in the kitchen; and outside the rain poured and winds went by howling. His presence imposed silence on the room. Twice had the old man raised his head and whispered: 'God pity them that's on the sea this night,' and twice his son had scowled at him. At last the old people went off, leaving him alone. He lingered for a few minutes, then taking a pine-splinter, and lighting it at the turves, he went into the little back room, lit a candle, as if he could see by its light, pulled the curtain down from the window, and sat wearily on the edge of the bed. He struggled to keep calm, but hot sweat came out all over him. Then he went cold and shivered. Worn out from stress of emotion, he would yawn in sheer exhaustion, would endeavour to calm himself, to sit still, to smile. But he could not. He rose and moved about; sat down and rose again, while the storm grabbed at his little house as if it would sweep it bodily over the cliffs; and every other moment he would stretch his ear towards the window, listening, jerking his head quickly about like a bird's. At last, muttering, he removed his boots, and was standing upright when, as if he had heard a noise outside his window, he sprang forward, quenched the light with one quick slap, flung open the window, and thrust his head, his blind head, out into the storm, whispering wild and yearning words of invitation and love. But the night was empty of companionship.

Chilled and angry, he drew back and threw himself along the bed, and grabbed at the bedclothes, rocking himself to and fro, sobbing out the one word – No! No! – over and over again, unwilling to confess defeat, unwilling to face the blank, loveless future. Yet in the end his words died away; self-pity clothed him all over with the warmth of tears; his passion ebbed, he slept.

The woman's sleep was different. Her they found next day, bedraggled, muddied, soaked, lying in a gully far back in the hills between Cuandor and Kilvonane, where her husband lived. She had been visiting her parents, had set off across the hills; the storm had overtaken her, had waylaid her. Her hands were torn, and she bled from the brow; she must have stumbled blindly on for many a mile in fright and fear. Perhaps she *had* skulked about John Donovan's house; this, anyway, was what he meant to suggest when in the crowd of gossips that gathered in Lavelle's public house discussing the event, he began to jest about the storm-birds that seek shelter from the storm at the lighthouse-keeper's window, how they do not have the courage to enter when the window is opened to them. The gossips could not understand; they stared in wonder at his bitter lips, his stony eyes.

THE WAGER

I

THE GENTRY weren't broken out of the country at that time; and some of them, most of them, did what they liked with us. When they were beginning to go down the hill, when the old times were gone, many of them had to content themselves with living in their own places, instead of in Dublin or London, and as often as they grew weary of the hunting, the dancing, the cards, would have to think of new pastimes for themselves.

At that time our sleeping place was a long loft over the workmen's sheds, over the smith's shop, the wheelwright's shop, and the weaver's. The weaver, though he was almost blind with old age and had a hump on his back, still gave no thought to anything except his trade. For hundreds of years, it was said, his people had been weavers; and he was terrified that he might lose some of the secrets they had left him. He was a bad sleeper, and any night at all we might hear him getting up and dressing himself and going down to his shop. 'Very well, so; very well, so,' we'd hear him repeating to himself as he rose, just as if he had been reluctantly compelled to accept the challenge of some voice within his brain – the voice of dead and gone Considines; and hours after his rising we might wake up again and hear the timbers of his machine luffing and swinging about and creaking, not loud and sharp at all, but drowsily in the stillness of the night.

Now, the last thing I remember that night was Sean O'Brosnan turning over noisily in his truckle bed, making its frame-work creak all over. 'Between them and him,' he said, 'there's no knowing night from day.' That night the Master had great company at the house, and we could hear them carousing and singing and breaking the glasses, although the full depth of the courtyard lay between us and the back of the mansion. As Sean said these words I was lazily watching the beams from the weaver's lantern striking up from the workshop beneath, striking up through the joints of the flooring, and nosing their way into the cobwebs under the rafters as if they would get at the sleepy spiders. That's the last thing I remember – Sean twisting and turning and snarling both at the weaver and the Master. And 'twould be hard to blame him, for he had given all that day to training the Master's racers, the two-year-olds – on the sands beneath the cliffs, a kind of work that leaves one sore enough and tired enough. My work that day had been snagging turnips in the sun, and a half-field of them still remained to be done – easy work if the weather held; and I was not greatly put out either by the chorusing or the weaving: my limbs were tired – thick and heavy, and I was happy enough staring like that up at the beams of light ferreting their way into the cobwebs while the pull and drag of the loom went on drowsily below. I went to sleep, and I awoke to hear somebody trying to undo the door of the loft. I thought at first that it was the weaver coming up to bed after working off his fit; but the fumbling continued rather violently, noisily, so I lifted myself on the point of my elbow saying, 'That's queer; that's not Peadar Considine at all,' because I knew Peadar, after his sixty years of handling it, could unfasten the rickety old contraption in his sleep. As I listened the door gave way suddenly, and in came the Master. It was a thing he had never done before. He stood there with his lantern raised almost as high as his mouth trying to find out the lie of the place. He did not know which of the nine beds held the man he was looking for. There were only six of us there at that moment: the two horse boys, the two jockeys, a labouring man who was a widower, and myself. The weaver was below in his shop, and the two herds were gathering the cattle for the fair in Dingle. 'Twas for Sean O'Brosnan, one of his jockeys, the best of them, he was looking; and he stood there, with his hunting coat still on him, swinging about, swaying, steadying himself, pouting out his heavy lips stupidly, his limbs still drunk but his mind struggling and struggling to master them. I do not know how it came into my head that it was Sean he wanted:

'Sean, Sean,' I whispered across to him, ''tis you he's looking for.' Sean was fast asleep, but even so, at my first word he was as bright as day. He sat up at once like a stag nosing the wind. He was that sort, a whisper would go through him, limbs and brain. He was thin and angular and had a lot of high-tempered steel in him; he was the Master's favourite, and he'd win a race or lose it as pleased himself.

'What? What?' he said, staring crossly at me, thinking maybe that he had found it hard enough to get to sleep that night. I jerked with my thumb towards the door:

' 'Tis the Master,' I said.

Sean stared in that direction:

'Is it me you're wanting, sir?' he said, with curiosity.

The Master couldn't easily find the voice; at last his eyes rested on Sean sitting upright.

'Don't rise,' he said thickly, and with that he came and sat on Sean's box at the foot of the trestle, and put the lantern on the floor, its light blazing up at Sean's face. It was a long, firm face, without a wisp of waste flesh on it. We felt it our duty to turn away. I thought of it first and the others followed my lead. 'Twas then the Master heard the luffing and creaking of the loom below: 'For God's sake, what's that?' he asked, and we overheard Sean telling him 'twas a common thing with the weaver to rise up and give a few hours in the calm of the night to his trade. The Master, we understood, gave no further thought to it. The two of them then began whispering together: it reminded us of priest and penitent; but after some time we noticed Sir Timothy's voice had become a cajoling whine while Sean's grew harder and harder: 'No,' he'd say, 'No,' or 'Let him,' or 'What's that to me?' and at last we heard him taking refuge in: 'We don't live twice, nobody lives twice.'

They were after forgetting all about us; likely for the two of them at that moment the world was a blank about them. 'Then I'm broke so, I'm broken out entirely,' the Master cried at last; and he took a step closer and put his blob of a hand on Sean's shoulder, as we learned after, and the whispering began again. 'We don't live twice,' was still Sean's unvarying answer. At last the Master grabbed viciously at the lantern and rose up: 'I'm deceived in you, Sean O'Brosnan, I'm deceived,' he snarled, and was turning away when a new thought struck him, for he looked down solemnly at Sean and said, 'There are Brosnans – there are Brosnans above in Kilvreeda and they'd do it for me – if only I could rouse them,' and he kept staring at Sean, we felt, for there wasn't a sound to be heard.

What did he mean by it? Kilvreeda is that bit of a graveyard above on the hill, and what he meant was that Sean was not as good a bit of stuff as his forbears. When we caught the words we were hard put to it to keep from turning towards Sean to see how he'd take it. He made no reply. What we heard was the poor daft weaver down below, and his working, we noticed, had neither quickened nor slowed down; it was as regular as a clock that might keep time for ever.

While we still waited for a sound from one or the other in swung the door again, this time with a swish, a clatter, as if now it was broken from the hinges entirely. In the opening we saw a second lantern swinging to and fro, gaily, recklessly. Old Sir Daniel O'Keeffe it was we saw there; and his five wild nephews, crowded behind him, were laughing and backing him obedient to his beck and call as usual. It was with him our Master was after making the wager. Sir Daniel was jubilant; he was making a sort of sing-song of Sir Timothy, he was 'Oh, oh-ing!' and 'Ah, ah-ing!' and 'Now, Sir Timothy,' 'Now, Sir Timothy,' as if he could think of nothing else. He held that he had won, that Sean had refused the jumping. He blurted out then, 'You're right, Sean,' although Sean had not spoken at all. 'You're right, there's a good many of them in it,' he meant in the graveyard, 'but not a man of them all would even try it, would even try it. There's not a Brosnan in Kilvreeda would try it, no, nor even in –' And now, look you, how pride and confidence will bring a man to his ruin. He was sure he had won the wager, the heaviest Sir Timothy had ever laid: people said afterwards it was all the land beyond the river – and he couldn't content himself with that nor with belittling the Brosnans in Kilvreeda, without going back to belittle the Brosnans in the Abbey in Killarney. What he said was: 'There's not a Brosnan in Kilvreeda would jump it, no, nor in Muckross!'

At that we all sat up, hiding our heads no longer. We looked at Sean. You will remember there is a great difference between the Brosnans who lie in Kilvreeda and those in Muckross Abbey. You might say 'tis only since yesterday, since they came down in the world, that the Brosnans are satisfied to lie in Kilvreeda. The Brosnans who lie in Kilvreeda were just poor common people like ourselves, but the ancient Brosnans, from time immemorial they had been laid in the Abbey with the MacCarthys, the O'Sullivans, the O'Donoghues, and the MacGillicuddys. Well, Sir Daniel had the great foolishness to say that even the ancient O'Brosnans in the Abbey wouldn't dare the jump in the wager! The last word wasn't out of his mouth when Sean himself was standing on the floor, fronting him, like a vision that was going to blast him.

'Without going back at all to them that's in the Abbey there's a Brosnan left here to jump it or drown in the boiling sea,' he said, and he turned to Sir Timothy and 'Is it now?' he asked him, civilly and respectfully. But Sir Timothy was frightened by that word, the boiling sea, and Sir Daniel was no better; he was swinging his lantern no longer, and his face was blank and cold. 'Is it now?' Sean asked again, looking from one to the other; and when Sir Daniel nodded, he began at once clutching quickly at his clothes to dress himself; and at once we all rose up in silence and began doing the same.

II

Here we are on the heights: look northwards now. To the right, making forward along the fall of the land, you can spy out the trace of the old road: follow it on and on and you'll find it stops suddenly at the edge of the cliff. In the old times, in that place, the rocks fell, making in one single night the ledge that's there to this day. It is about seventeen feet below the edge, sheer down below it; and is, it may be, twelve feet wide at the widest, a rocky bracket of irregular shape. Well, the wager was that Sean was to ride one of the Master's hunters from the stable door up along the old roadway, turn homewards then, keeping by the edge of the cliff, and as he came along jump sideways over the bit of protecting wall and land on the ledge beneath, steady his mount on it as best he could or, as he said himself, go down into the boiling sea – a true saying, for even in the height of summer, if one looks down from the table of rock one sees stretches of broken foam beneath, twisting and turning or diving with agony into the black depths where the rocks go straight down.

The company left us to dress there in the loft; and silently enough we went about it, not knowing what to say to Sean for he was never an easy man to make talk with. But this is a thing we have since often spoken about among ourselves: as we were dressing in silence, nervously, wondering if we were doing right in not stopping the whole caper, we heard the old weaver below passionately at work in the middle of the night! And it was at the selfsame moment we all found ourselves listening to his loom, and the selfsame thought must have struck into all our minds, for when Sean had finished dressing, when he had flung on his coat and blessed himself, he stood up straight and, as we all glanced at him, said with one of his strange looks: 'Very well, so, very well, so,' speaking quickly and quite suddenly, the very words the weaver used to say of a night-time when he rose up to the weaving. He then turned to go down.

Liam, the turf boy, had more presence of mind than the rest of us. He raced for the door and called after Sean: ''Twould be the best of your play to go and have a sconce at it,' meaning the ledge. But we heard Sean descending the ladder quickly and firmly.

'What did he say?' we asked.

'Not a word,' the boy answered.

For that matter, however, there was not a foot of the land that Sean did not know the look of and the feel of.

III

When we came out into the front courtyard we all stopped to note the sight before us. It was noisy and confused. Dogs and horses were everywhere. Some of the roisterers were already mounted, and others were doing their best to mount, blubbering, many of them, in a way that you'd pity. The two old coaches, one of them falling asunder, were wheeled out that the ladies might be taken to see the 'midnight ride' as one of them said with a snigger. Lanterns were swinging and moving, very ruddy-looking in the cold shadows hard by the walls of the courtyard: and all was life and bustle and riding off and yelping and yowling.

Sean was in the stables choosing the horse. He pitched on Litis, the Master's favourite mount. She was called Litis because she was a cold sort of white, without a tint of warmth in it. Litis is an Irish word. We stood clustered about the gates of the stables looking in at him examining her: and as he lifted one hoof after another making sure of her shoes, we heard him snarling through his teeth: 'Very well, so, very well, so.' The ancient Brosnans, as everyone knows, were the best horsemen in Corkaguiney. When we thought of this we went almost cold to hear their living descendant speaking to them in that hard and bitter way.

When he had finished he stood up and said: 'Send the Master in to me,' speaking like a chieftain giving his orders. Sir Timothy we brought to him.

''Tis Litis I'm riding,' he said. The Master pursed out his lips angrily, we thought, but then softened quickly: he was afraid Sean might draw back. 'Certainly. Anything you like. I'm thankful to you.' The word then went out that no one should go nearer to the ledge than the old *lios* which looks down over all the scene from the open hillside. It was afterwards settled, however, that the turf boy should lie in the heather by the edge: if he kept still in that position there was small fear that he'd frighten the hunter.

The company on their horses and the ladies in their carriages made out along the avenue for the roadway, and we crossed the lawn and hurried through the parkland on to the open slopes above the sea. After the darkness of the trees, the scene was dazzling.

The sun had gone down that October evening sullenly in dusky crimson and flaming gold; afterwards the clouds cleared and a frost had fallen. The wide stretches on the cliff-tops were white with it, the silent sheep were white with it; but wherever a streak of shadow was laid at all it was as black as ink, and sharp and strong. The moon was behind us, however, and only little jabs of shadow were visible: we were looking at a sharp-edged slope of white; beyond it was a grey mass, whether sea or sky one could not say except when out on the reef a run of foam would catch the moon's rays for a moment, wriggle silver-bright, like an eel caught in the hand, and then go out, leaving the darkness vast and vacant.

We made upwards across that white slope to the *lios*; and as we swept through the newly frozen grass and heather we left dark wet-looking tracks behind us. Far to the right we heard the gentry coming along the road. They met the herds driving the cattle to the fair in Dingle: the way was blocked by them, blocked completely, for three score cattle had been gathered together. Out raced Sir Timothy, wild with anger: 'Be off with yourselves,' he cried at the herds, and he ran his horse against them so viciously that they had to dive and juggle among the cattle to avoid him. 'Clear the road,' he bellowed, 'or I'll have your lives.'

They thought he had gone mad, shouting like that and leading all that rout with him along a half-forgotten road in a lonely land after the cocks had long crowed for midnight. The stock they goaded helter skelter into the bogs; and all the night afterwards we could hear the beasts crying and moaning, not knowing where they were.

We gathered to the *lios*, the gentry making their own of the raised ground within it. The Master then had all the dogs and horses taken back to the stables, fearing that some of them might make a noise or bolt off at the sound of the hoofs.

IV

'Stop that chatter,' the Master cried angrily at us, and I tell you we stopped it and held our peace. A bullock, far off, began to moan. 'Do you hear that, do you hear that?' he whined in agony.

'Is Liam below?' he asked later, and someone answered:
'You can see him.'

'I can't,' he snarled, putting an end to the talk. It was true that he could not see the boy, for we, who were younger, could hardly make out the figure on the ground, stretched out with his face almost over the edge of the cliff. If Sean did not jump, if at the last moment he took fright and raced on, 'twould go hard with the boy to save himself from the thundering hoofs.

After the lights and the yowling and the stamping of the horses and the quick, careless voices in the courtyard, the silence in which we had now to cluster together in that broken *lios* seemed to leave us without any defence against the chill in the air: we felt it settling down on our shoulders, like a cold hand; and the dainty ladies in spite of their wrappings began to shiver from head to foot.

But it was not long till we heard a lively daring galloping making up the rocky road behind us on the hill; we heard the hoofs smiting the rocky ribbings that run obliquely across that deserted roadway, and the whole wide night, as well as ourselves, seemed to listen to them as they rang out in the frosty air. Since Sir Timothy did not turn his head, we dared not do so, but even had we done so we could scarcely have seen the horseman.

Louder and louder the hoofs kept beating their rocky anvil until the crest of the hill was reached; then they softened, as if the rider was making a more careful descent.

At last we lost them; we knew then that Sean had turned in at the gap and was coming along by the cliff. It was a heavy thudding now that filled our ears. Soon we spied out what we had been peering for – a white mass bounding through the moonlit air.

That live mass suddenly seemed to burst through some veil; man and horse, at last we saw them clearly. With his long greyish stockings below his bleached corduroy knee breeches, with his white linen shirt, his fair head, he looked to be all as white as Litis herself. As they came more broadside on they shone out against the haze that covered the sea. They travelled forward with confident dash and swiftness, and the look of them was so fine that we lifted ourselves up forgetting our fear, forgetting the Master's commands. The pounding of the horse's hoofs was in our hearts. Our mouths were open, we heard a voice, masterful. The animal's head stretched out, threw itself up lightly. The white mass lifted itself, hung a moment in the air like a flower, then down it went, almost plumb. Not a sound then. We went cold to the marrow. The turf boy had not stirred. All our eyes were upon him. At last we saw him begin to wriggle rapidly along the edge, then to say something we could not catch – an excited voice. We strained to hear, and one of our ladies began to giggle losing control of herself.

'Stay where ye are,' whispered the Master hoarsely, and he broke from us and made down the slope. Halfway down he stopped suddenly. The turf boy had risen to his feet, was running along the edge, was crouched down again.

Then we saw Sean rise up above the top of the cliff. Quite still, erect, moon-bright, he stood with his back to the sea. From him the turf boy drew away, staring. Our Master, however, pulled himself together. He gave a wild view halloo and started to run down with his hand out towards his jockey. We all then started too to run down the slope, yet we were not certain of ourselves. For Sean stood still, erect, somehow proud, like a noble doorway awaiting a distracted mob and would find refuge within it. Breasting the full light of the moon he stood, white from head to foot, against the dull background of frosty air. His head was as high as he could hold it, and he took no notice of the Master's extended hand. So still he was he looked like a pillar stone erected in the old times on the edge of some ravine of wreckage.

We weren't surprised when the Master, drawing near, showed some confusion and unsteadiness; he even half turned to see how close to him we were. We gathered about him in kindliness. Soon we were all standing still, waiting, and then we noticed that that pillar stone of pride was trembling from head to foot. Our Master too noticed it, and in his confusion he straightway blurted out what he should have kept to himself: 'Where's the animal?' The trembling lips, pale and drawn, did not speak. Our Master's confusion got still more hold of him. He was a man of no character, and in such a one the least trace of submission in another will raise heat and arrogance; he now spoke quite boldly: 'I'm saying where's the animal?' Without a moment's delay he was answered:

'In the sea!'

And saying these words, the descendant of the Brosnans withdrew his eyes contemptuously from his abashed Master and strode through us all, noble and simple, as if we were so much dirt off the road.

V

It was all a bad night's work. The two great families fell out, Sir Daniel maintaining that the drowning of the animal excused him from paying the wager: and this falling out between them hastened their decay. The innocent boy who was the only witness of whatever wild thing took place between Sean and the horse on the ledge, a new look came into his eyes, into his mouth; as soon as ever he could he cleared away to America with his secret untold. And as for Sean himself – whoever knew a man that was happy and comfortable to carry his head in the air as Sean carries his?

THE RUINING OF DROMACURRIG

I T WAS A DESERTED-LOOKING PLACE between the main road and the sea, and because I could find no one to tell me of it, the whole countryside was so desolate, I took the by road that I thought must lead to it. I had not gone far when I found myself staring at a large old mansion set in a ring of stubborn trees. It was gone grey in colour, woodwork and all, and the three or four stone steps that led to the hall door had long since become unsettled; dandelion and tall grasses were growing up vigorously between the stones of them. The garden round about was a wilderness. Only with difficulty one followed the path in it. It brought me into some cobblestoned passages, also grass-grown, which were flanked with what was once well-set-out stabling for, it was clear, a large number of animals. Neither garden nor house had prepared me for such a range of stables, and I looked about me in some wonderment, noticing more particularly than anything else how utterly the southern sunshine and the winds from the sea had cleansed the place from any sign or smell of the horses: the stalls were shutterless, doorless, and looking at them one had the same feeling as when a person turns out his pockets to show us how empty they are.

I wandered round and round and at last discovered a sort of pathway that should, I imagined, take me again to the main road. I came on an old bare-headed man sitting on a bank as if he were a portion of it, as if he had been always sitting there. The look in his eyes told me he had been watching me all the time I had been exploring that broken dwelling place. It was he who told me of the ruining of the property, and something like this was his way of telling it:

'Tis only too well I remember every twist and turn of that long day, and the night that followed it. The news came to me maybe later than to anyone else, it was after three o'clock; and when I made over towards the house I came on the master himself, Richard Donegan, and he standing his full height in the midst of a crowd of them. I noticed how big he was, and that was but natural, for the rest of them were only a rabble of stable boys and horse boys and jockeys, jockeys in the making and jockeys that would never ride again, poor creatures that their misfortunes had twisted and broken. Tough they were, hardy and tough, but undersized, as was best for them. Himself was taking no heed of them. His eyes were glaring across the fields, out on the sea, and a flood of speech was gushing from his lips. 'I haven't looked at a horse for six weeks,' he was saying, 'I haven't mounted a back for two months – maybe ye don't know what I'm meaning by that?'

Well, we were hard put to think what was right to say to him, we were only poor hands at comforting a man in distress. Our voices and our way of speech itself were again' us. Some of us were saying, 'Yes,' and others 'No,' and others again only saying, 'Don't, Master' – saying it over and over again like what you'd say to a child. Maybe after all it didn't matter what we said, because 'twas little of it he noticed, his own flood of thoughts was that hot and strong within him. There he was staring over the heads of us across the pasture lands, not knowing how many of us were there nor who was absent. But 'tis often I thought since that the very smell of our clothes, the smell of the horses from us, and the look in our eyes, and our bony chins, and our big woollen mufflers, and our buttons, and straps, and leggings and all, were good for him in the way he was. For 'twas true what he said, that he hadn't flung a leg over a horse since his wife was given over. Indeed maybe he couldn't have a better medicine to relieve the poor foolish heart within him than the crowd of us to be there about him with the smell of the stables all over us. But that was a thing he didn't understand then nor indeed any of the rest of us either. He began to moan about his poor wife, saying that we could never understand what she was to him, saying that he knew he was a hard man and a wild man, but that his heart would now be empty for evermore, and that no one could comfort him. And although we knew he had some drink in him, as was only natural, we began to imagine that maybe after all he was not at bottom the harum-scarum creature we thought he was. He'd shake his head above us and cry out that his wife was always the flower of the meadowland – I remember the things he said quite well – and the star of the gentle dawn, and his treasure and his hope; and that she filled the day for him with sunlight, and many other curious sayings like that. And then he'd take a change and say that he was making too bold on us, and that we should excuse him, and that he was after having a great sweep, that is, a great blow, and that he wasn't master of himself, that he didn't know what he was saying nor where he was standing nor how he had passed the night. And at last he was for bringing us all into the house with him.

But the men around me whispered to me that that was the very thing the women in the house didn't want; that they were hardly done yet with the laying out of the corpse of his wife; and that they had asked some of the horse boys to take the creature out with them, and keep him away with them as long as they could. Yet in with him he would have us go, all of us, and we had to struggle hard to get the notion out of his head. At last I said to him that the house was the women's; that 'tis little they'd thank us to go in until they had the place ready for us; but that maybe he'd come down the yard with us to my place and take a bit of food there.

I made a mistake there. He blazed out in my face for thinking that he was such a beast of a man as to let a crumb of sustenance, even one crumb, and a crumb was a small thing, pass his lips at such a time. 'You mistake me, Jerry,' he said. 'It must be to sticks and stones I'm talking. 'Tis little ye understand a man like me. 'Tis little ye understand the nature of me. Ye know little of grief or sorrow if 'tis talking of food ye are,' and then again he'd call his dead lady the flower of the meadowland and the lamp that was quenched, and a lot more like that; and at last he turned on us as if he'd scatter us away from him in his indignation: 'Ye're telling me to eat up and drink up or my health will fail me. What health has that poor white face inside, and it so thin too, and the candles burning on the two sides of her and the flowers smelling?' And he told us, and maybe 'twas true and maybe it was not, that 'twas often he caught his own breasts and tore them down, mad because he couldn't share some of the great strength he had in him with the poor white-faced woman who had gone so woebegone and delicate. And then he'd say that the world was badly contrived to have the good and the beautiful going so soon to the grave and useless stumps like himself spared to encumber the ground. But at last I won him over. He said that God knew he hadn't the strength to resist me, that a child could lead him, the way he was, with his mind distracted and the comfort of his house snatched away from him. The slender one who brought him victory was dead, he said, and the column was broke, and the wreath scattered, and a great many other things that he remembered in the songs and ballads, they were gushing out of his mouth as if he hadn't to think of them at all, as if indeed he had a great store of them gathered up in his mind.

Well, I got my arm in his, and with my eye I told one of the older jockeys to keep close for fear he'd stumble on me, and with a look I told another to go back to the house and tell them where the master was gone. The rest of them followed us a little way behind and not a word out of them. He was moaning and groaning as we went along, repeating over and over again, surprising us with the names he was putting on the dead woman, surprising us all, because we knew he was no man for the books or the music. Indeed his business at that time was too big for him to have leisure for anything else. And it wasn't the business alone – though it was then at its best, with horses coming to us for training from the other end of Ireland, and from England too, because of those soft splendid fields we had and the sands below and the lonely roads that were as good to us as if the master owned every perch of them. The property is a sad sight now, a sad sight and a lonesome sight. But it wasn't the business alone, I'm saying, it was all the trouble he'd get into, he was that careless about what he'd say and what he'd promise – things he could never bring to pass – and 'twas only into court with him and out of court with him, from one case to another, and figures and names and accounts all mixed up in his brain. And besides that, we'd have accidents, and sicknesses, and losses, and victories, which were worse maybe than the losses, and lies told about us, and himself rushing up to Dublin and over to London to get the better of his enemies; and he coming home in a week or two in such a state that you wouldn't like to be looking at him – the big purple face of him so blue and shivery.

II

We got safely beyond the garden and were coming along a path through the fields when we all lifted our heads to the sounds of hoofs in the distance. It was a sunny afternoon in March, bright and clear, sharp enough too, and the roads were hard. The hoofs were far off when we heard them. All of us knew it was Robby Leddy bringing Starlight home – the hope of our stable – and a lovely thing she was – bringing her from the railway station; and we knew that he'd be making haste and that he'd be proud and high in his bearing, for he was after winning on her from a big field in County Waterford. In spite of the trouble and confusion on us all we couldn't help listening to the fall of the shoes and they so smart and ringing. Maybe the master himself was the worst of us all for that. He stopped up his rambling hullagoning, and when I glanced up at him I saw his big mouth and it hanging open, dead and helpless, like you'd see the clab of an idiot. He had the look of a man who climbs up a desolate mountain side and then sees down below him on the other side a shining scenery, something he didn't think to see. His head was flung up and his ears, as I knew well, were full of the music. Suddenly he stepped out from us, as if he was a new man, and across the field with him making for a gate where, he knew, the horse would have to pass. We all kept by him, of course, and when we had covered about half the ground he clamped his hand down heavily on my shoulder and began to say that Robby Leddy was a good boy, and that it was kind father for him, and that 'twas the pity of the world, so 'twas, that he had such an unfortunate day for bringing such grand news home with him. What use was good luck now to any of us, he said, or prosperity, and what was one horse above another or one jockey above another? But all the same, and he even saying the words, I knew he was listening to the beating of the horse's hoofs as well as any of us.

One of the boys, his name was Timsy Gallagher, he ran ahead of us; he took away the stone and swung the gate back into the field for us to go through. Our master was the first. When he turned east he stopped up dead. And we stopped up too. We saw him staring at a high trap that had been left standing beneath the bushes, the reins flung over one of the branches. ''Tis Denis's trap,' he said, frowning as black as night; and then he barked out at us: 'The news wasn't long travelling to them, I tell ye!'

But 'tis right for you to know that Denis Cashman was the brother of the woman who was after dying. He was the one man in the world that the master didn't want to see just then. He was tall and straight and hard; his mind as tough as his body. He had no talk in him, and no forgiveness. Soon after his sister married the master, the master made him a present of a hunter; but only a few weeks were gone by when Denis wanted to give the hunter back, so that he'd feel himself at liberty to tell the master what he thought of him and the queer people he was bringing to Droma-currig – visitors, a sort of company his sister was never used to. It took half the countryside to keep him from sending back the horse; it broke a leg soon after, and Denis, they say, grinned a smile when he lifted the gun to put it out of pain.

Well, we were clustered about the trap, and the master had his hand on the shaft of it when Robby brought Starlight swinging round the corner in a way that would raise the heart in you. He lifted himself up in the saddle to see us all there, master as well as the rest, to meet him; the poor boy's mouth was laughing, and we saw his white teeth shining. '*He* hasn't heard the news yet,' the master said, bitterly.

The boy didn't hear him; all the same, he saw that something was after going wrong, for none of us spoke a word of welcome or anything, nor raised a hand. I think the master would surely do so if the sight of Denis's trap had not put him out. 'Twas Denis he was thinking of, his sharp bony face, his close-cropped sandy hair, the thin weather-stained cheeks, the frost-bitten ears. He knew by the trap that he'd have to meet Denis in the house later on.

Horses are delicate, you know. You'd think that Starlight too knew that things were not all they should be. She was nervous, wheeling and snorting, arching her neck, tossing and champing. The boy was trying to hear what one of the jockeys was whispering up to him; and once or twice Starlight nearly flung him over her head. At last he understood. He twisted the horse about with a strong wrist, touched his cap, and said: 'I'm sorry for your trouble, sir.'

The master nodded three or four times in a dull sort of way. Whatever was the matter with Starlight, she flung out wild, backing, and twisting, and shaking herself, and all of a sudden she went up in the air, her forefeet battling above our heads. 'Stop it! Stop it! Stop it!' the master cried out all at once, as dark as thunder. 'Twas to the horse he said it. But again she went dancing on the road, scattering us. And again she went up in the air. The master snatched the whip from the trap and brought the lash down with all his force on the hind quarters of the animal; once, twice, three times he brought it down as viciously as he could. 'Stop it! Stop it! Stop it!' he yelled out every time he struck it, without any shame, and he springing about the road at the horse's heels. 'Twas getting rid of his anger he was. I then thought of crying out: 'Take it home, Rob,' and the horse was off like a flash.

We then saw Denis Cashman, bare-headed, cold-looking, coming towards us. Maybe he thought 'twas his own horse was in trouble until he saw Starlight rushing by. But the master didn't want to wait for him, I think he couldn't bear to wait for him. So he stepped off swiftly to meet him. He put out his hand to him:

'Forgive me. I'm excited. That animal excited me. It excited me. It maddened me. I cut it down. I lashed it. I'd kill it as soon as I'd look at it. What's one horse to me now above another? The flower of my meadowland is mown down – my meadowland is wasted. But you're after seeing her. My slender lily, my poor wife. 'Tis a sad spectacle.'

Denis Cashman was one without any nonsense in him. The wild mad look of the master confused him for a second or two. He glared at him and then said in a cold sort of way: ''Tis no time to be excited.'

To that the master answered:

''Tis not. That's true. 'Tis no time to be blazing out. But the animal maddened me. The way it showed off – there! there! There, in that spot; and that poor thing inside between the candles!'

And with that he covered his face with his arm. It made no difference. Denis Cashman answered – like stones falling in a well:

'What is done is done.'

And he kept a glinty eye sideways on the master, challenging him you'd think. The master turned to me and said: 'We'll go on now, Jerry.'

But mind you I had to catch him and put him in the right direction he was so bothered by the coldness of the other.

We made back into the field and although we did not turn around, for indeed we dared not turn around, we knew that Denis Cashman's eyes never left us till we were gone from his sight.

III

Now, we hadn't the master long sitting in the middle of us when, in spite of his fine words, he was eating and drinking too. Coming on nightfall the women sent over to say that the neighbours were gathering in for the wake, and that maybe 'twas the master's place to receive them. The oldest of us went back with him to the house then. I needn't say the place was crowded – his people are more than a hundred years in the parish, and her people – God only knows how many hundreds of years the Cashmans are in it – and of course there was plenty for all of us to do. We had to see that no one was neglected and that it wouldn't be in the power of anyone to throw a bad word at Dromacurrig afterwards. I stayed there till 'twas half-past two; and of course I'd stay the night, only that my wife's father, he was over seventy at the time, could hold out no longer. When I saw that everything was right the two of us came away. My wife's father, he was a living saint. Even as we came across from the house, there he was with the beads hanging from his hand.

'Twas a calm night with the moon shining full in on us from the sea. The air was lovely and cool and fresh after the heat of the rooms and the steaming glasses and the babble of voices, some of the farmers and the fishermen rising a little tipsy and inclined to sing only for the people beside them holding them in talk of the times that were past and gone. And do you know the thought that came to me and we coming along in the silence – that my poor old father-in-law with his handsome face and his bald head bent down by reason of his devotion – that he put a crown on the night entirely. Never a word passed between us till we reached the foot of the steps, when he blessed himself with the cross. Where we lived was in the middle of the stables, indeed there was a row of them beneath us. 'Twas for safety myself and one or two others were living above the horses. And a flight of stone steps led up from the outside to the couple of rooms we had. 'Twas when we got to the top of the steps, where there was a great big flag, that the old man and myself turned to look out over the harbour admiring the wonder of the night and the peace that was over everything.

Then I lifted the latch and went in. I knew the rooms would be empty, herself and the boys and girls were all helping at the wake. No sooner were we in than the old man let himself down into an old armchair he always made his own of, and I went groping for some matches on the mantelpiece. The moon was shining across the floor. I thought I heard something stirring out in the yard at the back. I stepped over to the window and looked out. The white-washed walls of the sheds and the tarred roofs of the stables and the polished cobblestones of the passages, they were all lit up with the brightness of the moon. I looked and I heard the sounds again, and when I looked better 'twas what I saw – the master himself and he crouched down and he fumbling at the lock of

Starlight's stable! I remembered then that just before we left the wake someone said the master had broken down entirely, and had had to go up to his room. Starlight's stable was the room he made for when the course was clear! He was vexed, it seemed; he was jabbering, and his voice would rise and fall in the dint of his anger. I was petrified watching him there. The patient old man, behind me in the armchair, kept still for some time, then he said:

'What are you doing?'

'Be quiet,' I said.

Of course he was puzzled then. He said:

'The candle, why aren't you lighting it?'

'Be quiet,' I said again. 'Sit there.'

He saw that I had some reason for being severe with him. He sat still, his two hands flat on his knees. But then he too heard the bits of speech coming up from the yard, and he could not contain himself:

'What's happening out there? Who's there at all?'

It failed the master to open the stable door. Maybe he hadn't the right key at all. He gave it up, he moved aside to the air hole: there were laths across it. He put his hand through the laths, far as 'twould go. And whether Starlight came over to the hand or didn't come, a great change came into the master's jabbering. 'Oh, ooh! Ooh!' he was saying like you'd pet a child of yours. And he was after forgetting the anger he was in. He called the animal his flower of the meadowland, and his star of victory, and every single thing he was after saying already about his dead lady! And mind you, 'twas a very different voice he had; you'd think 'twas a different man was there. There was music in his throat this time, I tell you, full of satisfaction and comfort. 'Twas that that set me on fire altogether – the same words to be sounding so different! I got red and angry. I drew away from the window. I couldn't help myself saying: 'Terrible, terrible.' I had forgotten about the old man. As old as he was he stood up.

'What's terrible? Who's abroad? Who's outside?'

I didn't answer him. I could only stride down the length of the room and back again.

'Is that the master's voice?' he said this time, because the daft creature outside was getting reckless, maybe he was after forgetting where he was or maybe the horse had come to his hand. I couldn't help saying:

''Tis.'

'Who is he talking to?'

I made him no answer, I stood still in the middle of the room with no idea what was the right thing for me to do. But the master was growing careless of everything now. Louder and louder he gave out what was in him, and over and over again, just as he was doing in the evening. The old man suddenly straightened himself up:

'Is he saying – slender lily flower?'

'He is.'

'Is he saying: star of victory?'

'He is,' I said, 'stop now.'

But he couldn't stop, and I wanting to think what was the right thing to do. He blazed out indignantly:

'Why, them's the words Timsy Gallagher told me he was saying about the lady is dead!'

That surprised me, and it frightened me, too, for I was thinking he could find no meaning in what the master was saying, that he would think it the foolish gabble of a tipsy man. Just then I heard Starlight whinny and clatter in the stall, and the noise somehow instructed me what to do. I caught a chair and I drew it along the floor heavily, so that he'd be warned someone was after coming in to my house. Sure enough he heard the noise. He started, and then I saw him bend down and scramble along the walls guilty-like, disgracefully. He got off through the wicket.

I turned to my old father-in-law.

'What's after happening, don't mention it to a soul.'

As if my words didn't matter he said:

'Is he a Christian man at all?'

'Christian or no Christian,' I said, 'don't mention it to a living soul. There was nobody heard him but ourselves.'

But there was, although to this day I couldn't say who. Because after his wife was buried, little by little it went about that the master had been fondling the horse and saying those things to it while his wife still lay above the earth. One morning he was no longer to be found.

Here the old story-teller stopped up; but I wanted to hear more.

'And was he dead?'

'No.'

'And did he come back?'

'No.'

'And why not?'

'Because, because those who met him in foreign parts many years after have this to say of him: that the marks of Denis Cashman's horsewhip are to be seen to this day on his neck and cheeks, and will be there for ever. So how could he come back? I needn't tell you the place went to wrack and ruin: 'tis little the lawyers could do to keep such a business on its feet and the owner of it abroad spending his substance in all the cities of France and Spain.'

THE SERENADE

I

THE CITY HE WAS BORN IN, yet had never seen, was mapped out in the brain of the blind man. On Monday his daughter, Maggie, a bare-headed girl of five-and-twenty, would lead him into the North Main Street, over the South Gate Bridge, westwards then towards the new houses and the new roads. His day's work would begin. Taking his fiddle from under his arm, he would tune it over his knees, clenching his teeth, for the keys were stiff; and while crouched down like that his head would sometimes swing up, and you saw his glaring eyeballs blankly reflecting the skies. Satisfied at last, he lifted himself to his full height, six feet two inches, flung backwards his massively domed head, hoisted the instrument, and in a voice surprisingly vibrant sent his song along the air. 'The Dear Irish Boy' was his favourite, but he had scores of others.

Tuesday he gave to the district called Sunday's Well: it is on the other side of the river. On Wednesday he took the streets that go zigzagging to the barracks on the hill. To the south side he gave Thursday. On Friday, mounting up Shandon Street, he dropped down into Blackpool. On Saturday he made along the quays, doing good business with the country people in the market square.

Of all those places Blackpool he loved the best. It was the poorest; and it swarmed with children. In the other districts he might have been a rock in the midst of moving waters, but in Blackpool the waters stood still to hear his song. He would feel little children clambering about his shaky knees; his daughter he would hear in deep and familiar discourse with some poor woman who, he was certain, had a child, limp and heavy with sleep, at the breast. Friday then, although a day of fasting, was his day of days. In hard coin he gathered there as much as in the richer places, while, at the

98

same time, his heart was filled with warmth and tenderness. Coming home from it, his knees might be sagging beneath his long body, but light streamed from his countenance.

II

On Tuesday evening as they made homewards from their rounds in Sunday's Well, he marched on in gloomy silence, his head aloft in the air. His daughter had told him that their total takings were two shillings and a penny. At last he complained in bitterness:

'I hear them going home, Maggie, going home they are.'

'They are; and why shouldn't they? Is it stop and speak with us they would?'

He sailed on in silence for a little space, and then, in a voice that was higher and still more bitter, broke out: 'They're a hungry lot. . .a hungry lot. And they have fine houses. Shrubberies. Lamps lit up. People waiting for them. But they're a hungry lot.'

Suddenly Maggie almost wrenched the arm off him. 'Hold up. There's the Riordans. There! You're all splashed again.'

'May misfortune overtake them for Riordans,' he cried out angrily, lifting his stick in a threatening, trembling hand.

'Come on, come on.'

'And why do we humble ourselves going up there at all?' he snarled. 'Why do we demean ourselves?'

His daughter's voice might seem unsympathetic, but to her all this was an old story, a little keener, a little shriller this evening perhaps.

'We must be careful,' she said, 'I never seen such traffic.'

She piloted him among the crowds hastening homewards after their day's labouring in the heart of the city. Suddenly again he broke out, and this time his utterance had become almost a chant:

'Beg from the poor, neighbours, let ye go beg from the poor! The poor! The poor! let ye go beg from the poor, neighbours. . .'

'Whisht,' she urged. 'Whisht, lave ye, and not be drawing attention on us.'

But he scorned her pleading; for he had found some passing solace in his rhythmic chant; and, his head swinging carelessly to its beating, he moved recklessly on. His glaring eyeballs sometimes caught the hard rays from the arc lamps on their high standards.

'Beg from the poor, neighbours! Let ye go beg from the poor. Don't demean yourselves with the mud of their motors. Beg from the poor, the poor.'

His daughter gave up trying to silence him; and they made forward, each in a different world. Because of her attention to what the old man was chanting out, the passers-by gave them just one uninterested glance and went their way.

The beggars reached the alley in which they had their little garret. A neighbour, a Mrs Walsh, greeted them, her words breaking from her:

'Ah, Michael,' she said, ''tis easily known 'twasn't in Blackpool ye gave the day.'

'Sing it! Julia,' he returned sharply. 'You may sing it for the truth. In Sunday's Well we were, the two of us, and 'tis there the misery's rooted in the hearts of them.'

''Tisn't long till Friday,' she said cheerily.

''Tisn't,' and then: 'But 'tis. And too long. To-morrow itself would be long. This moment I'd face for it if only Maggie wasn't so contrary and again' me.'

'Come in, come in,' Maggie uttered wearily, and turned a half-bitter smile on the gossip. The woman touched the girl on the arm and said, ''Tis hard to be dealing with the aged, child,' and went her way. But Maggie flung her head in the air and sent these words after her:

'We keeps Blackpool for the Fast Day, ma'am; the soft again' the hard, ma'am, and a fire on a cold night.'

Sunday's Well paid him less than Blackpool for his music and song, but, then, in the one place music and song were dull and stale, and in the other vibrant and strong – a lover's serenade.

III

On the next day, Wednesday, among the hillside and windswept streets about the barracks, he, without warning, turned bitterly on his guide:

'Come, come, let us go home,' he cried, 'home, I'm sick and tired of playing for them. Clankittane, Clankittane, there's not a house in it without bad English blood in it – so there isn't.'

'Whisht! Whisht!' she warned him, fearing the neighbours would hear him.

' 'Tis all whisht with ye,' he cried at her. 'Can't I give out what's in my heart? A stone itself will split in the frost of winter. Whisht! and God Himself knowing the truth of what I'm saying!'

'You'll bring confusion down on top of us if you don't hold your tongue.'

'Go away from me,' he roared out, snatching his arm from her grip. 'I'd rather be going the streets in my loneliness and going where I liked, than to be led like a dog.'

'Don't be foolish, only come on home.'

'Couldn't I?' he cried, as if she had challenged him. 'Couldn't I? There's not a step I don't know. There's not a street nor a crossing. I can sing out the names, none better.'

'Don't be gabbling like a poor foolish man,' she answered wearily.

While they quarrelled in the way of those who spend long hours every day in each other's company, her eyes were all the time calmly browsing on the life flowing on around her. It was her one solace; and she never dreamed how hard and cruel a blow she struck her father when, often in the middle of a verse, she would say carelessly: 'Come on now, 'tis time to be moving,' stopping him, not reflecting that all that passing pageantry meant little or nothing to him in comparison with the life within his song. As she went along, then, her eyes, sweeping from side to side, were filled with all the throbbing tide of life, its glitter, colour, sound, while his aged high-borne head went tracking a lonely path among the stars.

So came the morning of Friday, the lucky day when he begged from the poor in Blackpool, threading the little lanes and alleys in a fervour of love, his voice ringing with a timbre he himself could not account for, his wrist commanding a bow firm and strong, imperious upon the strings.

It was a bright day at the end of October. The sunshine came and went with spring-like frolic and nimbleness, bright clouds and dark clouds flinging onwards from the north-west. The walls, the chimney pots, the spires flashed out vividly, sharp-edged for a moment, and, the next, retired, gone grey again. The blind man answered to that blitheness in the air; his old limbs felt no weariness in their joints; his head tossed alertly, his features shone as his daughter led him towards the homely streets. All around them the gay stir of the forenoon rang brightly, and to it his spirit responded: his thoughts were become perhaps too eager: he drove manfully ahead, flinging out his long limbs. All at once he found himself whirled about, tugged at, shoved, dragged: and, staggering and groping, he found himself clasped in a dozen arms. All around him were noises – stampings, cries: 'Lift her,' 'Quick now,' ''Tis her foot,' 'Back the car,' 'Of course he'll go with her.'

'Maggie,' he cried out loudly. 'Where's Maggie from me?'

''Tis hurted she is. But 'tisn't much. Whisht now. You'll go with her in the ambulance.'

'If 'tis hurted itself she is, can't she talk to me? Ye're all deceiving me.' His voice outsoared them all.

They brought him over to her. He had to bend down; he then felt her fingers trailing on his cheeks:

''Tis my ankle, my ankle,' she said.

The little crowd melted away; soon only a few were waiting for the ambulance to arrive. To get the blind man – the six feet two inches of him – into a contrivance of which he had no idea, was more difficult than to get in the limp invalid herself. When they had failed a couple of times, irritably he stood up, fetching a breath:

'And my Blackpool day and all,' he sighed, not caring who heard him.

V

His daughter's foot was neither broken nor sprained; in a day or two she would be free again. She was certain the people in the lodging house would look after her father, and he, too, was anxious to get back to familiar surroundings. He was sent home from the hospital in a car. Arrived there, the neighbours gathered around him, and sitting on his bed, he gave them an account of the accident, making a picture of it from the remarks he had gathered in. They kindled his fire for him, spread his food, and left him preparing for bed. However, when they had gone, a great loneliness swept over him, chilling him. The memory of the bright morning recurred to him; it had been too fine, too careless, he felt; and suddenly he found himself on the verge of tears: he had looked forward to this one day more than ever before; he had during the week suffered in the waiting for it; it had come at last, and then everything in a second had gone wrong. He wrestled with himself; and, shaking his head, he impulsively rose up, got into his old street coat with the wide sleeves, pulled his hat down on his ears, took his fiddle from the top of the cupboard, and stole noiselessly and lightly down the creaking stairs. He knew the street door would be open: it was always open.

Bravely he guided himself along by the familiar walls. The wind had stiffened; he noticed this when he turned from the alleyway into the wider street. It was blowing in gusts. It held him back; but after a little while he got to know its ways, and so pushed confidently on. The corners, the crossings, gave him no trouble; he had been for more than forty years pacing the selfsame rounds, so that when the first nervousness had gone from him his feet of themselves seemed to pick his course for him. He could tell with exactness where he was, what shop or laneway he was passing by. But all the time the wind was rising; once or twice it had nearly taken him off his feet; at last he stopped, gripping an iron railing that protected an old-fashioned doorway. Stretching his ear he told himself the streets must be empty of people. Yet it could not be so late. He heard footsteps approaching; he awaited them, observing the sousing of the boots in the wetness:

'What time of night might it be?' he asked.

'After eleven. Isn't it late you're out?'

It was a strange voice, he felt glad.

''Tis late indeed. Maybe you're going up the hill?'

He released his grasp of the railing, and a sudden gust nearly whirled him off his feet. His right arm was gripped firmly, and the stranger's voice spoke again:

'If 'tis up you're going. . . Come on, come on.'

'Thank you, thank you.'

''Tisn't a kindly night at all.'

They made fair speed up towards Shandon. He would say:

'We're at Miss O'Sullivan's now,' or 'This is always a windy corner,' and once he said:

'Over there in O'Callaghan's there used to be a little red lamp – third floor, second window –'

''Tis burning there all right.'

'There's a holy picture above it. Do you know I used like to see that; and now I can't see it at all, I won't have a stim of the sight left me soon.' As a matter of fact it was Maggie's eyes that had seen that little red lamp burning on the third floor.

''Tisn't very easy to see anything to-night. There's a bit of the moon coming out now; and, look, 'tis flying it is – look at it.'

'Yes indeed, flying. Whew, there's a belt it gave me in the eyes – the wind, I mean. 'Twill be a bad night later on.'

They had reached Blackpool.

'We're at Merrick's now, aren't we?'

'That's where we are.'

'Isn't there anyone about?'

'Not a soul.'

'That's queer, queer for Blackpool, queer.'

'Who'd be out to-night?'

'Well, I'll be going this way. Thank you very much. No, you needn't. 'Tis only down here I'm going.'

'Mind yourself, 'tis dark, and very dark too: 'tis how the gas-lamp's blown out.'

'Good night.'

'Good night to ye, good night.'

In one moment the footsteps died away, and immediately the blind man felt weak and helpless and lonely in the mad whirlwind about him. The night was full of noises – noises close at hand, noises far off. The winds were bellowing, were hissing and snarling in the telegraph wires; water was falling in splashes; round the chapel's foundations there was the rush of a flood. He was tempted to stay where he was in the shelter of O'Mahony's potato store. But this thought he flung from him. He had often raised his song in a strong wind, and enjoyed it. In a moment he was standing in the exact spot where every Friday it was his custom to lift his first song in Blackpool. Up went his fiddle, his head; and then his heart leaped within him. His bow was dancing on the strings, swept from them in the eddying gusts. That didn't matter. He wouldn't give in. There was no one now to say, ' 'Tis time to be going.' His hand gripped his bow as if it were a sword. His song would outdo the winds, would enter those darkened houses to the very hearts of them. As soon as the people heard it they would open their windows, they might even. . .

VI

No one had missed him from his room, and no one had seen him return to it. When, later on, his daughter, alone, went the old familiar round in Blackpool explaining that her father was not well, would have to keep the bed for some time yet, and 'had they missed him at all?' – she was told they had, but that a lot of people were ready to swear that they had heard his voice in the middle of the storm, and not in one place only but here and there and everywhere, as if the gale was flinging him from post to pillar and from pillar to post. Nonsense, she said. The poor man was safe in his bed. But some sort of fever had come upon him, and he had cut his head and torn his fiddle strings all out. His hat was gone. But what value was an old hat? Maybe he flung it in the fire. He was very confused in himself all the next day. That was how she found him when they brought her from the hospital.

That night she told her father what the people in Blackpool were saying. He smiled, and she did not notice that it was the smile of a chastened lover.

THE STONES

I

THOUGH JOHN REDNEY'S HOUSE was far back in the glen his straggling farm spread out into the river valley of which the glen itself was, as one might say, a side pocket, narrow and secret. In all its winding length there was no other house: it was even more lonely now than when long years before John Redney had played in it, a companionless child.

When the sudden downpour of rain towards the end of August swept his newly gathered cruach of turf from the inches, leaving him without fuel for the coming year, he knew quite well that all down the valley, and on the heights as well, the farmers were shaking their heads over what had befallen him, were by adding this to that, proverb to proverb, memory to memory, strengthening one another's belief that such disasters did not overtake a man without cause. And the picture he made himself of them so grouped was a pain that almost overwhelmed the pain of his actual loss.

Only two days before, he had finished the ferrying over of the turf from the bogs on the other side of the river. He had thrown it out there loosely, not far from the bank, for, the very next day, he was going to cart it up the glen to the little rise where the Redneys had built their cruach as long as anyone remembered. That very evening he had sent his labouring boy over to Con Jer for the loan of his horse and man for the next day, for the one day only to help him in drawing the turf from the inches to that traditional ground. Con Jer had answered the boy that he came at a most unfortunate time, that he had never been so busy, that he couldn't think of letting him have even the horse not to mind one of his men as well. He said he was surprised that John Redney would not have thought of that himself. Innocently enough the boy repeated the words as Con Jer had spoken them. And so it was that the next day John Redney hastened down the glen, mounted a hillock at the mouth of it, and scowled at the swirling waters rolling his turf along the valley – good black turf, as firm a sod as he had ever cut, and a whole year's supply of it, and more.

The morning after, as he gazed at the drenched fields from which the sudden mountain floods were rapidly disappearing, he could not help recalling the very words the boy had brought back in his mouth from Con Jer, nor how they had set him on fire, maddened him until he had told him angrily that it might be a good thing for Con Jer to go up to Carrigavawring and have a look at his own effigy there. No, the exact words he had used were: 'Well, boy, Con Jer's effigy in stone, up there on Carriga-vawring, if Con Jer went up and had a look at it – one look' – and there he had stopped. It had been in his mind to say that one glance at it would leave Con Jer with only very little thought indeed for crops or cattle or fences or anything else that concerned this world of living men. This, however, he had not said and perhaps it was better so. The boy had, he was certain, truly reported the words, only half aware of the threat in them; and repeated in that broken fashion, they had, it might be, raised more confusion in Con Jer's mind than if they had been made into a frightful story. What did he care! Let them now come together, the farmers of the valley, stick their noses into one another's faces, make out that his turf had not been swept from him without reason – it was all one to him. Con Jer would toss and turn on his pillow for many a night to come, wondering if what the boy had reported was true and, if true, what would come of it.

More and more as he dully stared in front of him the river was reassuming its own true shape. Through the levels of the valley it curved from side to side with the light of the day, although it was a grey day, thick upon its surface, causing the pasture lands on either side to look dark and heavy. If the Nyhans had flung up a bit of a dam where the engineer had told them, there was an end to those sudden floodings; but no, the Nyhans hadn't it in them even to help themselves, when by doing so they would help another. The whole lot of them, the farmers on this side and the other, were against him.

II

It is a stony land. The name of it, Kilclaw, might mean either the Stone Church or the Stony Wood. Nobody now knows which. The woods were felled some hundreds of years ago; but felling the trees had not been sufficient, for, that done, even the roughest kind of tillage was not yet possible until the little patches first marked out for it had been cleared of the largest of the stones embedded in them. The roots of them were found to be tougher than those of the wild ash, the mountain fir, or the oak. Yet removed they were, dragged to the sides of the little fields, however they managed it, crop upon crop of them, year after year, decade after decade, century after century, until the stone mounds that now enclose the little patches of wheat or oats or potatoes take up as much, if not more, of the ground than the croppings within them. The boulders earliest removed were huge, huger than would now appear, for their bases once again are hidden deep in the ground. Halfway up their flanks, sometimes all the way, they are clothed with brown and silvery mosses, or with innumerable layers of the tiniest fern. On top of and around and between them thousands and thousands of smaller stones have been piled or flung; and these, more exposed to the winds and rain and sunshine, have not clothed themselves at all, remain still unclad, may remain forever unclad, unsoftened with verdure, bleached-looking, bare and stark. The people of the place fancy they see in them – those moss-clad boulders, those skull-like smaller stones that surmount them, effigies, images of their neighbours, never of themselves. A farmer using the *poirse* of a neighbour as a short cut for his turf or corn may suddenly behold, in some place that he has already passed by some hundreds of times, the rough effigy of one of the dwellers in the valley. If however, he be wise and of good heart he will keep his discovery to himself, for it bodes no one any good, this unexpected revelation of one's image in the stones.

John Redney never had been either wise or of good heart. His mind dwelt too much on things that were abroad in the air, in the darkness, drifting hither and thither. He was a poor lonely creature, living there in that unvisited glen, his the only house within it. His children were scattered far from him, were not writing to him, it was said, and his wife had become long since a poor sorry drudge to him. Having loosed that word effigy upon the wind, he went uselessly and restlessly strealing about his straggling fields more silent and gloomy than ever. He came to know that Con Jer had laughed at the threat, had said, 'And John Redney wants me to mount up to Carrigavawring and have a look at myself! I won't then. I have something else to do.' But Redney knew that if that laughter of Con Jer's was loud it was also hollow. He felt quite certain that Con Jer did not laugh in his heart when he laid his head on the pillow in the darkness.

III

At this time arrived one who had long since outgrown the beliefs of the hillsides – the ex-soldier, Jack Lambert, Miles Lambert's good-for-nothing son. He had slaved and tramped his way in England, had been in America, Canada, and Australia – and nowhere had done any good. He had found himself in the Great War, first in France, then in Gallipoli. Again and again he had come back to his father's house and again wandered off from it whither he would. He had been at home this time only a week or so when the news was abroad that he had been seen in Redney's company traversing the most hidden and ill-reputed places at unearthly hours. Even on nights that were stormy and wild and without a glimpse of either moonlight or starlight, the two of them were heard going by. On quieter nights the sounds of the footsteps of the two of them had wakened people from their sleep, had caused them to lift their heads to listen. Johneen Kelleher had been out in his fields before the dawn drawing the stooks together, making them ready for the help that was to come to him as soon as the sun had dried the corn – and those two misguided men he had seen coming down from the stony hills where there were neither houses nor tilled fields nor traffic, and they looked as if they had been abroad the livelong night! Over his story a dozen heads drew into a circle; and one and then another remarked how much Lambert was changing; how he had taken on strange airs, had been found staring intently into this man's haggard, and elsewhere, in a place where he could have had no business, had suddenly raised his head above a mound of stones. Besides they had all noticed how, whenever he chanced to meet them now upon the road, he would look through them as if he knew the very thoughts they were thinking. Yet it was not he they blamed. He they knew was but the empty book into which old Redney was writing all the perversity he had ever indulged in that crabbed brain of his. Larry Condon broke up their discussion with a free gesture. What was Lambert but a common bummer, sponging on Redney, who, fool that he was, God knows he was queer since the day he was born, had been glad to find anyone at all to strike up a friendship with, to drink with, to gossip with; and none of them could deny that Lambert was a man of fine discourse when he had swallowed down a glass or two of good whiskey. They all knew as well as he did that Lambert give no credence to those beliefs of theirs. Since they had often defended their beliefs against him this they could not argue against, whereupon, silenced for the time, they broke the gathering and went through the darkness each to his lonely house. But by the next night some other tidings of the two secret men would have floated into some farmyard or other and another discussion would take place around the hearth. The faces of the two of them, the look of intentness in them, began now to abide in the memory of all who crossed them. Whatever had come to possess them! the people asked one another. Were the two of them determined not to cease their searching until they had discovered the effigies of all the farmers of Kilclaw? Fear spread from house to house along the valley. There was not now a dweller in it who, if he spied the two of them coming towards him along the road, would not turn aside into some farmer's *poirse* to escape the peering of their eyes.

They were an ill-matched pair: Lambert, the ex-soldier, brazen-eyed, straight-lipped, withered-skinned, impudent, and with a reckless way of striding along: old Redney, shy and tongue-tied, looking out from under his shaggy brows, his head down, his left hand clenched across the small of his back, his right hand tight and heavy upon the knob of his stick. With quick, uncertain steps, he made forwards as if his secret knowledge was no happy cargo. The neighbours would see him hobbling along with Lambert, always a little in the rear. They would see him stop up, his stick directed across a valley or along the flank of a mountain while Lambert's eyes searched the distance indicated; or Lambert they would find looking back over his shoulder waiting for the other as he clambered clumsily over those fences of loose stones. And the same anxiety arose again and again:

'Are they burying the whole countryside of us?'

'And what will they gain by it?'

'Nothing except the pacifying of their own wicked minds.'

' 'Tis a frightful thing for a man to know that he is already in the stone, that he is there to be seen for all time. If you woke up in the dead of the night, a wild night or a night of hard frost, you wouldn't like to picture it. You'd feel the frost in your shoulder bones.'

But those who gathered of a night-time to Con Jer's were a quiet lot; Lambert and Redney might by dint of searching come on the images of the whole countryside and they would not lift an arm to prevent it. The younger men who met after the day in Dan Owen's were different. It was Pat Early, whose shoulder blow would fell a bullock, determined for that group what they should do.

The next day they loitered around the tumbledown cabin where their one smith kept his forge. Into its smoky background they retired, all of them except Pat Early himself, when they discovered that Lambert was coming along the road. From within they heard the approaching footsteps: they then heard Pat Early's voice: 'Lambert,' he said, with a rasping tone. 'Come over here.'

They heard the footsteps cease. Pat's voice they heard again:

'Come over here. I have a word to say to you.'

They could now see Lambert in the brightness of the doorway, his back almost towards them:

'Well?' he said.

'Did you hear Pat Nyhan is after dying on them?'

'I didn't: where would I hear it?'

Though he answered glibly enough, those within thought they saw him start when Pat flung the unexpected question at him.

'If you knew he was going to meet his end, sudden, and without preparation, you might have warned him: 'twould be a neighbourly act.'

They expected Lambert to deny, if only for safety's sake, any foreknowledge of Pat Nyhan's death; but the words they heard were:

'Is this a place for neighbourly acts?'

His next word then they felt would be either of old Redney's cruach of turf that the August flood had swept down the valley or else of the Nyhans' failure to build the rampart which would forever save the levels from the swollen river. Pat Early, however, gave him no time: he blazed out:

'Why don't you answer the question I put to you?'

'Question!'

'Did you know – did you know that something was in store for Pat Nyhan, some misfortune or other?'

'Two nights ago,' he answered after a slight pause and quite in a low voice, 'John Redney showed me him in the stone.'

They grew cold to hear him. And he had said the words in a way that showed that himself was no longer a mocker. Pat Early cried out quickly and with great strength and warmth, to their great relief:

' 'Tis a lie!'

Lambert, however, who had turned to go, was not disturbed either by the words or the force in them; he looked back and said in the same low voice:

'If he showed – the sight to me he can show it to you, that is if you care to see it, now the man's dead. Some people mightn't like to.'

113

The listeners gathered out noiselessly from the shelter of the forge, all of them; they feared that Pat Early was shaken, but again sturdily he answered:

'See what? A couple of stones! Do you think I believe old Redney has power over us?'

'But you'd face it?'

'I'd face a couple of stones anyhow.'

'We'd all do that,' John Morian added.

'By day or night?'

''Tis equal.'

'Very well; I'll tell himself.'

V

It was now the end of November. The night, it seemed, could not hold any more stars, nor the air any more cold. Con Jer's son, Tadhg, was one of the whispering group. Others were Pat Early, his brother-in-law, Michael Glynn, the smith's son, Larry Mehigan, and the teacher's son, Jim Carey, who had ventured without his father's knowledge. Morian was with them also. Larry Mehigan was delicate: the piercing cold had urged to rapid walking, and they had mounted Knockanuller at one spurt before they were suddenly aware of his gasping, of his effort to keep up with them:

'Are we going too fast?' Michael Glynn said.

'I'll be all right in a minute,' Larry answered; but immediately he had to turn aside doubled up in a fit of coughing.

''Twas the cold made us hurry: 'twas a queer thing for us to do.'

'But 'tisn't good to be stopping here; that's the devil of a wind for him.'

'There's shelter beyond.'

''Tis more than twenty years since I was up in these places.'

'Who'd come up here? What business would you have?'

'We'll be going on now.'

'How far up he came to find poor Pat Nyhan's image.'

They thought of him rigid in his bed.

' 'Tis a frightful night to be dead on.'

They did not laugh. Another time they would have done so at such awkward words, but dimly in the starlight they individually spied out shoulders of whitish rock and boulders that looked like massive ancient, long-weathered skulls. The little narrow path they were on was bordered by some of those immemorial pilings of stones, large and small. The mounds kept the wind from them, but the open spaces of the bogland would have been more welcome to them. 'Look, they're waiting for us.'

Sitting in the shelter of an upright slab of rock they saw the two figures; Redney's rigid grasp of the knob of his stick they noticed especially.

'Are ye waiting long?' Pat Early said, casually, he hoped.

'Mind ye,' old Redney answered, ' 'tisn't by my wish ye're up here at all; far from it.'

Pat Early thought he wished to put them off. 'If you can show us what Lambert said, 'tis right you should.'

'I can show ye that all right, since ye wish it.'

They all began to move forward. In the dim light the round water-worn stones in the *poirse* began to roll under their feet. Pat Early said:

'I see we would have done right to have our spectacles with us to see it.'

Only after a few moments the old man understood the words. He then said, calmly and coldly:

'There'll be light enough where 'tis. The moon's there already.'

As he spoke he raised his stick towards the brow of the hill, which was gapped and rugged with boulders and rocks. There the sky was becoming more and more luminous and the stars were gone. The moon they understood to be away towards the right. When they pierced through among the boulders they saw it suddenly, rising in splendour. Slabs of blanched stone, pillar stones of shadow, gaps of darkness – sharp-edged, were all about them in confusion. They felt astray.

'There's Pat Nyhan. The Nyhans were up here always.'

Even if, with his stick, he had not pointed out the particular group of stones in that long-deserted mountain farm ground they would have known it for Pat Nyhan. It was set up in a listening attitude, Pat Nyhan's attitude; just so he used to listen, his left ear advanced, for he had been for years a little hard of hearing. They recollected too having heard that the Nyhans had come from this place. As they looked they could swear they saw the stones stir. One or two of the men fidgeted, looking around. Others stared at the stones in a dull sort of way. They were conscious of a desire to strike old Redney or the ex-soldier, yet conscious also that that was not in the bargain. The ex-soldier stood a little apart from them, neither looking nor speaking. Suddenly Larry Mehigan with that burred and resonant consumptive's voice of his said:

'Up here too the Redneys were always. I heard tell of them.'

Their eyes swept from the image and fastened on Redney. He turned his back on them as if he would set off for home. Indistinctly he grumbled at them over his shoulder:

'Ye're after seeing what ye came to see.'

He put out his left hand and Lambert came and folded it in his arm, protectingly. They then began to move off, the two of them. The others hesitated. As soon as he had said the words, Mehigan had been taken with a fit of coughing. The stone desert was ringing with the sound of it, and the dogs in distant farmyards had awakened and were answering back. But the dogs' barking Larry heard no more than he heard his own coughing: his excited brain was working all the time; he would blurt out, not giving the spasm time to exhaust itself:

' 'Tis true what I say. Up here they were always, the Redneys.'

'Somehow that's true. I heard it said; 'twas said,' Morian gave his opinion earnestly.

They came closer together. They were thankful to Larry. His words excused them from looking around any more at the stone image, listening in the way that a tall deaf old man would listen.

Larry's cough had ceased, and they began to hasten after the two others. When they got within a short distance of them they saw old Redney stop up rather suddenly and raising his stick, point out something to Lambert. A word however he did not speak. The whole of them stopped up where they were. Individually fright fell on them. They did not want to know what the old man was pointing at. Lambert seemed vexed and impatient. They heard his whisper: 'Come on, come on.' But old Redney seemed not to be able to move nor to change his attitude. The moon poured its light on them all: old Redney with his stick stretched out, Lambert a little apart from him, waiting impatiently, and the other group still farther apart, puzzled and anxious. The cold was intense, and the sparkling earth was as silent as the starry heavens. The distant farm dogs had put their noses again upon the ground. It was their own stillness made the men aware of the benumbed stillness about them.

'Come on, come on,' they again heard whispered very hoarsely, and Lambert made a stride towards the petrified figure of his friend. As he neared it they saw the stick fall clattering to the frozen ground, and the next moment they saw Redney fling himself helplessly into Lambert's arms, a thin whimpering wail breaking from him into the silence.

'Look!' the boy Jim Carey cried; and right beyond the two clutching figures they saw old Redney in stone! The image was dark against the sky and immensely larger than the poor stricken thing in the ex-soldier's arms. It seemed to mock him, the head of it stretched out in unrelenting eagerness. One glance they gave it and without a word broke from the place.

Jack Lambert a few days afterwards was seen driving from the place, no one knew whither. Old Redney was missed. His poor bedraggled wife they would see driving the cows of a night-time to the inches. She kept her thoughts to herself. Only after weeks and weeks the men of the valley learned her husband had taken to his bed, awaiting his doom. In tongue-tied silence still he awaits it, his eyes staring out straight before him.

ON THE HEIGHTS

I

A STRANGER HANDED IN a little slip of paper at the door of the farmhouse in Acharas where I had been hiding for several weeks: within ten minutes of receiving it I was on my bicycle, was flying at break-neck speed down mountainy bohereens, one after another, crossing through water-courses without dismounting, and skimming the sharp corners of boulders by half inches or less. And yet I was all but caught! Only for their hooting, as their motor swerved from the main road, I had ridden into their arms. I caught that hoot! hoot! and flung from my path by very instinct; slap-dash in among the rocks and furze I went, went as far as I could, then threw myself off on the heather, and breathing like a swimmer after a long swim against time, could do nothing but wait, helpless. Puffing and panting on my knees, I could see them between the rocks: with frowning determination they were putting their heavy military motor at the hill, and I recognised the sergeant in charge. 'Mullery!' I gasped, and grabbed my handlebar again by instinct. If I fell into Mullery's hands, it meant five years: he was a man that would swear anything. When they had gone by, I mounted again, and swept into Gougane Barra by the back road, and was just making on for Keimaneigh when something spoke in my ear – perhaps it was the old Gaelic saints who lie there at rest – 'They will have set a watch in Keimaneigh: take the mountains.' And so, instead of taking the comfortable if heavy road through the Pass of Keimaneigh, I made straight for Coomroe, facing the great walls of rock that enclose that most impressive of mountain glens. I have never heard that any other mortal ever pushed a bicycle up the one thousand eight hundred feet of jagged rock that hangs above the inches there; but I did it, how I do not know, unless it was the vision of that dogged face in the motor car that kept me ever pushing on and on and up and up.

As I shoved, dragged, slided, lifted my wheels up the rocks, the sweat ran freely and warmly down my back and limbs. I gave it no thought, I felt no weariness. But when I reached the summit and expected to see the sun again, a cold sea wind struck me, refreshed me, and then, suddenly, chilled me; and up before me rose a wall of white mist. I looked for the mountain-peaks that used to guide me there, but none were visible in the cloud. Feeling it all around me, licking and stroking me, and remembering how warm it had been in the coom, I knew I was making into a night of rain; and there are no wetter hills in the whole of Munster. As I went forward I tried to recollect the whereabouts of the nearest house in those forlorn uplands, but all my landmarks were blotted out. I came suddenly on a close-huddled flock of black-faced mountainy sheep; they looked at me and scampered off into the mists with timid cries; they, too, seemed to be waiting for the rain. I felt lonelier than before. The pursuit was over and done with – years ago, it appeared. I thought of it no more. Could I make the Coomahola river before nightfall, was the only question that would rise up in my mind, as I pushed my bicycle now over the shale and then through growths of fragrant bog-myrtle. And it would come into my mind, too, that though I was making forward with fair speed I was doing no good, for I did not know where I was going. Yet somehow I feared to stop. I stumbled on and on, till suddenly I saw beside me a flat table of rock, about two feet high, as perfectly shaped as if stonecutters had worked at it. Before I had willed it, it seemed, I was sitting on it with a sense of delicious ease. 'I will think out exactly where I am and where I will go,' I said, comforting myself with a pretence of will power that I knew well was but a pretence. Then down came the rain, slanting from the south-west.

I bowed my head to it in sheer hopelessness – and that action it was that saved me. Beneath my eyes I saw certain light marks on the ground, not wheel marks – they were not more than two feet six apart, and besides they were not cut into the ground. I was instantly following them. I knew what they were. They were the marks of a 'tray', as the peasants of that place call it both in Irish and English – a sort of light sleigh on which they bring down the cut turf from places in the uplands that are too steep for horse and cart. These marks meant a house, sooner or later. With the greatest care I kept to them. And soon I began to come on other signs of human ways and strivings – a cairn of stones, a first effort at a clearance, then a crazy sort of boundary fence, long abandoned to its own will, then at last two forked stakes in the ground, a young ash sapling laid across them, closing a gap. I blessed the human touch: the pious hands of husbandry had made it! Then I struck the path.

The night thickened, and the rain thickened; but now with the path beneath my feet, all broken shale it was, I did not mind. I thought I might leave my bicycle there until I had found the house, which I knew to be somewhere in the darkness. I laid it in the dripping heather and made more swiftly on. (I recovered it next day, clean as a new pin.) A waft of turf smoke struck me. I breathed it in with wide nostrils. My spirits rose, I could shout out. Then in a pit of darkness beneath me to the right I saw the tiny little eye of a lamplit window, warm-coloured, and looking as if its kindly gleam had been peering out that way on the hills for thousands and thousands of years, so steady it was. I used no caution. I made for it through the blackness, and lost the path. I found myself stumbling down the side of a little ravine – I splashed through a leaping stream, I almost fell upon the door. I banged it with my fist. I heard movement within, a collie whined, voices whispered. I could not wait. I banged again, and the rain pelted my warm wrist. I caught the latch and shook the door. 'Open! Open!' I cried. Within, I heard the bolts being withdrawn.

A low-toned, uncertain voice spoke in my face:

'Who are you? What is it you want? Come in. You're all wet.'

A dull-looking, middle-aged man and his wife, a soft-featured, kindly creature, drew back from me, and continued to stare at me; I felt annoyed at their doubtful reception; there was no heartiness in it.

'I'm wet all right,' I said, trying to speak calmly; but then I added with a bitterness I could not help, 'There are more than me on the hills these times, and better than me.'

By these words I would give them to understand why I was on the hills.

The man's jaw fell; he looked at his wife; they stared at me helplessly, even more stupidly than before, I thought, and more frigidly. He came one step towards me and whispered:

'Maybe you'd speak low? Maybe you would?'

What did he mean?

'Draw up to the fire; take your coat off,' the woman said, handing me a towel to wipe my face.

'Why should I speak low? Is there anyone sick?' I said, looking at the poor staring creature that was man of the house.

'No, no; there's no one sick, thanks be to God; glory be to His Holy Name!'

He was smiling at me in an indeterminate sort of way, his jaw hanging. He was a weak-mouthed man, I could see. He went doddering away. His wife pointed to the door in the partition at the end of the room.

'The old man, his father – he's asleep within, and he's noisy if anyone wakes him.'

That then was why I should speak low. I understood. I had met such old men before – Lears, but Lears who get the best of the bargain, maintaining their rights of property to the very day that they have to step into the grave. We found ourselves speaking in whispers, all three of us, I trying to explain how I found the track to their lonely door and they wondering how I had missed the wider track across the hills. After all, they were a good-hearted couple and could enjoy a chat – if one carried it on in whispers.

The man raised his head suddenly: we all listened. The winds were coming up from Bantry Bay, they were roaring upon the roof. As we listened, in flew the door with a crash, the fire was scattered on the hearth, the sheep dog sprang from his sleep, planted his legs and howled at the storm. We all flung ourselves on the door. In the sudden tumult I forgot myself. As we got the door to I shouted with vast enjoyment –

'There! there! stay outside now – with Sergeant Mullery,' I added under my breath.

'Hush! hush! sir; lave ye.'

Both man and woman were terrified, it seemed. They were looking towards the end of the room.

I put my hand to my mouth, hunching my shoulders, and turning like them towards the unseen sleeper – how we leap at moments back into our childhood! But too late, too late. Three dreadful blows were struck on that partition towards which we were all looking, and an aged but vigorous and indignant voice cried out above the storm in ringing Irish:

'Am I to be kept always in the dark? Ever and always! Look at me, and I for the last hour killed with listening to your foolery – and dogs – and giggling – and the stranger's voice stunning me; and 'tisn't worth your while, Shawn, to come in with a little word.'

Man and wife were trying to smile at me; but I could see that they were used to getting the worse of it. They did not know what was best to do.

'I'll answer him,' I said. They clutched me.

'No, no,' they were whispering warmly in my face; 'no sir; no sir.'

I cried out in Irish as ringing as his own:

'You'd drive a stranger from your door, this night?' Half in jest, half in earnest, I spoke the words. The winds were roaring with a great voice; I could hear the cataracts pouring.

' 'Tis no decent person would be travelling the hills this night,' I was answered, and there was suspicion and challenge in the tones.

'There's a more decent person on your floor this night,' I answered back, and in spite of myself my voice was hard and rough, 'a more decent person than ever walked this hungry land since St Finnbarr left it, travelling to the east.'

'Left it and blessed it,' the voice answered me in triumph.

'I doubt it,' I answered, and my anger was gone; and there came swiftly over me a joyousness to think of the two of us shouting at each other there in that lonely land with the roaring storm outside, grandest of orchestras.

'I doubt it,' I cried, in a great voice.

'He did,' he answered.

'I doubt it.'

'’Tis well known; the authors say so!'

My heart opened to him! How often I had heard that or similar phrases from his like! '*Se adeir na h-ughdair. . .*'

'If he did, ye ought to remember it, and not drive a stranger from. . .'

'There's no one doing the like; but haven't I the right to complain if my son will not tell me who 'tis comes in or goes out? Come in to me, Shawn, and let you make the stranger his meal, Nora.'

Shawn went in to him, having first looked despairingly at his wife, who smiled back encouragingly. I felt I had not fathomed any one of the three of them.

'He'll be in his sleep in a moment,' she said to me in a whisper. 'You gave him his answer.' She was more courageous than the man.

III

I made free with the big teapot of black tea she made me, and with the lovely bread, laughing to myself and yet wondering. After a while Shawn returned to us on tiptoe from the old man's room, and, silenced, we could hear the deep and vigorous breathing of his father.

I began telling them of the detestable war bread the people in the cities and towns had to eat, and of the great scarcity of everything among them; they sighed over them, the poor creatures! And so the night passed. I began to wonder why they did not suggest retiring, for it was now near midnight. I began to yawn involuntarily, and to measure the settle with my eyes. I had often slept on one. They were again confused. At last the man, who was certainly an extraordinarily gentle creature, touched my sleeve shyly and said: 'The only place we have for you to sleep in is with himself,' he nodded towards the partition. I was just about to say, 'What about the settle?' when I thought suddenly that there were but the two rooms in the house; I glanced about and saw that the press on which the candle was lighting was of course a folded-up bedstead. Yet I didn't answer: I did not relish the thought of sleeping with a person I had just quarrelled with.

'You could slip in – quietly. He sleeps sound.'

I smiled at him.

'Go in,' I said, throwing myself erect, 'and tell him the police and the soldiers are on my track, and see what he'll say?'

I felt sure that anyone who kept the 'authors' in his thoughts would not refuse a corner of his bed to a rapparee. I was surprised how they took my words! Had they not known it?

'No, no,' they both cried warmly at me; 'not that way at all,' the man moved about the flags in trouble.

''Tis better say no word about the soldiers or police at all,' the wife urged; 'only that 'tis how a tourist is after losing his way in the fogs, a tourist was fishing in Loch Fada. Go on, Shawn, and tell him that; 'tis a story will do no one any harm.'

I consented, and Shawn went very timidly into his father's presence. We listened; yet there was no noise between them, no squabbling at all. He came out gesturing that the way was clear. About midnight I stepped very carefully over the old man's rather bulky figure, to take my share of the huge old bed.

'Out the candle,' he growled at me. Timidly enough I mumbled an apology, and did so. Outside, the winds shrieked among the upland gullies and the waters fell in them.

IV

I awoke with some dim feeling of annoyance. It was pitch dark and the storm was still roaring, but near by was an unceasing whisper, a sharp hissing of breath between teeth and lips: the old

124

man, hunched up in the bed, was praying. I dozed off again, and again I woke, and the hissing was still going on beside me. He was, I suspected, carrying out a practice of fifty or sixty years' standing. To the roaring winds outside he was deaf: he knew their voices better than I. I was listening to them, to him, thankful for the nest of warmth and peace I found myself in. I would occasionally hear the rattle of his beads, and from the sound could guess at their huge size. Dozing again, I heard him gather them up; and then I am quite clear I heard the words, '. . . and for the souls of all the men they put to death in Dublin!' His voice fell to a whisper, and a vigorous 'Amen!' finished his prayers, as with a clasp. He shrugged the clothes up about his shoulders, groped under the pillow, and settled himself to sleep. A sudden rush of thought and feeling swept over me. 'The souls of all the men they put to death in Dublin,' I repeated, and I thought of this lonely old man praying for them in this unknown cabin on the uplands. In the phrase of the people, I was glorified to think of it.

V

Yet presently I fell to wondering why his son and his son's wife had implored me not to tell him that I was a hunted man on the hills. I could not understand it.

VI

I awoke in the bright morning to find the old man's fingers touching and feeling my brow with great gentleness. He started when my eyes glared up at him. It was then I saw him for the first time with any distinctness. He had a fringe of white, wool-white, whiskers in under his shaven chin; he looked like a shepherd in an old play or in a picture; but there was a keenness and a sharpness about the brow – an alertness that made one forget this first thought of him. Seeing how he had started, I greeted him in good Irish. He smiled at me:

'You're no tourist was fishing Loch Fada,' he said, knowingly. I listened a moment; there was no stir in the room outside. I felt sure they had not yet risen, had not yet been speaking to him. The sun was bathing the hills, a robin was singing. Even in the little darksome cabin there was an air of freshness and gladness.

'What am I, then?' I said.

'You're no tourist,' he said again, with the same wise and, I thought, encouraging smile.

'But what am I?'

'I'll tell you: you're one of them!' He gave me a slow, antique wink; it was like a gesture. 'I was one of them myself and I young,' he added. He flung up his head.

'It wasn't I told you I was a tourist.'

'No, 'twas himself. But you, 'twas yourself, and no one else, told me – told me what I know. Brother,' he said, using the familiar word among the Gaels, 'you were dreaming. . . powerful dreams!' What wild foolery had I been crying out in my sleep! His eyes were full of vision – my dreams!

''Twill come to pass,' he said, 'the authors foretold it.' I had no reply, except to stare at him, his face aglow, bending upon mine.

'But isn't this a pitiful thing,' he grew mournful above me, 'that man outside, that son of mine – he's a thing without courage, he's like a sheep after being worried by the dogs, he is that! He'd be afraid to hang a bit of green on the door, or to keep a gun in the house. I'm sick and tired of him. But look, forgive me the welcome I gave you: these times there do be men in plain clothes going from house to house, innocent-looking slobs of men, gathering up information, and that pair outside, I must be watching them. 'Tisn't too much I'd tell them.' He repeated that solemn wink of his.

VII

I left him still in his bed, and I sat at breakfast with the two others.

'You got on all right with himself?'

'I did, I did, then.'

'He's a bit cross sometimes: he was a Fenian in the old days.'

'He told me so.'

They looked sharply at me. They were wondering how much he had told me. And in that state of mind I left them.

COWARDS

I

ROSSADOON IS A PROMONTORY on the Kerry coast. It ends in two blunt points that are not unlike the unshapely fingers of a giant's hand in a Scandinavian story, only that one of them, that on the northern side, is bigger in every way than the other, built up of huger cliffs, and so higher and freer of the winds and the clouds. Yet it was that northern point that the hardy people of old chose, when Christianity was still young in the land, to give to God, building their little stone church of four simple walls upon it, and burying their dead between that little church and the steep edge of the cliff. Of that early church only fragments of broken walls remain; hundreds of years must have passed since Mass was last sung there above the sea; but the crowded gravestones, many of them too neat, too new, tell us that the people of Rossadoon lay their dead of to-day with those that died over a thousand years ago. Too neat, too new, indeed, those shapely stones; and those on which one meets with such an inscription as:

Sacred to the memory of John O'Riordan, of New Inn... Erected by his son, Michael J. O'Riordan, of Portland, Maine, USA.

those are seldom in keeping with the place. Yet there, on North Point, among the crowded graves, will soon be erected a monument far bigger, far richer than any of those that American dollars have paid for. It will be set up above the grave of Tomas O'Miodhachain, and the inscription, in the purest of Gaelic phrasing, will tell how he died in Mountjoy Prison for sake of that land for which so many others like him have died in every age.

And so Tomas O'Miodhachain is gone home for ever to North Point, in Rossadoon—lying within ten fields of where he was born.

Colonel Hastings, too, has gone home, as if for ever, it seems, to his old grey weather-beaten house in South Point. And it was on the selfsame day that those two men of Rossadoon went home – the rebel and the colonel. But, as for that bright-faced boy – the colonel's only son, Edward Pendrift Hastings, who, in a certain way, saw them home – he had gone home before either of them, not, however, to South Point with his father, nor to North Point with the rebel: in a soldier's grave he rests, not far from Arras.

II

It was on a day of bright grey mists, those mists that seem to hide not one but many suns, that the poor wasted body of the rebel was brought by train, like any other dead thing, to Cappaban. There its guard of young Republican Volunteers from Dublin delivered it into the keeping of the local company of Republican Volunteers from Rossadoon. The funeral procession was soon faced to the west, faced against that straggling, winding, up-and-down hillside road of rock and shale, which, growing ever narrower and narrower for seven miles, passes at last, as a mere track in the heather, between broken walls into the graveyard on the Point. At the start there seemed to be three funerals rather than one: in the middle of the road the gathered Volunteer companies of the whole country-side marched evenly and compactly, far too numerous and too fierce-minded to take any check from the squads of silent, heavily armed police that were gathered at every corner of the road – marched with pipe music and draped drums and draped flags, the coffin in the midst of them, wrapped in the bright Republican colours, looking like an enamelled jewel-case against the hillsides, dim and grey in the mists. But on either hand of the steady, disciplined marching of the Volunteers there streamed along an irregular crowd of the people of the countryside: men, women and children, old and young, with here and there an old farmer from the hills on horseback, his brain alight and fiery with memories of other fights, other heroic deaths, other memorable funerals. Later on, those horsemen, and indeed the whole throng, would of themselves form too into processional order and take their place behind the drilled men about the coffin, but at the start the three bodies moved along the road in a silence that was full of hidden, fiery thoughts, as the mists were full of hidden suns.

The countrymen from Cappaban and Rossbuidhe and Rossadoon itself, although they gave every heed to it, could not march like the pale-faced men who had brought the body with them from Dublin; but ever since Tomas O'Miodhachain himself had left them two and a half years before, their drilling had been neglected; and many a one of them, now swinging awkwardly along, had a thought that the lifeless clay in their midst was conscious of this lack of training in their bearing, was somehow rebuking them. Yes, the Dublin men marched better; but it was not that alone that set them apart, not that alone but this: they had realised, unlike the men in faraway Kerry, what death by starvation in a cell in Mountjoy really means, had weighed it against the other deaths that are incident to rebels – death in a hot fight, death in the dawn, facing a firing squad, death on the scaffold – and come to feel that more than any one of them it tested the spirit within, the spirit itself, unaided and alone. As they marched now in unbroken silence, without the least glancing to right or left, their lips seemed uniformly thin and set, their brows uniformly pale and bent and hard, for each of them was marching on in the silence of loneliness. And somehow as the march went steadily on, climbing the hill with no abatement of speed or steadiness, this realisation of what death in prison really means, had meant to their own neighbour's boy, began to rule in the spirit of the whole throng, as well as in that of the men of Dublin, to unify them, to silence them, to stiffen them. Even from a distance one seemed to notice it, to yield to it, as to something severe and terrible and threatening; and then were it not for the relief and the release that was in the music of the pipes one would scream out.

Colonel Hastings, sitting high in his trap, did not notice it, did not cry out, did not even catch the wild music that was shrilling from sea to sea. He had been away from home for the past fortnight, had been to the War Office in London, was now making for home in a chilling silence. He would have driven straight on and into the procession, his road cutting across its road, if his man had not touched his arm:

'That's the funeral – the crowd passing –'

'What funeral?' The colonel was staring and frowning at the black mass streaming so earnestly forward.

'The Sinn Feiner's funeral,' the man answered, timidly. 'Tom Mehigan's funeral, the boy that died in Dublin, in prison. They wouldn't like us to break into them. . .'

Then, perhaps, the colonel did notice that strange stiffness, that severity in the marching.

'Why should I?' he whispered, in so strange a voice, so choked a voice, that his man glanced up at him from under his brows.

And so they sat there, the colonel two cushions higher than his man, while the funeral flowed by below them on the road. The discoloured leaves of the trees dropped their mist-drops noisily about them.

Were he half the age he was, the colonel might have stepped into the ranks of the pale-faced men and marched with them. Like theirs, his brows, too, were bent, his lips thin and set, his eyes as hard as steel. And the voice that had whispered so strangely went well with his look of inhumanity, so new to him. It was this star-like gleam, this aloofness from the common warm stir of life, that made him akin to the young men from Dublin. His man, daring to touch his sleeve, had expected from him an outburst of fury, at the least a snap of vexation. His mind was full of the last meeting between the rebel and the colonel. It was at the one recruiting meeting that was ever held in Rossadoon. The colonel had made his speech, had announced that he was sending his only son into the army, had asked the young lads of the place to step forward like men and join him. Not one had stepped forward.

How the colonel's eye blazed up, how he trembled with passion, how he flung his head in the air!

'I tell you what you are, you're cowards, cowards!' And then, his man remembered how, Tom Mehigan, in one spring, had leaped on to the fence beside the colonel:

''Tis the cowards that go!'

''Tis the cowards that stay!'

''Tis the cowards that go!'

''Tis the cowards that stay – by their dams!'

Too excited to catch up the phrase or its meaning, Tomas O'Miodhachain had then gripped the colonel's shoulder with his left hand, had flung his right towards the son who stood pale-faced by in silence:

''Tis he's the coward to go!'

''Tis you're the coward to stay – you and your men,' and the colonel wrenched himself free and raised his whip.

'Strike me!'

Then many men had leaped in between them, the police inspector led the colonel to his trap (this selfsame trap), his men formed themselves into a thick body around it, and the Loyalist party moved off, the whole meeting remaining behind them intact, holding the ground as won, and chanting in a single voice:

> Wrap the green flag round me, boys,
>   To die were far more sweet,
> With Erin's noble emblem, boys,
>   To be my winding sheet.

It was wise for Tomas to leave Rossadoon after that; he went to Dublin.

All this was present to the old man when he touched the colonel's sleeve; but as soon as he heard his master's voice, 'He's after hearing some terrible thing in London,' he thought, and he glanced timidly from under his brows at the frozen face.

It was to get some account of his son's death in France that the colonel had gone to London. It was thought he would even go to France. Here he was come back far sooner than expected, cold and silent and aloof.

Until they stopped up to let the crowds pass, the colonel had not spoken one word, had glanced neither to the right hand nor to the left hand. He did not even raise his eyes when, after long driving, his own place, still three miles away, rose up, like an old grey castle, against the rim of the grey sea. He had only stared straight ahead; and yet for all that would have driven into the midst of the crowds on the road if his man had not checked him. That old man, Maurice Dineen was his name, gave his master the true pity of the old retainer. Indeed he had to struggle with himself to keep his silence. He could have, and how willingly would have, broken out into a wild lament for the dead boy, in which there would be thoughts and words and phrases that no Hastings that ever lived could make himself for his relief. He had known the boy, had loved him, and loved him now the more for his hard fate, of which he had thoughts that must never be expressed.

Beyond count of time now, a tiny drop of rebelly Irish blood would suddenly leap to the surface in every generation of the Hastings. As in many another of the Garrison houses, their memoirs are parti-coloured. There's the story of one of them who fought for King James at the Boyne, of another who died fighting with the Wild Geese against the English at Fontenoy, of another who held lands in trust for the Papists when to do so was a high crime, of another who voted against the Union. And fortune has taken care that whatever there is of romance in these memoirs hangs around those wilder bloods that would not keep the safe path. When the young heir went to Trinity, what must he do but begin to learn Irish and lisp sedition! The old people at home shook their heads and smiled; 'A true Hastings!' they said. Then came the war; and the young lad was brought home and sent into the army. If he showed no inclination for it, he made no protest. Every other Garrison house in the country was doing the same. After all, that was the tradition. And, once in the army, he went through the mill of training with such high spirits and brightness that the old colonel, in his delight, used to read his letters to his visitors, slapping the pages with the back of his fingers and saying:

'A true Hastings.' But when the Rising came and the sixteen leaders, some of whom the lad had met with in the literary circles of Dublin, were executed, group after group, the colonel no longer read to his visitors the letters that were still coming to him from France, for they had become critical and snappish – and occasionally framed little lyrics and sonnets on Ireland – a true Hastings!

V

The procession had all but passed. Groups of women in black shawls and black cloaks were fussily making forward, five or six abreast, to be in time for the last prayers and the shots above the dead. They were too hurried for speaking. But a rough man's voice began to cry out, incoherently and indistinctly, so that it was hard to catch his words: 'I'm as worthy to walk as any of ye! 'Tisn't Tom Mehigan would reject me – the Lord have mercy on his soul. I'm as good an Irishman as any of ye, and Tom wouldn't deny that!' There was then but a mumbling, and then a cry more passionate than before: 'Don't mind me coat, lave ye! Don't mind it. Better men than me, they wore it and had to wear it. Don't mind it, lave ye.' There was again a silence, and the very end of the procession, old men limping on sticks and little girls hurrying them forward, went by, too earnest to notice the outcry of the drunken soldier. 'I'm as ready to die for me country as any of ye. But no, I'm rejected! The little boys, they wouldn't have me, I'd disgrace them! The old soldier would disgrace them!' There was wild indignation and surprise in the words.

The colonel's horse was now slowly, and with nervous forelegs, stepping down the steep road. The colonel saw the open road below him clear for a moment, but suddenly a huge, untidy figure in khaki, with a red, flushed, dribbling face, came headlong into the space; staring after the crowds ascending the road from him, his two arms wide in the air, he looked like a blind man on an unfamiliar road, groping and sprawling. He was returning on his phrases, 'Don't mind me coat, lave ye; better men than me had to wear it.' But the crowds were now too far from him; he turned and lurched to the corner where the roads met, and was about to fling himself there on the soft grass when he caught sight of the colonel. He drew himself up, steadied himself, and a strange and troubled look struggled in his eyes, and his poor dribbling lips worked a little. He saluted, and then, as if that was not enough, he quickly snatched the cap from his head and held it in his hands against his breast, as the people do when a religious procession is passing by. The colonel, grey and cold, still staring with fixed eyes, went on as if he had neither seen nor heard; but out burst the drunken voice again, warm and broken with sympathy: 'Don't mind them, sir; he was no coward; so he wasn't. He was no more a coward than that boy they're burying on the hill. He was a gentleman, he was, and good to the men, and if 'twas fighting for the ould land he was, by Christ, they wouldn't have to shoot him for cowardice!'

The colonel sprang bolt upright in his trap, blind and deaf and maddened. He clutched the whip and lashed his animal. He tried to speak to it. It was rearing in the shafts, its head tossing. 'Home, home!' he cried to it at last, hoarsely, hardly audible. The horse leaped forward and flew like the wind.

And so the colonel lies buried in the old grey house on the South Point, almost as deeply, it would seem, as Tomas O'Miodhachain lies buried in his grave on the North Point, or his own dishonoured son in his unmarked sleeping place in France. God be his comforting.

COLONEL MAC GILLICUDDY
GOES HOME

I

COLONEL MAC GILLICUDDY having been now laid to rest with his Gaelic ancestors in Muckross Abbey, my life, I trust, will soon again begin to flow into its old channels.

The memory of the colonel was becoming, perhaps, the faintest of all my memories – I had not seen him for years and years – when I chanced on this casual little paragraph in my morning paper:

> The lecture that Colonel Mac Gillicuddy was to give in Wexford Town Hall on 'Cromwell in Wexford' has been prohibited by the authorities.

Then the colonel is home from India, I thought. He had been wounded at the battle of the Somme, and these wounds, I knew, had unfitted him for further active service; I also knew that he had since then been put in charge of some commissariat department in India, and that he had had to make frequent journeys into the very heart of that vast land, as well as into Mesopotamia; but beyond this I knew nothing.

Anyway, he was now in Ireland and anxious to lecture in town halls – what had happened to him? To lecture, moreover, on 'Cromwell in Wexford', and in Wexford itself – whatever had happened to him?

Other colonels, it is true, had endeavoured to influence opinion in Ireland by lecturing on Irish themes: I myself had heard a colonel lecture on 'The Wild Geese' in quite a sympathetic way, and not without some show of learning; but then this was before the Rising in Dublin at Easter, 1916, and the colonel who had done so was by nature a flashy sort of person. Colonel Mac

Gillicuddy was different: a silent, brooding sort of man, some-what of a student, he would not be twenty-four hours in Ireland, his native land, without perceiving that all such methods of in-fluencing Irishmen had become useless, the temper of the people having changed so much.

I found a faint smile beginning to play about my lips. I thought of Mac Gillicuddy himself – a quiet, brooding man with pursed lips and a top-heavy brow – why, his very appearance on the platform would kill the life of any lecture hall in the world, though it were lit with a hundred arc-lamps and festooned with red and white flowers. And then his theme, 'Cromwell in Wexford'! What other picture could that bring before the mind than the slaughter in cold blood by the Cromwellian soldiery of the 300 noble women of the town as they gathered for sanctuary about the stone cross in the market place – surely an extraordinary story on the lips of a British officer! Then the place he had chosen – Wexford itself! And then the time – November, 1919, when the nerves of all Ireland were strained almost to the breaking point! Even as this thought flashed on my mind, I looked through the paper, and there, spread all over it, were stories of arrests, of midnight raids for arms, of prisoners hunger-striking in prison, of shootings, of jailings, of further proclamations of martial law. And I had only to look through the window to see soldiers marching by, armed to the teeth. Of the colonel's desire to lecture on 'Cromwell in Wexford' at such a time, in such a place, I could make nothing, except that something had happened to him.

II

I saw no other mention of that lecture in the papers; a fortnight afterwards, however, I received a short note from him, a fact surprising enough in itself, for during his two years of service in France and since in India – eventful years – he had not written me even one letter. His note made no apology for all this, neither did he make any enquiry of how these years had passed for me; he simply mentioned, casually it seemed, that he intended staying three weeks longer in Drogheda, *studying on the spot the details of Cromwell's massacre in that town!* How long he had been there already, why he had chosen to delve into these terrible things, and why he should trouble me with them – all this had not crossed his mind, it seemed. His postscript was queerer still: 'Have you seen Tate's book on "Kitchener in Africa"?'

That I noted. I had not heard of such a book, but since Mac himself had served under Kitchener in his African wars, it was likely to be authoritative or he wouldn't have referred me to it. 'Tate's "Kitchener in Africa"', I wrote in my notebook; and even as I did so a sudden thought jerked, *jerked* the pen from the paper: why, Mac himself must have witnessed some terrible slayings in his time, perhaps even taken a hand in them!

I stood up straight. I no longer smiled: his deadly earnest face, which now was all my vision, forbade it. I had to put away my work and go out into the streets. With a nervous, unrestful stride, that I found impossible to control, I went from hill-top to hill-top, without purpose. Fagged, yet quieted somewhat in spirit, I reached my lodging again about eight o'clock at night. A postcard stood against the foot of my lamp. I saw that it was Mac's writing. I turned the other side and read these words, 'Syed Ameer Khaldoun's book on India also.'

India! I could hardly touch the food they put on the table before me. And yet there was nothing like a definite thought in my mind – nothing, only the sense of a far-off background that I was afraid to examine, a background of outrage and blood and horizon-flames tonguing the distant skies; and against this background I would see, all the time, Mac Gillicuddy's brooding face, his top-heavy brow, his pursed lips, his gloomy eyes!

III

I had just settled down of an evening three weeks later on to resume the reading of Tate's ill-advised book on Kitchener in the

Sudan when the colonel was announced. I couldn't take my eyes from his face. He had changed, he had aged, withered, but these changes I might have looked for: he was verging on the middle age, and his life had been a hard one. It was not these changes in him that held me in wonder: it was a certain expression that would come across his face, chilling the air; and I could feel that he had somehow come on new standards and that he was now judging the world by them: at such times I would halt midway in a sentence, hoping he would not guess the conclusion I had intended! And often, until his whole face looked distorted, his right eyebrow would climb up his forehead, slowly, slowly; and the eye itself, so exposed, would then glare mercilessly into one's very brain! His very appearance disturbed me deeply. He did not speak of India or Egypt; his mind was too full, at the moment, of Drogheda and Wexford. Every detail of Cromwell's (or as he had taken to pronouncing the name, Crom'ell's) massacres in these places he had amassed, sifted, examined and arranged; and I could see that by dint of brooding on them, the terrible scenes, the locale of which he had been so familiarising himself with, had become alive for him, were burning as fiercely before his inner eye as if, like a poet, he had created them out of some central theme of human vileness. Noting how he would linger, involuntarily I was sure, on certain incidents – the killing of infants in the crypts of St Peter's Church in Drogheda, or the dragging with ropes of an old priest over the cobblestones – noting his rigid air of concentration at these moments, I could feel that the energy of his mind was exactly that of a poet's in the throes of creation: he was, I was certain, in the midst of passionate confusion, blood was flowing beneath his eyes, steaming, and the odour of it was in his nostrils.

I was really glad when, at two in the morning, he rose to go. I felt I should accompany him, for his ardour of mind was such that he might easily go astray or walk into the river, yet this I could not bring myself to do: he had exhausted my powers. When I shut the door on him I spread myself, dressed as I was, on my bed, forcing myself to think on anything, on everything, except on those wild scenes he had been speaking of like a living witness. . . I kept my eyes in the clutch of my left hand. . . After a long spell of this artificially nurtured coma, as it were, I sprang up suddenly, caught up Tate's book on Kitchener and hurled it into the fire, for an insidious, morbid craving to dip again into his horrors had begun to form itself in my quietening spirit.

IV

The next morning he called to tell me that he was starting at once for Kerry. Cromwell, I gladly recollected, had never visited Kerry, and I remember I said, ' 'Tis the very place for you – a charming land, wild, romantic, yet gentle, somehow, with mild winds from the sea. Besides, it is the home of the Mac Gillicuddys.'

'Yes; I have been told they were a branch of the O'Sullivans.'

'That is so.'

I was glad to find him in so contained a mood. I expected he would satisfy himself with south Kerry, with Kenmare, or Waterville, or Killarney itself, with its magnificent Macgillicuddy Reeks, the mountain land of his ancestors; but a few days later I had a few lines from him from Ballyferriter, which is in the north. Ballyferriter, he informed me, means the Town of the Ferriters, an old Norman family; and then he added: 'In Killarney I visited Cnoc-na-gCaorach (the Hill of the Sheep) where Pierce Ferriter, the warrior poet, the prince who was head of the clan, was hanged, a priest on one side, a bishop on the other, in the time of Cromwell.' I could not help muttering, 'Still harping on his Cromwell'; but I read on: 'From my bedroom window here I can see the whole of Smerwick Harbour; as I write the moon is shining on Dunanore.'

Smerwick! Dunanore! And not another word, only the two names – two names that I had almost forgotten. It was not for nothing he had gone to Ballyferriter! I could picture his gloomy eyes looking out on the still waters of that haunted bay. I should have gone with him.

The very next morning I had a letter from him which was, to say the least of it, incoherent. It puzzled me. There were lines in it, dashed down I could see, about Sir Walter Raleigh, about Lord Grey – terrible judgments; then there were homely phrases: 'Among the Irish-speaking people of this place I find the word for sixpence is *raol*, which surely is the Spanish word *real*.' Then following right on that: 'I hear screams in the dead night,' and then, 'Why does one become sometimes and quite suddenly possessed of a wild gaiety in such spots?' Every sentence in the letter, all but two, was quite intelligible, but as a whole it was without sequence: it was no more to be understood than the broken phrases a soldier, after a day of battle, flings from him in his restless sleep. It happened that I had just been reading Mügge's *Life of Nietzsche*, and I recollected how he tells that the incoherency of the philosopher's letters was the first hint his friends had of his approaching madness. I grew suddenly afraid. I picked up a timetable, and in less than an hour I was journeying towards Dingle, which is the nearest station to Ballyferriter.

V

I found him weakly struggling with his excitement. While eating the plain fare, the homemade bread, that had been put before me, I noticed that his face was becoming more and more haggard: the invisible fingers of a fixed idea were dragging at his cheeks. He could not help rising from the table to survey for the twentieth time the quiet bay outside, and he would scan its distances as anxiously as if he were fearful that an enemy squadron might at any moment round its rocky headlands. He was soon hurrying me along beside its gentle waters. For December it was a day of wondrous mildness, and never were any waters so limpid and beautiful in colour. They fell on the golden sands in just one long wave, that caught the mellow tints of the sky as it rose and broke lazily in foam. To our right, a black stump of a ruined stronghold stood a little way back from the waters. The colonel pointed it out to me, and told me how it had belonged to the Fitzgeralds, when they were overlords of all this land, and how one of them, when nearing his end, had asked to be raised up so that his last vision might be the waters of his beloved bay. The colonel spoke in a wistful tone, and I began to hope that this quiet country of St Brendan and many another life-forsaking hermit – so far from the turmoil of the world, might again win him to peacefulness. But the next moment, standing where San Josepho's Spaniards, three hundred years ago, had made their fight, he was, with an edge on his voice, pointing out to me the traces of the fort they had thrown up, and was showing me where Raleigh butchered the whole 800 of them to death, they having first surrendered to him their arms. Feeling that edge on his voice, I drew him unsuspectingly from the spot, and kept him pacing by the lisping and breaking waters almost till midnight, hoping that by first tiring out his body the great peace of the wide moonlight night might the more surely win upon his spirit.

I had just got into bed with a certain flattering thought that my ruse had not quite failed, when I heard him tapping hurriedly at my door. Before I was half dressed he was in the room.

'Look! Look!' He had flung up my window, his hand was stretched into the night: when I drew to his side I could see it trembling. Beyond it, was all the sweep of the bay, dreamy-looking in the moon, and quiet slopes of shadow were laid upon the hills. But, of course my eyes were fixed on that spit of land where Raleigh had done his slaughtering, for towards that the trembling moon-white hand, as I instinctively knew, was fiercely stretched.

'Ah, my God! my God!' he was breathing, and I could feel his limbs trembling. 'Horrible! horrible! horrible!'

'What? what?' I said.

'The cries, the cries,' he whispered. I could, by the sound of his voice, tell that there was no natural moisture left in his mouth; it was scarcely speech that came from him. He was hanging on to me, and his trembling shook me. Could it be possible that he was beholding in vision the murdering of 800 defenceless men? saw it as an artist would – in vivid groupings of destroyer and destroyed?

I peeped at him. His teeth were chattering, and his hands clutched my shoulders heavily, as if his legs were giving way; he was shrinking back from what he was glaring at. Yet the only sounds to be heard from outside were some sea-fowl quarrelling above a school of sprats (as I took it) in the mouth of the bay – sharp cries or melancholy, long-drawn and wailing. Was it these cries that were playing havoc with him? I felt my own ears greedily gathering them in, I felt myself yielding to them, I found them taking on some strange hurry and wildness. Bah! I shook myself. But he was trying to speak, and I thought it was the word 'cries' I again heard.

'Rather inadequate,' I flung out peevishly, thinking, perhaps, to break the spell that was on him; the cries of the sea-birds just then were very far away, and indeed, not unpleasant in the still night. How could anyone mix them up with the wild screaming of a massacre? But I had tugged at some tightened nerve in him. He leaped from me, back into the room, and the heaviness of weakness was gone from him. He was now all nerve and sinew. He was glaring at me:

'Inadequate! inadequate! That's just it.' He spoke as if the problem of his life had been solved.

'Inadequate! Laughable! Laughable, when you think of the horror of it! It is that that makes one reckless in such businesses. Wild, inhuman' (how he was glaring at me!) '– delighted to give the edge of the sword on a grey pate, or a soft breast, or a child! – "I will make them squeal," you say, you can't help saying it when the passion of slaughter is upon you, but you. . . *you can't make them squeal – loud enough!* and then, and then. . . my God! my God! Shut it! shut it! The curtains. Those also – Oh! my God! my God!'

He had flung himself on the bed, burying his face in the pillow. I knew he felt himself swooning off, dizzy; and seeing that he was beyond making any effort to get a grip of himself, I said no word to him, only gripped his limp hand firmly, firmly – there is no other medicine for such a crisis – until, little by little, the terror passed from him.

I was careful not to let him again out of my sight. As the death-still night went on – oh, what a land of holy silence it is! – he won back almost to his own self and tried to force me to my bed, protesting that it was not kind of me to treat him like an invalid. I shook my head, and there I sat until the inevitable reaction had come upon him, and he was sunken into an unrestful sleep.

The night was chilly, and there was no fire in the grate, and, not caring to rouse the household, my only plan was to slip into the room he had left and rifle it of the blankets and wrap myself in them; which done, there I kept vigil over him, like a shepherd in an eastern land. Sometimes the loud scream of a sea-bird would cut through the night, and I would glance at him to see if he stirred to it. But, no. Then the silence would deepen and my thoughts would follow the strong-winged bird over the wide waters. I began to recollect all that I had ever learned of the massacre Raleigh had made in this lonely land; and the slaughters that have been made by others in this country before and since, connecting one with another; and how it came about I do not know, but suddenly, with firm assurance, it came to me that Mac Gillicuddy was picturing all those terrible scenes in the light of his experiences in Africa and India and Mesopotamia! Certain phrases in his letters, certain words I had heard him use, certain enquiries he had been making of me, began to swarm back on me, one summoning another, and at last, I almost shouted out: I have it, I have it! – the fixed idea that is harrying him into madness!

With confidence I bent my eyes on the bed. He was whining, squealing like a young puppy in its first illness; but I didn't mind: I could cure him! Now he was still, quite still, seeming as if he were listening to things far away – that sense of strain, I noticed, never once went from him, asleep or awake.

Then little spasms of terror would cross his white features, which he would try to shake off. Yet still I did not lose confidence that now, understanding his disease, I could make a cure.

Of course we left Ballyferriter the next day. To catch the first train from Dingle we had to leave in the dark of the morning, and dark it was, the moon having sunken. A curious thing happened: in a wild, lonely place near Lord Ventry's woodlands, groups of silent-moving figures began to pass us on the road. The whole country, as everybody knows, was disturbed at the time by groups of armed men raiding in the nights. I grew timid.

'Who are these?' I whispered to the old driver.

'Whisht!' he snarled to me.

'But who are they?' I persisted.

' 'Tis little sense ye have, for an Irishman,' he said. I then said: 'Are they Sinn Feiners?'

'How would I know?' he growled at me.

The colonel had caught the words, 'Sinn Feiner', it seemed. He gripped the driver.

'Halt awhile, driver,' he said. 'I want to see these men; I won't be long.' He was just leaping from the car, when the driver, with some magic word he had, set the horse prancing. I caught the colonel's arm.

'Are you mad?' I said to him.

'Mad!' and he flung his head up; the horse was still rebelliously dancing along the road.

'Yes, mad,' the driver shot at him; 'them fellows would destroy you, and the likes of them clothes on your back!' The colonel was still in khaki.

The figures had vanished. We were recklessly rushing along through places where there was not the faintest glimpse of light of any kind upon the road.

VII

When I had him seated in the train I began to think of the remedy I would try. Since he was haunted by the vision of the reverse of the British Empire I would speak of its obverse. After all, one could make out a case for it. Had it not spread Christianity, I would say, into those wild lands, throwing some certain share of its wealth and its choicest children into the work? Then, its glorious pioneers – their gallant fortunes, their fame – might one quote of them:

Only the actions of the just
Smell sweet and blossom in the dust!

Then I would attempt to show what a blessing those vast hinterlands are to a mother-country, how they are as a very sporting jungle for the younger sons who, remaining at home, must gamble away the estates. Lastly, I would speak of the stream of wealth that has been for centuries flowing into England itself from those seemingly inexhaustible sources. Of that one could speak with confidence... So I would speak to him; but I would not begin yet awhile, for he was sunken into some deep reverie: he had not yet quite shaken off his wild visions of the night.

We stopped at a little place called Emlough, if I remember right, and resuming our journey I made an attempt to speak: but he raised his hand, motioning me to silence. Soon afterwards a crowd of English soldiers, very tired-looking, armed to the teeth, got into our carriage, and I thought I saw the colonel shudder. To start with a colonel a discussion on the two sides, the glory and the shame of the British Empire in a carriage full of soldiers might lead to the most unimaginable results as things were just then, so I was forced to hold my peace. And these soldiers kept us company until we reached home! I could see that their presence had made Mac Gillicuddy very excited. And there were other incidents as well to play upon him. In Tralee we saw groups of armed policemen lining the main street; presently we saw military motor lorries bringing some Sinn Fein prisoners to trial – young lads, they stood daringly upright in the hooded waggons, with bare steel all round them. We noticed how the people moved quickly through the streets in a sort of gloomy silence, peering into the hooded waggons as they passed in quick succession.

It was dark night when we reached the city. The next day I would make my first attempt to win Mac Gillicuddy from that fixed idea that was ruining his mind.

VIII

We were weary. I threw myself into a deep chair. The colonel seated himself at the table, opened the evening paper he had bought at the door as we entered, and became engrossed in it, it seemed. Presently he rose. 'Pardon,' he said carelessly, and went out, the paper still in his hand.

He spoke so calmly, as if by having at last made up his mind on some definite plan, he had crushed his excitement into quiescence, that I thought of questioning him as soon as he returned. But there was no sign of his returning! I went seeking him at once, with a growing agitation in my mind. He was nowhere in the house. Without a moment's delay I was rushing through the streets, sharply peering at all that I met or overtook. And the streets were crowded and uneasy. As in Tralee and Dingle they were swarming with squads of soldiers with their helmets and packs on them; and batches of heavily coated policemen, with white, strained faces, went silently and swiftly about whatever business they had on hand. Military motors and military lorries were recklessly tearing through the dimly lit darkness. And the people seemed hurrying too, and silent.

For fully three hours I dived hither and thither through wide and narrow streets – through squares lit by arc-lamps and through filthy passages where there were no lamps of any kind. In an alleyway a poor beggarman was singing; his hair was long and matted, he had a thick, unkempt beard, he wasn't four feet in height, an old overcoat that he was wearing soaked water from the muddy ground. Yet he was singing heartily, and the name, Ireland, was in every line:

> 'Tis Ireland, 'tis beautiful Ireland,
>> Ireland, the gem of the sea,
> Oh, my heart is at home in old Ireland,
>> And I wish that old Ireland was free.

He had a pair of nigger's bones in his right hand, he flourished them to the rhythm. I don't think I should have noticed him, but in three different places I came on him that night. I began to think in

147

the end that maybe he was not a beggarman at all.

Exhausted, I again reached my lodgings in the market square; how wide, free and airy it was after the narrow streets! The moon held half of it in a white still light, the other half was black with shadow, in which a few odd lamplit windows glimmered very warm and mellow, contrasting with the wan moonlight.

'My friend has not returned?'

'No, sir; there is no trace of him. Johnny, here, saw him going out.'

'Well, send in whatever you have; I'm fainting.'

'Yes, sir; and there's the paper.'

I had little mind for it, but as it lay there on the table, I saw in scare headlines:

MASSACRE AT AMRITSAR!
2,000 INDIANS SHOT DOWN BY THE ENGLISH
500 KILLED OUTRIGHT.

There was little other information except the name, General Dyer. I must confess I did not cast one thought on those murdered Indians, nor on their murderers; my one thought was Mac Gillicuddy. This was the news he had been so intent upon; it was this dreadful story, come so pat upon its hour, that had sent him out – and he had gone so calmly out! Though the paper trembled in my hand, my weariness had fallen from me. I was sweaty and cold, yet anxious to be up and doing; the shock those three lines of print had given me had called out those reserves of spirit that in such moments so dominate the mere body.

'I must find him,' I said. I swallowed some cups of tea, one after another, and rose up to make again for the streets.

At that moment I heard steps on the stairs, and in flung Mac Gillicuddy himself, quickly and nervously! An appalling wistfulness was in his features, his eyes were wide and pale, his lips weak. He threw himself into a deep chair and buried his head in his hands. And these hands, too, seemed so pale, long-fingered, sweaty!

'What has happened?' I said.

Without removing his hands from his face he shook his head. He wouldn't speak.

Meanwhile, outside, the whole city seemed to have gone into riot; that it was in train for it I had noticed in my rushing through it. The tramp, tramp of soldiers went by, the rattling of their horses and waggons. Far away a rebelly song was being sung firmly and defiantly. Suddenly we heard cries and screams, and hundreds of voices:

'Release the man, release him!' 'Shame on ye, ye ——' 'Shame!' 'Shame!' 'Shame!'

I listened to it all, still staring at the broken figure sunken into the chair. Again I heard the cries, 'Release him, release him!' and 'Let him go, ye ——' And then all the cries, shouts, running, singing, seemed to gather up into one long, loud, triumphant roar. I leaped to the window, I saw a great crowd below, a group of policemen in the centre, buffeted by the people, and a wild, squirming little figure in their grasp – my little ballad-singer, I thought. They were all in the moonlight; but a different crowd were surging into the square from a far-off angle, singing; and it was their coming that had caused the cheering. The little prisoner squirmed more than ever, and at last the policemen had to let him go. They then formed up into a dense mass, and began to fight their way back towards the opening they had come from. All was confusion; stones began to fly through the air, glass was broken. Little knots of people stood still, clutching one another, and others began to whirl around the knots, like currents in a rock-strewn river. Presently, other shouts, yells and screams, screams of terror, arose in another corner of the square; very shrill, they were, very high-pitched; and at once the whole crowd broke into a wild stampede: an armoured car had entered from a side street at a tearing rate and was encircling the square; the place emptied itself in a flick of time, lay again open to the moonlight and to the broad shadows. Still the car tore around it, circling it three times. At last it stood still. At its first coming Mac Gillicuddy had dragged himself wearily to my side; together we had watched its antics; now we were staring speechless at it, as it stood there, throbbing in the moonlight in a pool of shadow; it seemed to look around to see where next it should make a spring. We saw two young heads rise above it. They laughed. They spoke. If Mac

Gillicuddy caught the words, I did not; but he raced from the room as if struck by a whip. I leaped after him. I flew down the stairs. He banged through the glass doors. I opened them. I saw him making headlong for the car. The two heads turned towards him. Then down they went. He leaped at the car, crying out – I know not what. A succession of revolver shots rang out, seemed to fly everywhere. Then the car blew a cloud of smoke and moved. He was all limbs, right in front of it. I could see nothing for a moment – only a lifting cloud. Then in, beneath, that little cloud I saw a figure crawling slowly on all fours, like a beast, stupidly, heavily – a most ridiculous posture. It only went a little way, when down it flopped, kissing the ground. And all the time the car circled the square. It swerved to escape the bundle that now lay in its path, and then shot swiftly out of sight by the side street it had entered from. There, in the middle of the moonlight, lay Mac Gillicuddy, dead, with his secrets.

It seems he had gone to the Sinn Fein headquarters and laid certain plans before them for the wrecking of the British Empire, offering his services in the carrying out of them. They would not listen to him. It was then he returned to me, a man who had suddenly given way to despair.

He sleeps in Muckross Abbey. Hundreds of other Mac Gillicuddys – soldiers also – sleep there, too. Considering the story of his life, the manner of his swift death, it is curious to try to imagine how those old Gaelic warriors received him, their kinsman. With aloofness? or with kindly welcome?

I, who knew him so well, I can picture him only as a poor abashed and tongue-tied figure, shrinking away from their hard gazing, their fierce brows. May he rest in peace.

THE PRIEST

I

BECAUSE FATHER REEN had been reading all day the rain had
meant but little for him. Since breakfast time he had
not been disturbed, his housekeeper even had not entered,
and he had reached an age, he was sixty-two, when a day of
unbroken quiet was the best of holidays. Yet any more of the
quietness might have taken the edge off his pleasure. In the
afternoon, just in good time it seemed, an uncertain sunbeam
floated tremulously across the pages of his book; quite unexpectedly, it had stolen in through the still streaming window
panes. Father Reen, his mouth suddenly opening, raised his head
and stared with his blue eyes, large and clear, across the river
valley towards the mountains. He noticed that, even as he looked,
hedgerow, branch, and rocky height were emerging through the
saturated air, were taking form, unsubstantial still, yet no longer
broken in outline. His house was in a good place for the afternoon
sunshine; it stood on a rise of ground above the river and looked
to the south-west. The soil was sandy, the paths in the garden well
kept and kind to the feet; before long, in the mild November
sunshine, he was pacing to and fro the full length of his little place.
Between this pleasant place in the sun, and the study he had just
come from, he had grown into the custom of passing nearly all his
free time – too much of it, as he often told himself, for it meant
further and further withdrawal from the life of the village, the life
of his parish; but then where in the parish was such life to be come
upon as he could profitably make use of? He was conscious that in
this parish of his, as in many another round about it, there was,
speaking from either social or cultural point of view, neither an
upper class nor even a middle class – there was only a peasant
class that had only comparatively recently emerged from penury,

a class that needed spurring, that needed leadership, and that was not finding it. He had long since reasoned out that the time had come for the building up of a middle class, an upper class too, on native lines, to take the place of those that had failed; but as often however as this thought came to him he smiled, for he certainly was not one of those who get things put to right. Now, however, breathing the fresh air, which was chilly enough to make quick walking necessary, he fortunately was free from the thought of all this. Beyond the feel of the fresh air in his nostrils he was free almost from sensation. Film after film of moisture he saw lifting, dissipating themselves in the effulgence of the sun, leaving the wide river valley, the hundred thousand rocky scars and ridges that encumbered it, sharply drawn, one against another, if as yet without colour, a succession of grey tones. But the swollen river made no response to the light above it, for its waters had become stained, were heavy after the scourings from the fords and inches. He could see it tumbling along.

Whenever in his pacing he faced the west his eye traversed not only the river but the village beyond it. He saw the evening smoke of its homely fires ascending, each spire of it alive with the sunshine streaming through it. He had been so long in the place, first as curate and then as parish priest, that he had got into the way of whispering to himself such pet phrases as: my valley, my river, my river, my hills. This afternoon, the ascending smoke spires taking his eye. My people! was the phrase that possessed his lips. It seemed touched with the memory of emotion rather than with any living warmth. He had scarcely uttered the words when he stopped up in his pacing, for in that single patch of open village street that was visible to him, he saw a horseman swinging steadily along, making, he was certain, towards the bridge, towards this hillside, towards this house of his.

II

In less than a half-hour Father Reen was riding alone across the bridge and through the village, faced towards the west, towards Kilmony, a ploughland ten miles away on the farthest edge of his far-flung parish, where, the messenger had informed him, an old man was nearing his end.

Anyhow there would be no more rain. The sky was clearing, the wind was swung round towards the north. Now the sun was hidden behind a barricade of cloud, cold grey in colour, and thick, that rested all along the horizon, shafts of rich light ascending from behind it to the height of heaven. The sun would not show itself again; and the moment it was gone one would feel how hard the night was turning to frost. Father Reen was conscious of this as he made on at a good pace. Yes, the air would become colder and colder, the landscape barer and barer, harder and harder in its features. The village, which he had come through, was windswept enough, was hard enough and niggard enough in all its ways, yet it did not lack for trees in various groupings, nor for clipped bushes, shapely hedges, flower plots. And he remembered how, as he passed through, he had heard an outburst of reckless laughter from the stragglers in the forge – their meeting place as long as he could remember. He knew he would come on no other group of gossips as loud-voiced or as merry as they: nor on hedgerow trees or clipped hedges or any flowers. Already he was aware of the denuded character of the landscape about him, every feature of it sharp and bare; he foresaw all the long roads and byways, little cared-for, stone-strewn, with their surfaces swept away, deep-channelled by the rain torrents from the hills; and, very insidiously, uneasiness intruded on his peace of mind, not induced so much by the discomfort of the roads ahead of him as by the thought of Kilmony itself, to which they led – a place where the people were still living in wretched cabins, on the poorest fare, without a notion of giving attention to, or spending a penny on, anything except the direst necessaries of life – a place where he hardly ever remembered an old person to die without the lust of property troubling the spirit almost to the beginning of the agony. Against the fear that this foreknowledge aroused in him he struggled; he shook his head at it, he set his teeth, he grasped the reins more firmly, consciously giving himself to the onward rhythm of the gallop.

Already, he felt, there was thin frost forming on the pools

beneath his horse's hoofs. And what a bite in the north-west as it blew across the marches and the reedy lakes! Soon the stars would begin to come forth sparkling with frost. Everywhere now slabs of rock, pinnacles of rock, hillsides of rock; and not a tree anywhere, not a bush even; scarcely a sign of humanity, hardly a human being. On an upland farm he had seen a boy driving a few scraggy beasts diagonally up a sloping field to the stall. Now, across the inch, he saw an old man bent under a huge mass of bogland cow-fodder, making for a gap – and between man and boy there were miles, it seemed, of rock and heather, of such desolation as hindered the growth of any community spirit, which, of itself, would little by little, induce a finer way of living. My people! My people! he thought, so good, so sinless, even so religious, yet so hard, so niggardly, so worldly, even so cruel; and again he blamed himself for not starting, for not forwarding some plan or other – sports or story-telling, or dancing or singing or reading or play-acting – anything that would cut across and baffle that lust of acquisitiveness which everywhere is the peasant's bane. My people! My people! My people! and then: If only I were young again! But this, he chided himself, was but self-deception. What was really wrong with him, he told himself, was that he had unconsciously withdrawn himself from them, with those hard ways of theirs. They were leaderless, at least in the social sense. They had no initiative – yet he had left them to themselves lest – yes, that was it – lest – he was like a doctor falling into age, afraid to use any except the safest remedies – lest complications might ensue – yes, that was the phrase. But it was true he was ageing. And the best day he ever was he had not been one of those blessed people who get things done. Anyway, his duty as a priest – that, O thanks be to God, he had never neglected, so far as he knew.

It was dark night when he turned up the hillside on the ridge of which lay Kilmony – a place where every household was inter-married with every other household. Pluckily his horse stepped up the broken ground, his forehoofs smiting the rocky shelvings, impatient for footing. When the ascent became a little easier Father Reen raised his head and saw the crest of the hill swarthy and sharp against the grey cloudless sky, darker than it, full of roughnesses, of breaks and points, a restless line running east and west with here and there a bright star fallen upon it. He knew he was at the right place. Beyond that ridge, he remembered, were immense slowly-rising uplands abandoned to nature, miles on miles, where sheep were driven to pasture at the end of spring-time, and left to themselves the length of summer, where turf was dug out, but where no attempt at tillage had ever been made. On his right he now noticed a haphazard group of gables; some of them had once been whitened, and these helped still to separate the whole group from the beetling background. He heard a gate opened, and dimly he made out a tall figure in the middle of the road – it was indeed little more than a rough pathway – standing against the sky awaiting him.

III

'Am I at Miah Neehan's?' he asked.

'Yes, Father. You're better get off here, the yard isn't too clean in itself.'

He dismounted, and already he felt the wind cold on his sweaty limbs.

'I'm in time?' he questioned.

'Good time. In good time,' he was answered, and then he heard the voice raised:

'Isn't it a wonder one of ye wouldn't hold a lamp for Father Reen?'

There was but a dull glimmer of light in the interior of the dwelling: he saw it reflected in the dung pit which, in the old-fashioned way, occupied most of the yard. By peering he made out the causeway of large boulders running through the mire to the doorway. All was just as he had expected. It was one of those places, now happily rare, over which the spirit of the bad old times, as the people say, still seemed to brood, a place where necessity was served, and that only. Among the dark figures in the doorway he saw movement – the effect of a harshly spoken word of his guide – and he was glad, for the sweat was chilly on his limbs. He saw now a flannel-coated middle-aged man emerge, shielding the lamp from the wind with a corner of his wrapper. He made towards him, and by the time he reached the threshold the figures were all withdrawn again into the interior. There were both men and women, but the faces of the women were so deeply hidden within the hoods of their cloaks that all he could see of them was a pale gleam. They were seated by the walls, but the men were standing haphazardly about or leaning their shoulders wherever they could find support. Tall and spare, a mountainy breed, their heads were lost in the darkness that hung beneath the ancient thatch. The fire on the hearth was uncared for; and not a word was passing among those present. He saluted them, his hat in his hand, and waited until the lamp had been again hung on its accustomed nail.

'Where is he?' he said.

There was a slight pause before the reply came: 'Inside, Father.'

Before he entered the lower room, the only other room in the house, he turned towards where the voice had spoken, saying: 'Are his affairs settled, are they in order?'

No answer coming, he turned towards the man who had held the lamp for him, looking at him questioningly, but he, throwing down his eyes, slunk away into the midst of the others. He raised his voice then:

'Are his affairs in order?'

Just then, the man who had welcomed him on the roadway, he had since been seeing after the horse, entered hurriedly, looking like one who had been anxious whether those within might not have been scanting the courtesies. A voice in the semi-darkness, a woman's voice, met him:

'Father Reen wants to know are his affairs settled?'

'Oh yes; that's all right. In good order. In good order. You needn't give yourself any uneasiness about that, Father.'

He spoke loudly, challengingly, the priest felt, to those about them in the room. Indeed he had scarcely finished when one of the tallest of the men flung himself from his place and strode across the room to the doorway where he took his station, his back to

156

those within, his eyes staring out into the black night. 'Sit down, sit down, Jack. Be easy.' He who had answered the priest's question it was who spoke, with the carelessness of contempt, it seemed, rather than in any spirit of good fellowship. But the man in the doorway answered him, flinging round his head suddenly and angrily:

'I'm all right here – just here where I am.'

It appeared to Father Reen the two were fairly matched. 'Very well, very well. Please yourself. Come on in, Father.'

A woman's voice said:

'Tim, you'd want a second candle within.'

'You're right. One is a poor light on these occasions.' He soon had a lighted candle in his hand, showing the way.

'Come on in, Father. Everything is ready for you. Quite ready.'

IV

Father Reen was alone with the dying man. In the squalid room, the rickety contrivance of a bed, the ancient coverings, the stained walls, the tainted air, he again found all he had expected to find. Above all he found his thought realised in the head thrown weakly back upon the pillow, the eyes of which had fastened on him at the moment of entrance. He could feel how grimly the old man's will – he was ninety-one years of age – had been exerted, had been struggling against the craving of the worn-out body for rest, for the lapse of unconsciousness. He drew near to the bedside, seated himself at its edge, and noticed how the old eyes were searching the spaces of the room; he then heard the dry and wearied voice speaking with a distinctness that of itself alone would acquaint one with the triumph of the will over every other faculty in the old man's soul:

'Whisper, Father, is that door shut?'

The priest rose, made certain that the door between them and the crowd of descendants and relatives outside was fastened, then seating himself again said:

' 'Tis all right.'

'Whisper,' the old head was reaching up to his face, 'I'm destroyed, destroyed with them, with them in and out to me all day, all night too, in and out, in and out, watching me, and watching each other too.'

It was a long time before he was satisfied he had done all he could, and could do no more, for that struggling soul, which, he was sure, would enter the next world before the night was out. But the moment he had caught sight of the old face, the tight wisdom of it, the undefeated will in it, the clasp on the lips, the firm old chin, and then the hard-shut fist like a knob on the scraggy forearm that would lift and threaten and emphasise – he knew what was before him – that he would have to call up all the resources of his own brain and will, having asked help from on high, and wrestle, and wrestle, and wrestle to dislodge that poor old peasant's handful of thoughts from that which had been their centre and stay for seventy or eighty years – the land, the farm, as he called it – a waste of rock and shale, bog and moor, that should never at all have been brought under the spade. He had more than his farm to stay his thoughts upon: as earnest of his long and well-spent life he had his dirty bank-book under his pillow with eighty pounds marked in it to his credit. No sooner was Father Reen aware of this than he knew that it would be easier almost to wrench one of the rocks in the fields abroad from its bed than to wrench that long-accustomed support from the old man's little world of consciousness without shattering it to insanity. Yet this at last Father Reen felt he had succeeded in doing; he thought he found a new look coming into the old man's eyes, overspreading his brow, some expression of hard-won relief, some return of openness, of simplicity, that may not have been there since early manhood; in the voice he thought he found some new timbre, some sudden access of tenderness, of sweetness; and, more surely telling of the new scale of values suddenly come upon by that old battler in a rough world, a flood of aspirations broke impetuously from the trembling lips: 'Jesus Christ, O welcome, O welcome; keep near me, I'm not worthy, I'm not worthy, but welcome. O Blessed

Mother, pray for me, now, now' – a flood onward and never-ending once it had started at all; and Father Reen noticed how the two fists, twin knobs, equally hard and small, were pressed fiercely down upon the brows, side by side, covering the eye sockets, hiding almost the whole of the rapt countenance, except the moving chin. Limbs and all, the old peasant had become one knot of concentration, and the thought of what he was leaving behind him was not any longer its secret.

V

When Father Reen re-entered the larger room, the living room, he found the crowd in the selfsame positions as when he had gone from them; and he felt that not a syllable had passed between them. Tim, that master mind of the group, the man who had led him to the old man's bedside – he was one of the old man's grandsons – had the middle of the earthen floor to himself. He blurted out, almost with a touch of levity in his voice: 'You had a job with him.'

A murmur of sudden and indignant surprise broke from those against the walls. Father Reen shot one glance at the speaker, he could not help it, the fall from the plane he had been moving in was so terrible – and the man, suddenly realising his fault, made some hopeless, mollifying gesture with a limp hand, speaking no word, however. His wife, as Father Reen perceived, came forward, saying: 'Would Father Reen take some little refreshment? We could make a cup of tea? 'Tis a long journey is before you.'

He motioned her from him, making for the door: he wanted with all his heart to be in the saddle and away under the stars.

VI

It took some little time to get the horse ready. He then had to lead it down that steep decline beneath the crest of the hill. As he did so he noticed a glimmer of light above him on the right-hand side. He had noticed no house there when ascending; he would not have noticed it now only that he caught a high-pitched babble of talk above him, and, looking round, had spied the dim gleam of a window. As he looked he saw a flash of light – the door had opened – and he heard an angry passionate outburst: 'I'll have the law of him! I'll have the law of him!'

The door was suddenly shut to. There remained the angry onward confusion of talk and the dull glimmer in the tiny window. It was a son's house or a grandson's house, surely; and there was many another house in the neighbourhood thinking the same thought this night. Law, yes, and years and years of it over those stony fields and that dirty bank-book. But this much, he told himself, he had known from the moment of entering that crowded living room.

The remembrance quickened his blood. With almost a touch of savagery he urged his beast forward the moment he found his legs gripping its belly. The hard roads invited it. They, with the frozen pools all along them, were bright enough to see by; there was also the tangle of starshine hanging somehow in the middle air above the landscape. For one no longer young he rode wildly, but then the Reens from time immemorial had been eager horsemen. When he came down on to the level ground he broke into a hard gallop; and when, after an hour's going, he had won to the better-kept road beside the lakes he rode as if for a high wager. He was flying not from Kilmony so much as from that fund of reflections all he had witnessed there had aroused in him. That terrible promiscuity of rock, the little stony fields that only centuries of labour had salvaged from them, the unremitting toil they demanded, the poor return, the niggard scheme of living; and then the ancient face on the pillow, the gathering of greedy descendants – he had known it all before; for years the knowledge of how much of a piece it all was had kept his mind uneasy. He knew he would presently be asking himself: Where do my duties end? And this hard riding of his was but an effort to baffle that inveterate questioning. He rode like a man possessed. If the rhythm of the riding, the need for alertness, the silence of the black, stark landscape, the far-stretching lakes, the mass of starshine in the air, weakened at moments the urgency of the question, it overwhelmingly leaped upon him, that question did, whenever he passed a lonely farm-house clung against its slab of protecting rock at the base of a cliff, or espied one aloft on some leaca or other, betrayed to the night by the lamp still dimly burning. Each and every one of them seemed to grab at his very heart pleading for some human succour that their inmates could not name. And all the time the hoofs of his animal were beating out from the frozen road in perfectly regular rhythm: My people! My people! My people!

A LOOTER OF THE HILLS

I

I TOLD THE WOMAN that her little girl was now recovered and that there was no need for a further visit. In quiet thankfulness she accompanied me down the rickety stairs, and suddenly, and entirely by way of impulse, said: 'Doctor, there's another poor patient here, and you ought to have a look at him. His name is Phil Donaghy.' With that she tapped on a door I had not noticed in a sort of recess at the bottom of the stairs. As if she had expected no reply she had put her fingers on the handle when the door opened: she said at once:

'Oh! I didn't know you were with him, Nora. I'm after asking the doctor here to have a look at him: 'twill do him no harm.'

Nora, a decent-looking soul, started and gaped at us, and I, knowing the pieties of such people, said at once: 'The room will do well enough. And himself, too.'

Of late I have been noticing that so surely as that close-wedged mass of tenement houses, crouching there in the shadow of St Michael's, rises to my memory or actually comes into view from some terrace on the hills, it is this Phil Donaghy, the patient I was then to become acquainted with, that emerges from it as an individual. That network of lanes and alleys, lying in the skirts of the bleak-looking ungainly church, is his background. They are scarcely six feet wide, these lanes, and the houses in them are so high in the old-fashioned way, that they feel even narrower still. The houses cling to one another in ramshackle groups like a lot of tipsy sailormen, some of them tossing their heads, some of them gone in the pins, others sodden and dull, while others again are gay with all manner of patchings, stains and weatherings. The footpaths by which one navigates the district are hardly a foot in width, paved with cobblestones, as also are most of the lanes themselves; and when you leave these pathways and turn into the hallways you find but little difference. One trusts oneself to a dark twisting passage along which one feels with the feet cautiously; flooring, soundless with rottenness, is beneath them, or flags, or, it may be, common earth. They are so long, these passages, they shoot forward so fiercely, turn sharply aside, shoot forward again, that one imagines oneself as burrowing under the old church itself, for piles and piles of crazy masonry seem to surround one on every side and to be over the head as well.

The room I was led into was large enough, very ill-lighted however. The window was hidden away behind driftings of lace curtains that had gone the colour of a negro. I gingerly put one of them aside and saw that the little yard into which the window looked was like a dripping well sunken into that mass of bur- rowed masonry. The sky I could not see, but an expiring gleam of light falling down the greenish mouldy walls hinted of it. That yard was indeed a dismal prospect. I turned from it and found my patient hunched over a lifeless bit of fire in the grate. When he raised his undetermined face to me, the eyes melancholy, the brows lifted, I could think only of an empty shop.

'Stand up, my man,' I said; and when he did so, resting limply on the back of a chair, I noticed the huge limbs, the huge awkward-looking trunk, and I knew for certain there was peasant blood in him.

'Out in the air,' I said, cheerily, 'out in the air is the place for you – what else have you to do?'

His eyes sharpened, searching me with some effort at keenness. Not only that, but the kindly creature who had been tidying the place for him – she was his brother's wife, and lived on an upper floor – looked up quickly at me as if I had said some surprising thing! In a moment she was all words: 'That's what I tell him, Doctor. He should rouse himself!' And she caught him by the sleeve: 'You should rouse yourself, Phil. Isn't that what I'm always saying to you? A thousand times, Doctor, I said as much to him myself. And what harm but there's not a foot of the country that he doesn't know by heart. He used to be forever scouring it, ever and ever; but that was before his mother died on him.'

The lump of manhood turned its slow eyes upon her and said – I know not what.

She looked from his face to mine:

'Yes, Doctor, that's right. 'Tis long before 'twill be forgotten – how we buried her, the flowers –'

I knew then where I was. That very funeral, six months earlier I had come upon it as it threaded the lanes. Crowds of people followed it, with some sort of hidden excitement playing through them, and the coffin was entirely hidden in flowers and greenery – not the fast-bound wreaths, shapely and meagre, that florists supply to order, but a wild profusion of branches, flowers, and leaves, heaped and gaudy.

II

Only for that his mother had come from the heart of the country she could never possibly have lived to be over eighty years of age in such surroundings. Up to that age she had been a busy woman, attending to the housework, shopping, going to Mass, taking her place in all the doings of the laneway. Then she had a stroke, as the people say, losing control of her right side, more or less. From that out the dark room, with the bed in the corner, was her kingdom. No more housework, no more shopping, or Mass, or Retreats, or Missions, or anything. Then, as will happen, the recollections of her simple childhood came more and more to the surface. To her overgrown half-wit of a son she would say:

'There's no knowing the damage a goat will do. The goat we had, it went into Colonel Seeve's place one morning before a soul was up, and it tore down and destroyed all the lovely shrubs in the lawn! What did it care about handsome places! And it came home and laid down, and had a lovely sleep for itself! Look at that for you! And not a mortal knowing where it was after spending the day. But when 'twas found out – Oh, then there was murder!'

Or she might say to him – to him who was true child of the city's heart:

'Sheep's milk is so thick you couldn't drink it without putting water in it. Now there's lots of people don't know that sheep have any milk at all. The people of this lane now, Betty outside, or Johnny Mahony, they never saw sheep's milk at all. Sitting there they were, and they downfaced me when I said that people used to drink sheep's milk and goat's milk too.'

Or again, although his world had never been any other than the laneways and the wharves:

'Up in the dark of the morning we'd be, boiling the potatoes for them. And maybe then someone would say, "Do you hear that? That's the Linehans." 'Tis the way we'd be listening to know if the others were taking the road. And one after another we'd hear them coming from all quarters. You'd think some of them hadn't gone to bed at all at all. Away to the fair with them then: into Macroom; and 'twould be the dark of night when they'd come back. Over the mountains they'd go: there are places there would frighten you to look at them.'

At another time she would be still further back in her child-hood: 'Gathering brosna in the wood we'd be; and we'd be all right so long as the daylight held; but the place would get cold and still, and we'd be listening to know if anything was stirring; and we'd say we had no right to stay so long, and we'd run home with ourselves. But all the same maybe we'd stay longer the next evening or the evening after.'

As if to aid her in this recovery of her childhood's far-off life in far-off places the film on her eyeballs thickened, more and more hiding away from her the dismal surroundings into which her many years had narrowed. When, unconsciously, she had ceased the struggle to keep tally of what was going on about her, when her eyes had gone utterly dark, her head lifted itself higher and higher, the features relaxed, her face brightened, took on the appearance of a sky in which the winds have died and the clouds vanished – frank, open and serene, lighted from within.

Beside her was another simple nature, this gom of a son of hers, who was lucky if he poked out two days' work in a week. Only when there was a rush of shipping at the jetties did the stevedore beckon him to take his place in the run of corn-baggers or timber-heavers. For the most part, he loitered in his mother's room drinking in her chatter of a world he had never known. Who could say what images he made himself from the rambling gossip! Anyway he began to explore the countryside round about, one day taking to the hills on either side of the city, on another threading the river valley to the west. It was not long until in that darkened room buried under, lost among, those piles of crumbling masonry there were to be heard two voices instead of one speaking of the green hillsides: 'Little lambs they were, jumping about their mothers. Lively. Awful game. Look! Look, can't ye!' And if the aged eyes could no longer actually see his clumsy antics, his six-foot friskings, they could most certainly make themselves pictures of lambs that were as white as snow and pastures that were green and deep. Or it might be a braver vision he had raised for her:

'At the top of the field he turns them round. . .'

'The headland, Phil boy, the headland.'

'Turns them round; and the tackling and chains goes rattling: "Whoa! Hack! Back you! Back, I tell you!" And one of them puts his head up in the air. And he opens his jaws. You'd think he'd take a bite out of the air or the clouds! And the other fellow puts his head down, down, into his chest, like a magistrate in the court. And he drags them round like that – "Whoa! Come out of it!" And all the seagulls and crows!'

'But 'tis hard work, ploughing is,' she'd answer, 'and after a day of it, if the ground was heavy, you'd be only fit to throw yourself in the bed, like a log of wood. Isn't it often I seen them! Often and often!'

Because his nature was simple and passionate it was his way to act out his thought; and, listening in the dim passage outside the door of their room you might hear coming from within, the swish of a scythe or the whirr of a reaping machine or the gossip of a group of gleaners or the unrestrained argument of a group of cattle-dealers at a fair. For, little by little, he had ventured farther and farther from the dens of the city and grown knowledgeable of the life of the countryside. It was a common thing with him now to rise long before the dawn that he might enjoy the spectacle of a fair. Sometimes he was paid a couple of shillings for assisting in the driving of the cattle, at a headlong pace, into the city to catch a steamer or train. But indeed, whatever he thought of it himself, it was not for the sake of the odd shillings he hung about the earnest bargainers like that: it was rather to find food for his own hungry mind and heart that in turn he might feed that other hungry mind and heart imprisoned in the slumland of the city. She as well as himself had benefit of all he saw and heard in his excursions.

One day he had lain stretched for hours on a grassy bank gazing lazily at the mowers in the meadow. That evening his mother grabbed him to her suddenly and buried her nostrils in his clothes:

'That's a good smell. So 'tis. So 'tis. A good smell. A good smell.'

After a day of cattle-driving the smell of the beasts was to her a delight, as indeed was anything at all that renewed for her the impressions life had made on her virgin soul eighty years before. He began to loot the hillsides for her sake. Armfuls of wild flowers he brought her, whole branches of blossoming trees or masses of trailing woodbine. In autumn he came garlanded with boughs of crab apple, tangles of fruity briars or even half a sheaf of corn. She would bury her nose in them, play with them, plucking the fruit and thorning her fingers while she did so.

III

Late one night in the springtime her daughter-in-law heard stirrings in the old woman's room. She went to her: 'Mother,' she whispered through the darkness, 'what's the matter? Is it how ye can't sleep or what?'

'Nothing child, nothing is the matter. What a goose you are! Don't be rising like that getting cold for yourself.'

The voice ceased suddenly, the stirrings had again begun. The young woman groped on the table and lit the candle. She found a live lamb in the grip of the old woman. The animal was struggling to escape from the claw-like ancient hands.

Things had gone too far; there was a scene. The half-wit had only little to say while they threatened him with the law.

'I'm no robber. I never stole anything. I was going to take it back. Nobody would miss it. I gave it milk. I covered it with my coat. I never stole nothing!'

After that the two of them, mother and son, had again to fall back on the wild flowers, the hawthorn and crab blossom, which fortunately were now plentiful along the hedges. Into the midst of the lane-dwellers as they sat at nightfall at their doorways, the harmless giant would break, his basketing arms letting the wilful blossoms fall as he moved along with odours in his wake. They would raise their nostrils and smile, sometimes wistfully, or shake their heads, remembering old times and places.

IV

Of a morning in autumn Nora roused her husband impatiently. As her custom was she had, first thing, gone to the bedside of the old woman. She was now returned:

'Something is after happening,' she said to him.

'What's up with you? Is it Nanny?' Then he sat up quickly. 'You're shaking.'

'The two of them is missing!'

'Merciful Father!'

When he had dressed himself, was come with her to the empty room – litter of bird cages, of withered boughs, of branches dry and crackling as it was – she said to him: 'I knew they were up to something. They had their heads together. That's what they were planning. And sniggering. Laughing at us.'

'I'll break his neck for him! I keep a home for him, and that's the thanks I get. Nothing but annoyance and trouble.'

The room soon filled with the neighbours, councils were held: the police, it was decided, had better be sent for. They best could trace them. In the police station telephones were set ringing; telegrams dispatched; hospitals communicated with. All, however, without result. Alone or accompanied by a young policeman, Tom went from place to place, everywhere noticing as soon as the matter had been explained, a thinnish sort of smile break over the faces of the officials. And he felt ashamed of himself.

'You have tried them all, you say?'

'Every one of them; and the Poorhouse too.'

'Well, there's the river.'

Tired out, embittered too, he came home and told his wife what the police sergeant had said.

'Don't say it – don't say it, Tom,' she said, her finger on his wrist, ''tis before my mind the livelong day! We were hard on them; we were hard on them!'

'No, no. We gave them their own way in everything, too much of it.'

Towards nightfall they heard an authoritative voice in the hallway; tremblingly they opened. It was the same sergeant. He looked at them – as his habit was – for a long time steadily and in chill silence. They felt miserably guilty. He asked them many sidelong questions, as also was his way, before explaining to them the simple matter that a horse and cart had been stolen from a farmer's yard a mile outside the city. No one in the lane, however, had heard any sound of a cart; and anybody else might have taken it as well as this half-wit of theirs. The telephones, the wires, were, however, all at work again, so he informed them; and before long they would surely have news. Yet no news arrived.

Late that night Tom and his wife and a neighbour sat in silence, dispirited, fearful of they knew not what. The neighbour had tired of urging them to make their minds at ease, to go to bed, to be ready for whatever would be sent to them; no more than that could he say to comfort them. Yet the silence irked them all; so that at last the wife rose up and began to set about some homely task. Tom too raised his head from his long brooding. 'Do you know, I think I can tell where they're gone to? Come, Dinny, come with me. We'll get the ambulance from the Corporation.'

The sleeping Corporation watchman did not wish to set out on a wild-goose chase. They had to threaten him; if the aged woman was found dead from exposure her death would be laid at his door, he would hear about it.

The motor ambulance drove through the silent streets, making a great clatter. Into the country with them, mile after mile. Towards the west they made, then northwards, cutting into the heart of the hills. Yet in spite of the excellent lamps they had they could make only slow progress, for none of them knew the country when they were a score of miles distant from it; all they knew was the direction. The steady whirr of the engine comforted them, and they began less and less to fear the unforeseen. They wondered at the great silence, the great blank spaces of the sky as the darkness drew away. The sun rose up on their right, and they saw wisps of mist hanging from juts of rocks or laid astray along the hedges. The increasing warmth of the sun was sweet to them, yet Tom widened his eyes as he caught the tumultuous singing of the birds. Their morning rapture promised that everything would be the same, but he was quietly saying to himself that nothing ever again would be the same, and his look was piteous.

At last they quenched their lamps: the landscape was flooded with brightness. They climbed along the side of a straggling belt of ruined woodland; they made the ridge; descending, they swung round on to a bridge that crossed a foaming torrent diminished after the summer yet still very loud. Before them lay a broad valley with wide meadows and sloping fields of corn, unexpectedly rich and soft-looking in the heart of those craggy hills. But their eyes had scarcely scanned its features when they noticed down below them in the middle of the dust-white road a solitary farm cart standing perfectly still, its shadow laid sharply upon the dust. So still the picture they made – horse, cart, shadow, and the solitary clumsy figure gazing towards them as if he had heard the noise of the car from afar off, it struck them the group must have been as stilly as that for hours. Without a word they slowed down as they approached. The poor fool looked at them as if he had expected them. He gave them no time to question him.

'She was all right, not a bit afraid, talking, talking, asking me everything. She never stopped, only asking me everything. I'm telling you she was as game as paint till she heard that river there and it giving tongue out of it.'

What could they say to him?

They brought her home and never again did the gift of consciousness descend upon her. After seventy years of absence she anyway once again had breathed her native air, had heard the voice of her native vale, its birds and its waters, enough perhaps to give her blind eyes to see its fields heavy with harvest, and its households as she had known them in her childhood.

Her son – the melancholy fit will pass. He will again take to wandering on the hills, gazing at the flowers thick-strewn in the hedges, or gaping at the young things playing about their dams, his mind all a confusion, yet not uncomforted.

THE RETURN

I

WHERE ANKLE LANE joins Blarney Street there are four high houses, dark-looking and very old, of that sort lane-dwellers call 'fabrics' or 'castles'. The number of inhabitants varies from day to day: tricky-men in for the races will stay two nights, cattle-drovers only one; in periods of idleness a group of coal-porters sometimes attains to a certain solidarity – the same figures go in and out the doors day after day – but, just as happens in a factory, change sets in with prosperity; new faces come and go; and the next period of idleness sees a new colony, the same in its general characteristics, though made up of quite different individuals, repeat the fortunes of the last.

The largest, the darkest of these four houses was kept by a widow named Tynan; Bonnety Tynan she was called, from a wisp of a bonnet that clung to her scanty hairs; the other lodging-house keepers wore shawls. Her face was crabbed, shut like a fist against craft, reduced to its smallest and toughest by dint of years of hard-dealing. And her bonnet was equally shorn of its beams; this, too, was now not much bigger than a fist, but the legend still held that it was the lodging-house keeper's money-box. Sometimes she would have as many as thirty men under her roof, most of them idle, so her hardness, her aloofness were needed. How else could she have managed them? The law? – it was too complicated; and besides, she kept too irregular a house to care to invoke it. She had laws and ejectment-processes of her own. Sometimes she conceived suspicion of a lodger; she waited till his back was turned; then she would slap a few buckets of water over his bed; he returned to find it sodden; and she went on with her washing while he stamped and cursed.

In the beginning of winter one evening towards six o'clock, as she shuffled in along the dark hall, she was surprised to see a glare of firelight breaking out towards her from the kitchen; she had been out of the house for some hours and hoped for nothing better than a spark in the bottom of the grate.

Opening the squeaking door she was still more surprised: a great figure, a darkness, sat on a stool before the fire; she noticed the curving width of his back; the huge head bent forward – he was asleep. She went silently up to him, bending to see his face: it was tanned; she glanced at his hands: they were dark with tar, knobby, and had blue rings and flags tattooed on them; but it was the hard, exaggerated-looking creases in his serge clothes that spoke his trade most clearly – these clothes had been folded tightly for weeks, perhaps for months, in the bottom of a seaman's chest. She shook him: 'Come on now – wake up, who are 'oo? who are 'oo?'

He growled; then his voice softened; he rose and stretched himself, very much at his ease; a light came into his sea-bleared eyes; he examined the old woman's face with interest, with amusement apparently. 'You're not changed a ha'p'orth,' he said, 'not a ha'p'orth.'

She stared up; he was handsome in such a place.

'Sit down,' she said, 'I can't call to mind what your name is – 'tis after escaping me memory.'

With a seaman's licence he put his great arm about her, drew her towards the glowing fire, and said again:

'You're not changed a ha'p'orth.'

'I don't know you,' she snapped out, breaking away.

'If you don't there's not a soul in Cork to say who I am – I'm Jim Daunt that was.'

A memory or two, quite unimportant, stirred in her brain:

'So you are, so you are; you're welcome; how long will you be staying?'

'Till half-past eleven, anyway,' he said.

'Where's the boat – Queenstown?'

'No – the Jetties,' he answered, 'and I must be aboard for midnight.'

She treated him well; she gave him a couple of eggs and many rounds of bread; yet for a seaman he made but a scanty meal.

'You're not doing well?' she said.

'If I only had it yesterday,' he said, 'you'd see the death I'd give it.'

She moved about in the silent way of a woman who is accustomed to keep people at a distance. It was he who spoke:

'Isn't this a quare thing,' he said, 'I was never a bit lonesome wherever I was on sea or land – thousands of miles away – never a bit lonesome till this evening sitting there on that there stool.'

She believed him; for she knew these sailormen well; and how any shelter that has the look, or even the name of home, stirs them.

'You were a great long time out,' he continued, half complaining.

'How did I know you'd be here?'

'When did you leave the house?'

'Near four, I expect.'

'Well, now, look at that,' he said. 'You mustn't have been well round the corner when I came in; and here I stopped, for I couldn't go away again – couldn't go away. Was I asleep when you came in?'

A lodger they called Brother entered; Mrs Tynan made the two men known to each other. The sailorman wanted drink to be sent for; Bonnety, however, wouldn't have it: there was plenty of time, and, besides, drink was no food for a man after a day's work. Brother seconded her; Saturday Night would be coming in soon, and he was the best of company; 'twas company a man wanted after being shut up for months in a wind-bag, 'Wasn't it, matey?' he said, taking the seaman's hand. A radiance had come into Brother's face: unexpected joy is straight from the hands of the gods: exhausted, heavy in all his limbs from climbing with a laden hod forty-foot ladders from early morning – terrible work – he had hoped for nothing beyond a single drink in Miss Nora's, and lo! the pleasures of a revel were emerging in his imagination.

'Have you enough of it?' he said.

'Of what?'

'The say?'

'God knows an' I have,' said the sailor, with unexpected earnestness, 'but isn't it a quare thing to say that I was never a bit lonesome till this evening sitting there on that there stool?'

'How so?' said Brother.

And then with lingering detail the sailor told how he had kept watch while Mrs Tynan was down in Miss Nora's.

III

Saturday Night came in after a few moments; in every feature, in every limb he had become misshapen by dint of combat; his most restful attitude challenged; yet in Brother's words he was the best of company: spirit is spirit.

Brother, introducing the men, mentioned the sailor's former connection with the house: 'There's no house like the old house,' he said, and Saturday Night, gripping the sailor's hand, told him that though he had never met him before, he felt they were old friends already: 'There's something draws me to you,' he said, and the sailor answered: 'A fellow don't hear words like them from foreigners.'

And three minutes afterwards he told Saturday Night that he had never known what it was to be down-hearted till that evening, sitting on that there stool before the fire. And, indicating Brother, 'Himself will tell you,' he answered Saturday Night's look of enquiry.

Again he wanted to send out for drink; but again the landlady blanked the proposal: What hurry was there? Wasn't the night long enough? Couldn't they wait for Johnny Swaine at least?

Instead of Johnny Swaine came Katty Sullivan, saying as her first word:

'Isn't Johnny here?'

'Not yet,' and they bade her sit down.

'By James, I might as well,' she said: the form of swear she had invented herself, and its use seemed to lift her above the common throng; yet she needed no such aid; by nature she was above her surroundings. Strong and happy, with full, firm flesh, her face coloured like ripe corn, her eyes blue and bright as the skies that go with it, she was large-hearted, and merry and frank because of her fearlessness, of her consciousness of power.

'Here's a lonely sailorman wouldn't object to a bit of company,' said Saturday Night, and ''Tis a thing no wan objects to,' she answered, in a tone that had as much daring as pity in it. Her words seemed to take the sailorman off his guard; the impudence in his face withered before her eyes. She had laid her spell on him; but everyone saw that some weakness of spirit denied his rising to it; he looked like a sick sportsman who, on a morning of sunshine, suddenly discovers that he is unable to lift his body from the bed. The moment's unrest was swallowed in a whirl of words, for Katty Sullivan was one they all liked to talk with. She was one of those who, though they might give a man a 'wipe' across the mouth, never get on their dignity, an attitude that takes all heart out of a night's merriment. Soon Johnny Swaine came seeking Katty, even as she had been seeking him; and the sailor saw at once that he was her accepted lover, and with the knowledge a touch of daring came back into his look; his eyes, in spite of himself, as it were, would now find themselves resting on Johnny's face. Brother was sent for drink; he returned with two friends; ''Twould go to me heart to refuse them,' he explained to the sailor.

The sailor drank nothing but raw whiskey, and it soon appeared that his loneliness had gone from him; so, too, had his hold on himself. He became aggressive; when Brother was telling his champion tale of a sailor who, having deserted, signed on again in the selfsame ship under stress of drink, the sailor stopped him halfway, and in his mouth the story from being a mere fill-gap became wild and thrilling. And almost without a pause he went on to tell the story of a parson's daughter of Adelaide, the girl who hid herself in a ship's hold for the sake of a young captain – how she might now be met with in the cities of the South American seaboard, in Buenos Aires or Rio – the sailors speak of her as the

Australian Rose. He had seen her himself. His voice became higher and louder; he seemed to be talking against time, and his eyes shifted continually from face to face. He twitted Brother on his powers of drinking; he joked Saturday Night on his wounds; yet somehow his merriment was not contagious; and they all sniffed trouble when he began to raise bad blood between the lovers, for they could see that Katty's eyes were rife for mischief.

Johnny, she said, would have gone sailoring himself only for the wetness of the sea and his love for his mother; anyway, he wouldn't like to be pickled as well as drownded and, by James! she wouldn't care to see him pickled herself; 'he'd be a terrible sight!' Then the sailor, with great concern, asked her what would she do if Johnny went off with another girl? She laughed, bent with laughter at the idea, and the whole room laughed uneasily with her. And so Johnny Swaine, made scapegoat for the company, sat by the girl's side, looking with glum eyes at his unfinished drink. But at the end of a bout of merriment the sailor stretched his hand to him saying that a joke was a joke; Johnny would not even look at the proffered hand. 'Anyway, fetch us the measure,' the sailor continued with some diplomacy; and Swaine, thinking of peace with honour, rose from his place and made for the gallon. Without a sound the sailor sprang into the vacant space at the girl's side, and Johnny, turning, found him there. A roar of laughter addled him, maddened him. He flung the gallon about the floor, squared out, and his voice rose above the jubilee: 'Stand up, if you're a man.'

'Miss Sullivan,' the sailor's voice was heard saying in the sudden, expectant silence, 'isn't it lovely weather?'

'Stand up, I say.'

'A beautiful night?'

'Will you stand up?'

And the girl's eyes danced to see such spirit in her lover.

'You won't, won't you?' and Johnny's open hand met the sailor's cheek with a ringing blow. In a flash the two men were dancing at each other, the sailor all activity, his voice jerking out the best known of all the chanties:

Ranzo was no sailor;
Ranzo, boys, Ranzo.

And every time he came to 'Ranzo' in the refrain – the word on which the rope is dragged as they hoist sail – he struck or rather touched Johnny's face or side or ears: he played with the landsman, dancing round him, tipping him wherever he wished.

Ranzo was no sailor;
Ranzo, boys, Ranzo.
The mate he was a good man;
Ranzo, boys, Ranzo!

The company seeing that he did not mean to punish his man let their mirth loose; they began to cry out: 'Go it, Johnny, go it, old man.' But after some time the sailor became over-confident, became careless; Johnny, on the other hand, had recovered his self-possession. Seeing a chance, he stood statue-still for a moment; then, making a wild charge, struck full in the sailor's face. The sea-blood fired up; song and dance ceased; with swift, careful drives he drove Johnny back, back, almost into the fire-grate. The room had become silent. Both men seemed to be fighting for life. They panted; their feet scraped the floor. Katty stood up: 'Sir,' she said, in a breathy voice that was scarcely audible, 'Sir, sir'; but neither fighters nor onlookers heard her at all.

Suddenly shuffling steps were heard coming in the hall, and 'Police,' whispered Brother; for policemen walk into such houses in the same manner as factory-inspectors enter factories. At the word the sailor's face went white; he turned half-round from his man towards the room door; and Johnny, who had not perhaps heard Brother's warning, battered him right and left with great will.

'Wait awhile,' said the sailor, all confusion, still staring at the door.

'Come on,' shouted Johnny, wondering what had happened.

All faces were on the door; some of the men were gripping others by the shoulders. It was old Ned Mulcahy, the mason, who stuck in his head. The next moment the sailor was dancing once more around Johnny.

> He gave him five and twenty;
> Ranzo, boys, Ranzo.

His terror had lifted; he resumed his antics, and soon he had Johnny hemmed into a corner, where he kept him until he had his nose pumping blood. Then the combatants were separated.

'He's a game fighter, anyway,' said the sailor, releasing him; and Katty Sullivan, passing the defeated man a handkerchief, thought in her heart of hearts that she wouldn't give him for all the tanned-faced sailors on the sea.

IV

It was now high time for the sailor to be going if he was to make his ship by midnight; yet he dawdled to hear the end of a story, to turn a joke, to look at Johnny's nose. He lingered too long; for Saturday Night suddenly began to tell the tale he always reserved till he had become quite emotional in his drink. They were unloading the *Cyclamen,* he said, and the first glimmer of dawn was coming on the river and, merciful God! he saw a woman floating down the tide, her golden hair spread out on top of the water. They got her into a boat – the handsomest woman he ever laid eyes on, and he tried to persuade the men to say nothing at all about the matter, only just take the corpse up to Burnt Lane on a shutter and give her a decent wake with candles, and Christian burial in the Gardens; but they wouldn't, they were afraid of the law; and the police came, and the first words the sergeant said were (and Saturday Night wept to repeat them): 'What do you know about this *person*?' 'What do you know about this *person*?' Saturday Night spoke the words again, turning towards the sailor; and 'Was that what he said?' the sailor gasped out, but his voice was so strange that the whole room on the instant forgot the story; the sailor's jaw had become locked, his neck rigid, his head looked as if carved in hardwood, the eyes unskilfully painted – a blank stare. But he lifted himself up, and 'I'll be late,' he said, in a voice that beseeched them not to question or hinder him; he had broken down; he could not explain himself – at least, this is what they would think.

'Good night,' he said, putting out his hand to Katty Sullivan in a sudden, jerky way, his eyes meanwhile turned away from all the faces. She took no notice; she let on to be speaking to Johnny, who was now once more at her side. Without another word the sailor vanished from their midst.

After a pause the old woman spoke in her hardest voice: 'Did any of ye see that fellow coming in here?'

No one spoke; in the silence Brother cracked a match on the bowl of his pipe.

'He said he came in here to-day after I wint out.'

'And sure he might.'

'I'd like to know,' the old woman rejoined, and she lit two candles – a signal for them to retire.

'He said he was asleep,' she added, 'he was no more asleep than I was.'

'Holy Mother!' said Katty Sullivan, as she rose to go. 'I'm sorry I iver laid eyes on him.'

V

Now, I think that the sailor, as he stumbled down the deserted hillside streets towards the river, shook himself and stood still a moment here, stood still a moment elsewhere, saying at every pause: ' 'Twill be all right – what a fool I am!'

Anyway, he got to his ship; made to walk up the plank with his head in the air, and – who knows how the end came?

But the next day they brought up two dead bodies from between his ship and the quay-wall; one of them, the second mate it was, had a knife-wound in the right lung and another in the back below the lung; the second body, bearing no signs of struggle on it, was our sailorman, Jim Daunt; and it was proved by the stopping of their watches and otherwise that one body had been a couple of hours longer in the water than the other. Saturday Night says that as he went up the plank maybe he heard a voice saying 'What do you know about this *person*?' but Brother says that 'tis how he threw himself in, for he saw that the whole race of men were turning against him – look at how Katty Sullivan, with no reason at all, *couldn't* shake hands with him. Johnny Swaine says they all came well out of it, as if a murderer has evil spirits at his beck and call.

But what brought the sailorman up to Bonnety Tynan's at all? Was he trying to prove an alibi? Or was it that the word Home was ringing in his brain?

REFUGE

I CAME TO UNDERSTAND afterwards that the women in the house, or rather on the second floor of it, were the old man's sister-in-law and her daughter. They were poor struggling people who, although the old man had really no claim on them, looked after him as well as they could in their poverty. What was really the matter with him was old age and its debilities – that and trouble of mind. Trouble he had been having all his life, I understood – mostly with his wife, whether his fault or hers I did not learn, so much of it that at last she went off and left him, taking their two children with her: they were just of an age, it seems, to be of use to the household. Up to that time he had held on to some clerkship in a bacon-curing factory. After that he was rudderless, living from post to pillar. When he was stricken down by illness, the sister of the woman who had left him came to the rescue, as I have said, herself and her daughter. And they had kept him with them since. They knew as well as I that nothing could be done for him. He knew as much himself. Indeed it was himself suggested, insisted on, my being sent for, to save trouble, he said, when his time came: if he dropped down on the floor, for instance, well, they didn't want an inquest over him, did they?

I found him cuddling over a bit of fire, hunched up in a deep old chair, his head sunken into his shoulders, his two hands, ever trembling, resting on the top of his stick, a heavy stick with thorns along it. I put my hand lightly on his shoulder:

'What's up?' I said heartily. He slewed round a little and raised his eyes to me. God help us, they told of many things that were up with him. After a moment, and with a little shaking of the head – he was very old – he said the one word:

'Everything!'

I thought there was some cynicism in the accent. But it was true. Not an organ was sound. And so I pitied him. It must have been many years since he had had freedom from pain. I thought of hospital treatment for him. I mentioned it. But the old woman, wisely, as I now know, thought he wouldn't listen to such a thing. She said I didn't understand. And saying so she drew me aside. While we whispered he rose, and without a glance at us or a word crawled into the next room and closed the door behind him. I can recall the bent-down figure, the scraping feet, the uncertain stick poking in his right hand, the left, extended, balancing him – I see the stretched fingers of it, long and frail, white as chalk.

It was a ramshackle sort of room we were in. It is in one of a group of very old tenement houses which, squeezing together, rise mightily up from a narrow quayside to bend themselves, it almost seems, over the waters of the river – the Shannon itself. The group looks very picturesque at a distance, weather-beaten, tall and grey; close at hand, however, one is conscious only of a general decay, slatterliness and unpleasant smells. No other part of the old city is so poor.

As I watched in silence his slow going from us into the next room, I became aware that the old house swarmed with people. Up the stairs and down the stairs they banged or slided or shuffled; their feet scraped, and by the eager voices one knew they moved in groups. A snatch of whistling, a fling of a song, a name called, again and again and again – and the traffic seemed to be part of the place, for I noticed that neither the old man nor the old woman, nor the daughter, who kept all the time in the background, had taken the least notice of it. Indeed in the room itself there was, in spite of the manifold and curious noises outside, a sort of silence, a stillness anyhow; and as I wondered at this, and indeed also at the never-ending traffic, I felt the eyes of the two women resting upon me. They were ashamed, I think, of the rather discourteous way the old man had treated me. Then suddenly from the next room, into which the old fellow had retired, I heard with some surprise a run of speech start up and continue without pause. I turned towards the woman. I saw that she also had leant an ear to the speech. Then she nodded, not to me though, but as if she would say, 'That's it,' and casting a glance at her daughter she began to move about.

'You mustn't mind him, Doctor,' she said. 'He's after his share of trouble.'

'Who's with him?' I said.

'No one,' I was answered. ''Tis excitement makes him talk like that.'

'How?' I said. 'Like what?'

'When the talk begins he forgets his troubles. You know he was waiting for you all day. No. No. You have your calls to make. We understand that, Doctor. But he's impatient. And 'twas a strain on him. He's not such a care as you think.'

'But you'd imagine there were three or four people talking with him?' I said.

She smiled, a chilly sort of light wavering in her features.

'There are,' she said, and then added, the helpless little smile still within her eyes:

'There's old Kilrenan, and young Kilrenan, and Phil, and the Young Lady.'

She stopped suddenly, and suddenly nodded towards the room:

'There she is – the Young Lady.' She listened. We all listened. I could hear a curious sort of whispering, all sibilants, it seemed.

'She was drowned, you know.' The phrase was intended to explain everything.

I turned on her with some indignation in my glance.

'Oh,' she said, ''tis all in a book. Everything about them, the Kilrenans, and about the Bunratty country, and this place, too, but 'twas different then.'

'Is he reading it?' I said.

'Not at all.'

'Has he the book by heart?'

'No,' she replied, in an off-hand way – and then went on:

'This is the new book. But they're all in the old book, too.'

'Who?' I said.

She jerked her head again towards the room.

'The people talking.'

184

'I don't understand. The new book, the old book, what do you mean?'

'The old book is the book he wrote.'

I could not credit it. I saw the poor creature in my mind. She added immediately:

'Of course 'tis fifty years since he wrote it. I'll get it for you.'

The daughter remained silent in the background; and I found myself listening with new interest to the changing voices from the next room. I should never have associated them with the poor decrepit creature I had seen disappear into it. They were so various, so swift – with life.

From across the landing the old woman returned, bringing the book with her. It was bulky enough. Its cloth cover was a dull red; its edges were black with filth, were rounded at the corners: its pages the colour of snuff. The title page was loose. I read on it –

THE WRAITH OF THE KILRENANS
BY
MAURICE PRENDERGAST.

The date on it showed that it was published in 1885, and in London. I thought the name rather pretty, though I had never heard of anyone named Kilrenan in County Limerick or anywhere else, but writers, of course, often invent such names for their characters. I held it gingerly enough in my hand, it was so dirty.

'And where's the new book?' I said.

'Ah, where?' she answered, with a very patient lifting of her head, and she went on:

'He never asks for the ink now. 'Tis years since he asked for it. But he says he has it all in his head. And he'll write it all out some day. It amuses him, I suppose. Sometimes he's quite silent: we don't hear a word out of him. 'Tis only when he's excited he runs on like this. Other times he's like, like a thinking man, not a word out of him; but he comes out to us then looking very glad, very glad, you wouldn't believe it.'

'And what's the new story about?' I said.

'Oh, the same as that. 'Tis how 'tis, the end of everything is to be explained in the new one. But he'll never write it. I don't think he will.'

She made me take the book with me, although she impressed on me that no other copy of it was to be had.

I exposed it to the bright sunshine for some days, and in the sunshine in my garden I read it. 'Twas quite a nice story, a bit romantic. There were old castles in it, and banshees, and lights on the Shannon, and very dark nights. I am no great judge of literature. I don't have time to study it much; but I couldn't see anything wrong with it. At any rate when I got into it, I wanted to see how it ended; and that's a good sign, I take it. And then I knew so many of the places referred to in it that I couldn't help taking a special interest in it. I think I have read other stories like it – old stories: I hardly remember them. But I'm sure I have often come on poorer yarns. He could make his people talk in a well-bred sort of way, perhaps a little too well-bred.

When I handed the book back to Mrs Dereen I slipped her a pound note. After all I had never seen another author in the flesh.

'Isn't it queer,' I said, giving it back, 'one never hears any mention of that book or the name of the writer?'

She seemed surprised. She looked at me for quite a long time. She was thinking of something, I could see. We were coming down the rickety stairs, and again I noticed the crowds of people who seemed continuously going up and down them, mostly unemployed young men, one thought. They took no notice of us. There was a sort of eagerness in them all that I couldn't understand.

'Do people know about it?' I said.

She smiled. We were standing at the street door.

'Do you see that old green gate?' she said.

'Yes.'

'That's the Dog Club – St Mungret's. Well, there's not a dog in their lists that doesn't come out of that book.' She had it still in her hand, she was weighing it. She went on:

'Did you never hear of Kilrenan the Fifth?'

'I did; certainly I did.'

'And Kilrenan the Sixth?'

'Surely.'

'And Mickey Weeping?'

'Right. That's right.'

'They're all in the book.'

'That's so.' I recalled the names.

'But there's one dog now they call Monaster. That's wrong. It should be Moncaster.'

'That's so. Ralph Moncaster.'

'They're forgetting.' She was a little indignant.

As we spoke young men in twos and threes, idle young men, I'd say, were passing in and out; they were full of youth, full of life, their eyes were bright. We could hear the old stairs creaking and doors banging.

'And what does himself,' I said, 'think of all that – giving the names to the dogs?'

'Oh, we never mention it to him. I heard one time that he didn't like it at first. He said they didn't know better. But that's a long time ago. But really they mean no harm. Anyway, the present generation scarcely know he's there at all – and sure that's just as well. And they don't know where the names came from.'

He had refused to see me on that visit, and I have not since been sent for. But to-day as I passed over the bridge in my car, a news item I had read at my breakfast made me slow down so that I might rest my eyes on that group of old tenement houses he lives in. The news was that Kilrenan the Seventh, after winning the Clontarf Cup in Dublin yesterday, had been sold for four hundred pounds to an Englishman from Cheshire: it was also stated that the dog had been purchased in Limerick six months before for thirty shillings. Kilrenan the Seventh, four hundred pounds for thirty shillings – great news, yes, but I had some difficulty in spying out the towering old houses at all, for their heads were more than half lost in one of those wandering mists that thicken so often above the waterways of the ancient city. The ramshackle huddle seemed very retiring indeed – stilly, shy, and very grey in tone. But surely, I thought, there must be great coming and going about that green gate to-day, for glory is glory even if thirty shillings is not four hundred pounds; yes, and what great trafficking must be leaping up and down the stairs of that old house where such a crowd of the dog boys hive themselves. If on my visits there in quite ordinary times I had found their eyes with such light in them, how they must sparkle to-day! And to recall them was again to hear their swift feet on the steps of the crazy stairs, their calling voices, the banging doors. Great excitement indeed. But then I suddenly recollected the little group I knew of – silent in the midst of it all. By this the stir of that noisy excitement must have edged its way into that inner room, I thought; must have jangled the wits of the old writer so much that, even without knowing why, he cannot but have flung himself headlong into swift converse with the shadows in his brain to escape it all and the world it comes out of. I was tempted, but I hadn't the heart to go and see. I earnestly hoped that my thought was wrong. God grant, I prayed, that he is having instead one of his silent days, that he is hunched into some old chair or other, his chin on his breast, and his face full of quiet joy as he moves his puppets about, making the pattern happier.

THE EYES OF THE DEAD

I

IF HE HAD NOT PUT IT OFF for three years John Spillane's home-coming would have been that of a famous man. Bonfires would have been lighted on the hill-tops of Rossamara, and the ships passing by, twenty miles out, would have wondered what they meant.

Three years ago, the *Western Star*, an Atlantic liner, one night tore her iron plates to pieces against the cliff-like face of an iceberg, and in less than an hour sank in the waters. Of the seven hundred and eighty-nine human souls aboard her one only had been saved, John Spillane, able seaman, of Rossamara in the county of Cork. The name of the little fishing village, his own name, his picture, were in all the papers of the world, it seemed, not only because he alone had escaped, but by reason of the manner of that escape. He had clung to a drift of wreckage, must have lost consciousness for more than a whole day, floated then about on the ocean for a second day, for a second night, and had arrived at the threshold of another dreadful night when he was rescued. A fog was coming down on the waters. It frightened him more than the darkness. He raised a shout. He kept on shouting. When safe in the arms of his rescuers his breathy, almost inaudible voice was still forcing out some cry which they interpreted as 'Help! Help!'

That was what had struck the imagination of men – the half-insane figure sending his cry over the waste of waters, the fog thickening, and the night falling. Although the whole world had read also of the groping rescue ship, of Spillane's bursts of hysterical laughter, of his inability to tell his story until he had slept eighteen hours on end, what remained in the memory was the lonely figure sending his cry over the sea.

And then, almost before his picture had disappeared from the papers, he had lost himself in the great cities of the States. To Rossamara no word had come from himself, nor for a long time from any acquaintance; but then, when about a year had gone by, his sister or mother as they went up the road to Mass of a Sunday might be stopped and informed in a whispering voice that John had been seen in Chicago, or, it might be, in New York, or Boston, or San Francisco, or indeed anywhere. And from the meagreness of the messages it was known, with only too much certainty, that he had not, in exchanging sea for land, bettered his lot. If once again his people had happened on such empty tidings of him, one knew it by their bowed and stilly attitude in the little church as the light whisper of the Mass rose and fell about them.

When three years had gone by he lifted the latch of his mother's house one October evening and stood awkwardly in the middle of the floor. It was nightfall and not a soul had seen him break down from the ridge and cross the roadway. He had come secretly from the ends of the earth.

And before he was an hour in their midst he rose up impatiently, timidly, and stole into his bed.

'I don't want any light,' he said, and as his mother left him there in the dark, she heard him yield his whole being to a sigh of thankfulness. Before that he had told them he felt tired, a natural thing, since he had tramped fifteen miles from the railway station in Skibbereen. But day followed day without his showing any desire to rise from the bedclothes and go abroad among the people. He had had enough of the sea, it seemed; enough too of the great cities of the States. He was a pity, the neighbours said; and the few of them who from time to time caught glimpses of him, reported him as not yet having lost the scared look that the ocean had left on him. His hair was grey or nearly grey, they said, and, swept back fiercely from his forehead, a fashion strange to the place, seemed to pull his eyes open, to keep them wide open, as he looked at you. His moustache also was grey, they said, and his cheeks were grey too, sunken and dark with shadows. Yet his mother and sister, the only others in the house, were glad to have him back with them; at any rate, they said, they knew where he was.

They found nothing wrong with him. Of speech neither he nor they ever had had the gift; and as day followed day, and week week, the same few phrases would carry them through the day and into the silence of night. In the beginning they had thought it natural to speak with him about the wreck; soon, however, they came to know that it was a subject for which he had no welcome. In the beginning also, they had thought to rouse him by bringing the neighbours to his bedside, but such visits instead of cheering him only left him sunken in silence, almost in despair. The priest came to see him once in a while, and advised the mother and sister, Mary her name was, to treat him as normally as they could, letting on that his useless presence was no affliction to them nor even a burden. In time John Spillane was accepted by all as one of those unseen ones, or seldom-seen ones, who are to be found in every village in the world – the bed-ridden, the struck-down, the aged – forgotten of all except the few faithful creatures who bring the cup to the bedside of a morning, and open the curtains to let in the sun.

II

In the nearest house, distant a quarter-mile from them, lived Tom Leane. In the old days before John Spillane went to sea, Tom had been his companion, and now of a night-time he would drop in if he had any story worth telling or if, on the day following, he chanced to be going back to Skibbereen, where he might buy the Spillanes such goods as they needed, or sell a pig for them, slipping it in among his own. He was a quiet creature, married, and struggling to bring up the little family that was thickening about him. In the Spillanes' he would, dragging at the pipe, sit on the settle, and quietly gossip with the old woman while Mary moved about on the flags putting the household gear tidy for the night. But all three of them, as they kept up the simple talk, were never unaware of the silent listener in the lower room. Of that room the door was kept open; but no lamp was lighted within it; no lamp indeed was needed, for a shaft of light from the kitchen struck into it showing one or two of the religious pictures on the wall and giving sufficient light to move about in. Sometimes the conversation would drift away from the neighbourly doings, for even to Rossamara tidings from the great world abroad would sometimes come; in the middle of such gossip, however, a sudden thought would strike Tom Leane, and, raising his voice, he would blurt out: 'But sure 'tis foolish for the like of me to be talking about these far-off places, and that man inside after travelling the world, over and thither.' The man inside, however, would give no sign whatever whether their gossip had been wise or foolish. They might hear the bed creak, as if he had turned with impatience at their mention of his very presence.

There had been a spell of stormy weather, it was now the middle of February, and for the last five days at twilight the gale seemed always to set in for a night of it. Although there was scarcely a house around that part of the south-west Irish coast that had not some one of its members, husband or brother or son, living on the sea, sailoring abroad or fishing the home waters or those of the Isle of Man – in no other house was the strain of a spell of disastrous weather so noticeable in the faces of its inmates. The old woman, withdrawn into herself, would handle her beads all day long, her voice every now and then raising itself, in forgetfulness, to a sort of moan not unlike the wind's, upon which the younger woman would chide her with a 'Sh! Sh!' and bend vigorously upon her work to keep bitterness from her thoughts. At such a time she might enter her brother's room and find him raised on his elbow in the bed, listening to the howling winds, scared it seemed, his eyes fixed and wide open. He would drink the warm milk she had brought him, and hand the vessel back without a word. And in the selfsame attitude she would leave him.

The fifth night instead of growing in loudness and fierceness the wind died away somewhat. It became fitful, promising the end of the storm; and before long they could distinguish between the continuous groaning and pounding of the sea and the sudden shout the dying tempest would fling among the tree-tops and the rocks. They were thankful to note such signs of relief; the daughter became more active, and the mother put by her beads. In the midst of a sudden sally of the wind's the latch was raised, and Tom Leane gave them greeting. His face was rosy and glowing under his sou'wester; his eyes were sparkling from the sting of the salty gusts. To see him, so sane, so healthy, was to them like a blessing. 'How is it with ye?' he said, cheerily, closing the door to.

'Good, then, good, then,' they answered him, and the mother rose almost as if she would take him by the hand. The reply meant that nothing unforeseen had befallen them. He understood as much. He shook a silent head in the direction of the listener's room, a look of enquiry in his eyes, and this look Mary answered with a sort of hopeless upswing of her face. Things had not improved in the lower room.

The wind died away, more and more; and after some time streamed by with a shrill steady undersong; all through, however, the crashing of the sea on the jagged rocks beneath kept up an unceasing clamour. Tom had a whole budget of news for them. Finny's barn had been stripped of its roof; a window in the chapel had been blown in; and Largy's store of fodder had been shredded in the wind; it littered all the bushes to the east. There were rumours of a wreck somewhere; but it was too soon yet to know what damage the sea had done in its five days' madness. The news he had brought them did not matter; what mattered was his company, the knitting of their half-distraught household once again to humankind. Even when at last he stood up to go their spirits did not droop, so great had been the restoration.

'We're finished with it for a while anyhow,' Tom said, rising for home.

'We are, we are; and who knows, it mightn't be after doing all the damage we think.'

He shut the door behind him. The two women had turned towards the fire when they thought they again heard his voice outside. They wondered at the sound; they listened for his footsteps. Still staring at the closed door, once more they heard his voice. This time they were sure. The door reopened, and he backed in, as one does from an unexpected slap of rain in the face. The light struck outwards, and they saw a white face advancing. Some anxiety, some uncertainty, in Tom's attitude as he backed away from that advancing face, invaded them so that they too became afraid. They saw the stranger also hesitating, looking down his own limbs. His clothes were dripping; they were clung in about him. He was bare-headed. When he raised his face again, his look was full of apology. His features were large and flat, and grey as a stone. Every now and then a spasm went through them, and they wondered what it meant. His clab of a mouth hung open; his unshaven chin trembled. Tom spoke to him: 'You'd better come in; but 'tis many another house would suit you better than this.'

They heard a husky, scarce-audible voice reply: 'A dog-house would do, or a stable.' Bravely enough he made an effort to smile.

'Oh, 'tisn't that at all. But come in, come in.' He stepped in slowly and heavily, again glancing down his limbs. The water running from his clothes spread in a black pool on the flags. The young woman began to touch him with her finger tips as with some instinctive sympathy, yet could not think, it seemed, what was best to be done. The mother, however, vigorously set the fire-wheel at work, and Tom built up the fire with bog-timber and turf. The stranger meanwhile stood as if half-dazed. At last, as Mary with a candle in her hand stood pulling out dry clothes from a press, he blurted out in the same husky voice, Welsh in accent:

'I think I'm the only one!'

They understood the significance of the words, but it seemed wrong to do so.

'What is it you're saying?' Mary said, but one would not have recognised the voice for hers, it was so toneless. He raised a heavy sailor's hand in an awkward taproom gesture: 'The others, they're gone, all of them.'

The spasm again crossed his homely features, and his hand fell. He bowed his head. A coldness went through them. They stared at him. He might have thought them inhuman. But Mary suddenly pulled herself together, leaping at him almost: 'Sh! Sh!' she said. 'Speak low, speak low, low,' and as she spoke, all earnestness, she towed him first in the direction of the fire, and then away from it, haphazardly it seemed. She turned from him and whispered to Tom:

'Look, take him up into the loft, and he can change his clothes. Take these with you, and the candle, the candle.' And she reached him the candle eagerly. Tom led the stranger up the stairs, it was more like a ladder, and the two of them disappeared into the loft. The old woman whispered:

'What was it he said?'

' 'Tis how his ship is sunk.'

'Did he say he was the only one?'

'He said that.'

'Did himself hear him?' She nodded towards her son's room.

'No, didn't you see me pulling him away from it? But he'll hear him now. Isn't it a wonder Tom wouldn't walk easy on the boards!'

No answer from the old woman. She had deliberately seated herself in her accustomed place at the fire, and now moaned out:

'Aren't we in a cruel way, not knowing how he'd take a thing!'

'Am I better tell him there's a poor seaman after coming in on us?'

'Do you hear them above! Do you hear them!'

In the loft the men's feet were loud on the boards. The voice they were half expecting to hear they then heard break in on the clatter of the boots above:

'Mother! Mother!'

'Yes, child, yes.'

'Who's aloft? Who's going around like that, or is it dreaming I am?'

The sounds from above were certainly like what one hears in a ship. They thought of this, but they also felt something terrible in that voice they had been waiting for: they hardly knew it for the voice of the man they had been listening to for five months.

'Go in and tell him the truth,' the mother whispered. 'Who are we to know what's right to be done? Let God have the doing of it.' She threw her hands in the air.

Mary went in to her brother, and her limbs were weak and cold. The old woman remained seated at the fire, swung round from it, her eyes towards her son's room, fixed, as the head itself was fixed, in the tension of anxiety.

After a few minutes Mary emerged with a strange alertness upon her:

'He's rising! He's getting up! 'Tis his place, he says. He's quite good.' She meant he seemed bright and well. The mother said:

'We'll take no notice of him, only just as if he was always with us.'

'Yes.'

They were glad then to hear the two men in the loft groping for the stair head. The kettle began to splutter in the boil, and Mary busied herself with the table and tea cups.

III

The sailor came down, all smiles in his ill-fitting, haphazard clothes. He looked so overjoyed one might think he would presently burst into song.

'The fire is good,' he said. 'It puts life in one. And the dry clothes too. My word, I'm thankful to you, good people; I'm thankful to you.' He shook hands with them all effusively.

'Sit down now; drink up the tea.'

'I can't figure it out; less than two hours ago, out there. . .' As he spoke he raised his hand towards the little port-hole of a window, looking at them with his eyes staring.

'Don't be thinking of anything, but drink up the hot tea,' Mary said.

He nodded and set to eat with vigour. Yet suddenly he would stop, as if he were ashamed of it, turn half-round and look at them with beaming eyes, look from one to the other and back again; and they affably would nod back to him. 'Excuse me, people,' he would say, 'excuse me.' He had not the gift of speech, and his too-full heart could not declare itself. To make him feel at his ease, Tom Leane sat down away from him, and the women began to find something to do about the room. Then there were only little sounds in the room: the breaking of the eggs, the turning of the fire-wheel, the wind going by. The door of the lower room opened silently, so silently that none of them heard it, and before they were aware, the son of the house, with his clothes flung on loosely, was standing awkwardly in the middle of the floor, looking down on the back of the sailorman bent above the table.

'This is my son,' the mother thought of saying. 'He was after going to bed when you came in.'

The Welshman leaped to his feet, and impulsively, yet without many words, shook John Spillane by the hand, thanking him and all the household. As he seated himself again at the table John made his way silently towards the settle from which, across the room, he could see the sailor as he bent over his meal.

The stranger put the cup away from him, he could take no more; and Tom Leane and the womenfolk tried to keep him in talk, avoiding, as by some mutual understanding, the mention of what he had come through. The eyes of the son of the house were all the time fiercely buried in him. There came a moment's silence in the general chatter, a moment it seemed impossible to fill, and the sailorman swung his chair half-round from the table, a spoon held in his hand lightly: 'I can't figure it out. I can't nohow figure it out. Here I am, fed full like a prize beast; and warm – Oh, but I'm thankful – and all my mates,' with the spoon he was pointing towards the sea – 'white, and cold like dead fish! I can't figure it out.'

To their astonishment a voice travelled across the room from the settle.

'Is it how ye struck?'

'Struck! Three times we struck! We struck last night, about this time last night. And off we went in a puff! Fine, we said. We struck again. 'Twas just coming light. And off again. But when we struck the third time, 'twas like that!' He clapped his hands together; 'She went in matchwood! 'Twas dark. Why, it can't be two hours since!'

'She went to pieces?' the same voice questioned him.

'The *Nan Tidy* went to pieces, sir! No one knew what had happened or where he was. 'Twas too sudden. I found myself clung about a snag of rock. I hugged it. I hugged it.'

He stood up, hoisted as from within.

'Is it you that was on the look-out?'

'Me! We'd all been on the look-out for three days. My word, yes, three days. We were stupified with it!'

They were looking at him as he spoke, and they saw the shiver again cross his features; the strength and warmth that the food and comfort had given him fell from him, and he became in an instant the half-drowned man who had stepped in to them that night with the clothes sagging about his limbs.

''Twas bad, clinging to that rock, with them all gone! 'Twas lonely! Do you know, I was so frightened I couldn't call out.'

John Spillane stood up, slowly, as if he too were being hoisted from within.

'Were they looking at you?'

'Who?'

'The rest of them. The eyes of them.'

'No,' the voice had dropped, 'no, I didn't think of that!' The two of them stared as if fascinated by each other.

'You didn't!' It seemed that John Spillane had lost the purpose of his questioning. His voice was thin and weak; but he was still staring with unmoving, puzzled eyes at the stranger's face. The abashed creature before him suddenly seemed to gain as much eagerness as he had lost: his words were hot with anxiety to express himself adequately:

'But now, isn't it curious, as I sat there, there at that table, I thought somehow they would walk in, that it would be right for them, somehow, to walk in, all of them!'

His words, his eager lowered voice, brought in the darkness outside, its vastness, its terror. They seemed in the midst of an unsubstantial world. They feared that the latch would lift, yet dared not glance at it, lest that should invite the lifting. But it was all one to the son of the house, he appeared to have gone away into some mood of his own; his eyes were glaring, not looking at anything or anyone close at hand. With an instinctive groping for comfort, they all, except him, began to stir, to find some little homely task to do: Mary handled the tea ware, and Tom his pipe, when a rumbling voice, very indistinct, stilled them all again. Words, phrases, began to reach them – that a man's eyes will close and he on the look-out, close in spite of himself, that it wasn't fair, it wasn't fair, it wasn't fair! And lost in his agony, he began to glide through them, explaining, excusing the terror that was in him: 'All round. Staring at me. Blaming me. A sea of them. Far, far! Without a word out of them, only their eyes in the darkness, pale like candles!'

Transfixed, they glared at him, at his round-shouldered sailor's back disappearing again into his den of refuge. They could not hear his voice any more, they were afraid to follow him.

THE OLD MEN HAVE A DAY OUT

T HOUGH THE FIRST WEEK of April was almost gone it was still March weather, cold and sleety. Then, quite unexpectedly, there came a day of brightness, of sunshine and caressing breezes. It was good to be alive and out of doors. The old men of the city – pensioned-off policemen, pensioned-off teachers, railway men, tradesmen, old soldiers – pensioners of all kinds – they all came forth, resuming their custom of daily Mass and daily saunter round. They stopped before the fronts of newly built houses, pointing to them with their heavy sticks, inspecting them with great care, condemning most, passing some. One another they examined, too; were surprised to find ominous changes in old cronies they had not seen since the winter set in; were surprised also to find others stepping out more briskly than ever, a discovery that rather dismayed them, for some reason or other. And having had their airing they all faced again for home, tired but elated: they had found themselves sound in wind and limb, and with God's help there was a long summer before them.

Old Stephen Roche, one of them, reached his house, or rather that of his daughter-in-law, in nice time to sit at dinner with her and her husband.

'John didn't come yet?' he said.

'No, not yet; he won't be long now. You're after having a fine day anyway.'

'A great day. Great! Great! But I'm a bit exhausted after it. And I have reason. Old Millerick I saw first. He's not long for this world, I'm afraid. But he's as straight up as ever; and the dainty steps of him – sergeant-major, you know. Well, he was very angry.'

'Angry?'

'Yes, quite put out. And no wonder. He was after parting with, with – that fellow Bradley. He could hardly speak to me, he was so disturbed. He's after putting down six weeks in the infirmary, the old complaint, and he's only pulling up now. Well, you know, Bradley is a most impertintent man. No doctor would ask a fellow the questions he asked old Millerick. How was his appetite? What was the rate of his pulse? Did he never count it? Had his breath a bad smell? Imagine that! Where was the cough catching him? Used his feet swell at the end of the day? Was there laudanum in the stuff the doctors were giving him? And a hundred others. All the time, you know, he was vetting the poor man. He left him at the last gasp. When he had told me all this I took his arm and pointed out the new buildings to him and the new railings at St Joseph's. 'Twas no use. He'd stop up, and he'd bring out all the horrid questions again; and whenever he came to one that was worse than the others he'd let out a volume of – of good wishes to friend Bradley that would terrify you, terrify you. Well, I could see plainly 'twasn't much good his turn in the sun was after doing him. However, I cheered him up a bit, and I left him sitting on the window-sill of his daughter's house with his two hands on the knob of his stick, and his two poor feet very flat and heavy on the ground, tired out. 'Tis a nice sunny spot, that is, and he said he'd stay there till dinner time.

'And what happened then, do you think? I hadn't gone a hundred yards when my brave Bradley steered himself round Tim Sullivan's corner and breasted me like a ship of state, without a smile or a good-day. There was no escape, I was after floating into his very arms. I shut my mouth, telling myself that 'twasn't much he'd get out of me even if he stayed at it till nightfall. But it was old Millerick he began talking about. "The old sergeant-major is done," he said. I kept my peace. "He keeps up a good appearance from the front view," he said, "but 'tisn't by that I judges a fellow, 'tis by the back of the neck: when that falls in under the base of the skull, the next thing is: 'What's the length and breadth?'" Mamie, I'm giving you his very words. Did you ever hear the like? The base of the skull! 'Tis what you'd hear at a murder trial, or an inquest. And worse still was what he done. Old Millerick is a straight up, independent sort of man that always looks his enemies in the face. Well then how did Bradley get a view of the back of his neck, you'll ask. This way. He edged him from his position until he got him up against a shop window and there in the glass he feasted his eyes on the base of poor Millerick's skull and he not knowing it at all! How's that? How's that for trickery? I was disgusted with him. I was listening with my head turned from him, but whatever glance I gave, what was he doing all the time only examining myself, riddling me through and through! He's a most impertinent creature. His face is like a bit of old board – flat, just flat. But how did he find out about that little touch of a stroke I had last Christmas?'

'Did he mention that?'

'Not by name. But he might as well. He told me that people of a certain age, a certain age, should be careful, should take things calmly, that the arteries, the arteries, cannot be expected to hold out for ever. Imagine that! I didn't contradict him, of course. I just kept on saying yes, yes, because you know he doesn't bother one bit to take in what you're saying to him; he just will bring out whatever he wants to ram home into you. He's a sort of pile driver. I thought I'd never get rid of him; so that, in the long run, I had to tell him that I had the hill to face and that he had no hill. No sooner was it out of me than I knew I had given him his chance. He shook hands with me: to see how my circulation was, of course; and he turned off; but I knew all right that as soon as I started the hill-climbing, he would just put his back against the wall, resting himself, and survey me at his leisure and I struggling up against the height. There was a predicament!

'Well, I had to do it. I plucked up courage. "Here goes," I said, and at the back of my mind I struck up that marching tune the pipers rattle off coming home from a funeral. 'Tis a great tune, you know, for keeping a fellow going. They give the big drum a terrible wallop at the opening of every single bar; and I gave the pavement just a nice lively little touch, just a sharp, smart little rap with the ferrule of my stick every time my left foot shot out. And up I marched. I knew, of course, his eyes were nailed to my back. I could feel them. What could I do only keep a stiff neck? The base of my skull is as well upholstered as ever, thanks be to God, so he could look away. Up, up, I marched, keeping great time; but I didn't feel too good at all getting on to Carey's. I always stop there; 'tis nice to look down and see the buses flying by below. And I was just thinking of turning round as usual, when I took hold of myself: "If I stop now," I said, "that fellow will have it all over Cork before nightfall that I was winded before I was half-way up the hill." Isn't that what he'd say? So I stuck it out. I kept the music going within me and I tapped the pavement, lightly you know, lightly, like a three-year-old; and when I was as far as Miss Conary's, "Right turn," I gave myself, and the whole band right turned and in with it, drums beating and colours flying.

'But that was all was in me. That old black-leathered bench she keeps in the snuggery, down into it I flopped. 'Twas a haven of rest, I can tell you. She's a good poor soul, Miss Conary is. "What's up with you, Mr Roche?" she said. "You're puffed." 'Twas true for her. I hadn't a gasp in me. And then she said: "Who's after you?" Ah, 'twas that put the fright in me. If he had followed me, if the door opened and that old sign-board face of his ghosted in and stared down on me stretched in my weakness! Cold! I went cold to the marrow. And poor Miss Conary wondering what was wrong and I not able to explain to her. "Rest yourself," she said, and indeed 'twas little else I was fit for. Anyway, the door didn't open. After a while I recovered, and the bottle of stout was a beauty. She keeps it good.

'But do you know, just as I came in that door there a thing old Millerick said came back to me. He was reckoning up that Bradley has two good years on himself and three on me. He's eighty-two, Bradley is, if he's a day! When we had made that out, old Millerick said: "Stephen, you'll see that old boy's coffin going by one of these days and the old sergeant-major giving it the salute—did you notice the pallor that's on him?" Well, do you know, Mamie, I'm after remembering that Bradley's father went pale like that a short time before he went off, and suddenly enough, too, he went off. 'Tisn't right to wish evil to any man, but if Stonewall Bradley comes up to me to-morrow with any of his croaking about arteries or skulls, I'll just read his face all over, pallor and all, and I'll inform him nicely and quietly that it does no one any harm when the great age is on him, eighty years or so, it does him no harm to put his affairs in order. That's all I'll say to our old cock-of-the-walk. He won't have so much prate then about the base of any fellow's skull or his arteries either, I think. Mentioning such things a day like this, and one able to be out in the sunshine meeting people and getting the news from them.'

'Sit in, now, I hear John coming.'

Shaking his head, confirming his own convictions, he put his stick in the corner and sat in: 'We'll let John get through his dinner, anyway, before we'll say a word about it,' he said.

SELECT BIBLIOGRAPHY

Averill, Deborah M. *The Irish Short Story from George Moore to Frank O'Connor*, Lanham, University Press of America, 1982

Hutchins, Patricia. 'Daniel Corkery, poet of weather and place', *Irish Writing*, vol. 25 (1953)

Kiely, Benedict. *Modern Irish Fiction: A Critique*, Dublin, Golden Eagle Books, 1950

Lucy, Seán. 'Place and people in the short-stories of Daniel Corkery' in Patrick Rafroidi and Terence Brown (eds.), *The Irish Short Story*, Gerrards Cross, Colin Smythe, 1979

O'Faoláin, Seán. *An Irish Journey*, London, Readers Union/Longmans Green, 1941

Saul, George Brandon. *Daniel Corkery*, Lewisburg, Bucknell University Press, Irish Writers Series, 1973

NOTE

The stories in *Nightfall and Other Stories* have been selected from the following collections:

A Munster Twilight, 1916

> The Ploughing of the Leaca
> The Return
> The Stones
> Storm-struck

The Hounds of Banba, 1920

> Colonel Mac Gillicuddy Goes Home
> Cowards
> On the Heights